B

Murder in the Mind

Detective Inspector Skelgill
Investigates

LUCiUS

1

Kindle edition first published by Lucius 2016

Paperback edition first published by Lucius 2016

Cover design by Moira Kay Nicol

For more details and Rights enquiries contact:
Lucius-ebooks@live.com

EDITOR'S NOTE

Murder in the Mind is a stand-alone crime mystery, the sixth in the series 'Detective Inspector Skelgill Investigates'. It is set primarily in the English Lake District, a National Park of 885 square miles that lies in the rugged northern county of Cumbria, home to England's highest mountain, Scafell Pike, and its deepest and longest lakes, Wast Water and Windermere.

THE DI SKELGILL SERIES

1. MIDSUMMER MADNESS

Fishing. For a person seeking inspiration – whether it be a mathematician pondering the probability of a parallel universe, a writer striving to wrestle a recalcitrant octopus of a plot from the cavernous depths of his subconscious, or indeed a policeman charged with unravelling what he suspects to be a mare's nest of a mystery laid upon his lap by an impatient superior – then *fishing* is a good word to begin with. Never one to shy away from ending a sentence with a preposition himself, Skelgill has muttered, "No point staying in," and this Sunday dawning in early July finds him afloat upon Bassenthwaite Lake with a comparable purpose in mind.

Why he has contemplated staying in *at all* – when the love of his life beckons omnipresent just a few short miles from his bed, and when no other commitments compete for his soul – can be deduced from the condition of his boat. Not a man to be influenced by congruency, Skelgill has implemented certain modifications, and at a glance – and viewed from a distance – a Chinese junk springs to mind. A capacious if dilapidated olive green fishing umbrella is unfurled above the stern of the craft, its shaft secured in a sawn-off section of steel pipe bolted to the gunwale, and in the bow, perched upon the forward thwart, is a small tent-like contraption fashioned from a section of stained tarpaulin and a wooden orange crate with two of its three front spars knocked out. Skelgill even has his own verb for this kind of Heath Robinson inspired mischief, *to mackle* (*v.t.* to adapt, improvise, rebuild or repair in such a way as to achieve the functional objective at the minimum of cost, with little or no regard for the appearance of the finished job). As such, he carves pike lures from wooden paintbrush handles, suspends fishing rods from his garage ceiling with redundant neckties, and has a replacement aerial for his car radio bent from a wire coat-hanger into the shape of a fish. All prime examples of mackling.

The deduction that can be made, of course, is that it is raining. Britain is experiencing one of its damper summers. After a promisingly dry and sunny April, May became unseasonably cool; in June the mercury refused to budge much above sixty, and the jet stream resolutely declined to slide northwards. Presently the country is the recipient of a succession of depressions, queued up over the Atlantic, each waiting its turn to make a dash at England's western seaboard. Cumbria being first in line to greet these unwelcome visitors, and mountainous to boot, it is living up to its damp reputation, and retailers of cheap cagoules are making hay while the sun doesn't shine.

Skelgill's attitude towards rainfall, however, is no more nor less than ambivalent. While it poses certain challenges from an angling perspective – coloured water, surface disruption, death by lightning – he subscribes to a philosophy borrowed from the long-suffering Scots, that there is no such thing as bad weather, only the wrong clothes. Thus, when this morning the steady drum of raindrops upon his roof had summoned him gently from his slumbers, his determination to brave the elements had been bolstered by the expectation that he would probably have Bass Lake to himself.

Apart from Cleopatra, that is. She – a middle-aged spinster – snores contentedly from within the mackled kennel clamped in place in the bow. And while he generally prefers to fish alone – not least for reasons of uninterrupted contemplation – an aspect he has discovered as a relatively recent dog owner is that being caught talking aloud to oneself is much more easily covered up when one has a canine in tow.

This morning, however, he need have no fear of eavesdroppers. As he has predicted, fair-weather sailors and bank anglers have remained in their beds, and he may converse freely without recourse to his piebald pet. The rain is steady though not especially heavy. The surrounding fells are truncated

– a couple of hundred feet of shadowy forest disappearing into grey mist – and even the further reaches of the lake are invisible. Of wind there is barely a breath – the main reason that his umbrella rig is feasible – although in lieu of complete silence there is a faint sibilance as precipitation meets meniscus, a soft hiss punctuated by the occasional plaintive birdcall.

He is fishing in a somewhat sedentary style. The canopy is a constraining factor, militating against regular cast-and-retrieve methods, and so he has settled for laying out a couple of dead baits and lying in wait. That he constantly fiddles with his box of cooking kit suggests that he is only wiling away the time until he can reasonably adjourn to a suitable stretch of shingle for the purposes of breakfast.

But he does have a conundrum to mull over. And while there is a professional aspect (though nothing so auspicious as murder or terrorism or organised crime), curiously it also concerns the topic of angling.

Cumbria Police have this past week hosted a major national conference showcasing the latest developments in forensic science, which includes such varied disciplines as bloodstain pattern analysis, ballistic fingerprinting, and DNA profiling. It is uncertain why the provincial force was awarded this honour, although cynics among the ordinary ranks have drawn attention to the breath-taking Lake District scenery, comfortable country hotels, and the best gourmet food outside London. Striding briskly about HQ have been glimpsed unfamiliar delegates sporting rarely seen uniform insignia, alongside sundry eccentric academics trailing letters after their names like untidy luggage.

With attendance restricted to grades well above that of Skelgill's, his connection is entirely indirect. On Saturday evening the event culminated in a sumptuous farewell dinner of local fare and not so local vintages, its climax being a consequently well-oiled charity auction. As a precursor to this grand finale, on Friday afternoon Skelgill – along with several of his peers – had been hauled before the Chief to be confronted with the demand: what could they supply to boost the presently unsatisfactory catalogue of lots? One officer – quick to find favour – had immediately piped up that his sister runs a B&B in Ambleside, and speaking on her behalf donated a free off-peak stay. A second nominated an uncle with an abattoir near Greystoke, and suggested a lamb might be available (dressed, butchered and frozen, naturally). And a third – elbowed unceremoniously by a colleague in the know – was obliged to admit that his better half is the (dubiously) talented artist whose quirky acrylics adorn many Lakeland souvenir shops; thus a suitable landscape would be forthcoming. DI Alec Smart, the sharp-suited and slick-tongued Mancunian – never slow to ingratiate himself with the Chief (and who Skelgill believes had advance notice of this request) – clearly considered that he trumped all with the offer of a scenic tour of the Lakes in his brand new convertible roadster, followed by a candlelit meal in a *Michelin*-starred restaurant. This prompted one inspector present to quip that DI Smart seemed to have someone in mind; reinforcing Skelgill's suspicion, Smart had smirked brazenly, though offered no further explanation.

The room had turned to Skelgill. Not to be outshone by DI Smart, and under the steely gaze of the Chief, and – it must be admitted – in something of a panic being entirely unable to think of a suitable offering, in a moment of midsummer madness he had blurted out his proposition.

'A thirty-pound pike.'

When the ironic laughter had died down, and only expectant stares remained, laid upon him like the swords of victors in battle, he had elaborated.

'A weekend's guided fishing – I'll guarantee they'll catch a thirty-pound pike.'

And thus Skelgill has his paradox this morning. Many times he has eschewed the suggestion that he could make a living doing what he loves most. Why fish only in one's limited spare time, when you could do it every day of the week? His answer, however, is consistently unequivocal: "I'll tell you why." Because, for Skelgill such an occupation would be the ultimate busman's holiday – or rather the converse of this – for he recognises his passion would become relegated to the level of a chore. Instead of the freedom to roam as he might wish, to go with his whims, to drift with the wind, to talk to himself, to consume outrageous portions of charred sausage; instead of the freedom to *not* catch fish... there would be all manner of pressures. Never mind that the precious commodity of solitude that angling bestows upon him would dissolve forever: from where would he draw his inspiration?

And he might not like his clients. Indeed, substitute *would* for might! Recalcitrant, capricious, truculent and obstinate, and far too self-absorbed ever to make a good servant – this is Skelgill, and, secretly, he knows it! His customers – well they would be cack-handed, scared of fish, afraid of the water, apprehensive of the weather, rude, demanding, expecting to be entertained and – most of all – anticipating a catch with every cast – when the reality is that a blank day is odds on. (Especially with a "bloody amateur thrashing about" in the boat.)

The thought pains him that, once strangers were admitted aboard, he would be trapped for the day, obliged to humour them, to make conversation, to listen to stories of their uninteresting exploits – when he'd rather tell them about his! Even worse – it could be someone who thinks they know better than him – or, heaven forbid, the impossible-to-contemplate scenario – someone who actually *did* know better!

As he ponders variations upon these unpleasant themes, his features draw progressively into an anguished grimace, and it is just as well that his dog is asleep. As the only other person here present, she would wonder what misdemeanour she has committed. But Skelgill is simply regretting that, in the heat of the moment, beneath the Chief's burning scrutiny, he had reacted to the gauntlet cast down by DI Smart. Why hadn't he come up with something that didn't involve him personally – perhaps a prize of a fishing rod (he has plenty to spare – several hooked free out of the lake – loth as he would be to part with any), a box of hand-tied flies, or some wild trout from his freezer?

But, no. He had opened his big mouth, the words had come tumbling out, and – it must be said – there was a glint of approval in the Chief's eyes (as if this were exactly the kind of money-can't-buy lot she sought, knowing the habits and hobbies of her predominantly upper-middle-class male audience). There was no going back. Indeed, the luminaries' dinner has been consumed, the auction duly executed – and deemed a financial success – and the Chief's ultra-efficient PA has already electronically notified Skelgill that the thus far anonymous winner desires to take their prize next weekend.

So now, rather ironically, he is compelled to allocate a measure of solitude – in order to contemplate and plan – to agonise over, to vicariously prepare for – not a heinous crime or a horrible murder – but the *waste* of a weekend on the water. For he must deliver – there will be feedback to the Chief. A thirty-pound specimen pike was what the auctioneer sold – and that is what the successful VIP will expect.

2. POLICE HQ

'I'd forgotten Jones was off.'

'No problem, Guv.'

This exchange takes place in Skelgill's office – DS Leyton has brought the teas for the regular Monday morning catch-up meeting, a task normally entrusted to his ever-willing female colleague. As is also customary Skelgill overlooks a thank you, and hence DS Leyton's subtly sarcastic response – not that Skelgill seems to notice. He takes a gulp from his steaming mug and scowls disapprovingly – though it cannot be that DS Leyton has made a lesser job of it, for the canteen has a consistent output of the scalding beverage. DS Leyton, with a groan, lowers himself into his usual seat opposite his boss, while Skelgill squints at a map of the British Isles pinned upon the wall above his sergeant's head.

'Can't think why she's gone to Norfolk – flat as a pancake – little strip of scenery and a whacking great empty sky.' He takes another swig of tea. 'You might as well be at sea.'

DS Leyton is blowing at the surface of his mug, trying to cool down its contents. Without looking up he twitches his broad shoulders.

'Flat's the reason, Guv – her Ma's not so good and her old Dad's in a wheelchair – so's they can get out and about.'

Skelgill turns a sceptical eye to his window. Rain streaks the glass; there has been no indication of a break in the weather, and the early-morning forecast on the radio for the week ahead had only words of pessimism.

'What's wrong with the prom at Blackpool? That's dead level – and it would save the journey – there's no proper roads lead to Norfolk – it's the back of beyond.'

DS Leyton calls a temporary truce with his tea and lifts the mug up onto the cabinet beside him. He stretches and yawns.

'Suppose there's some good views, Guv?'

'Views? You can see five countries from the top of Skiddaw – that's a view.'

DS Leyton does not appear convinced by this statement – it smacks of the hyperbole that he suspects often infects such proclamations. Skelgill detects his subordinate's dissent. He makes a tally on his fingers.

'Scotland, Wales, Northern Ireland, Isle of Man... England.'

DS Leyton frowns and his thick eyebrows meet above a deep furrow.

'I didn't realise you were counting the Isle of Man, Guv – nor England. Thought you might have meant France.'

'France! Leyton, it's a good view – but not that good.'

DS Leyton cranes around to gaze at the map – in the very bottom right-hand corner a ghostly sliver of apparently unimportant territory contains Boulogne and Dieppe. He gives a shake of his head and looks suitably chastised. And if he is tempted to highlight the difficulties attendant in pushing a wheelchair up Skiddaw, he refrains – which is perhaps just as well, for Skelgill's stock reply would be to refer to the great Alfred Wainwright, who notes that the popular tourist path has been derided as being *"for grandmothers and babies"*. Instead, DS Leyton takes what he must consider is a more endearing tack.

'I hear that bigwigs' auction was a success, Guv – according to George there was a bit of a ding-dong over your fishing jaunt.'

Skelgill casts a doubting glance at his subordinate.

'How come George knows – I thought it was all hush-hush?'

DS Leyton shrugs casually.

'He's got a niece works in the bar at the hotel – she was serving after-dinner drinks.'

'So – who bought it?'

Now DS Leyton shakes his head, his jowls following with a marginal delay.

'She don't know – they had bidding cards with numbers on – but it seems you got the best price of the night.'

Skelgill's features remain stern, but he can't hide the glint of triumph that lights his eyes.

'So I beat Smart.'

'Sounds like it, Guv – George reckons the Chief's cock-a-hoop.' DS Leyton rubs the fingers of one hand against his thumb. 'Maybe it's a good time to ask for a pay rise, Guv.'

Skelgill dismisses this suggestion with a scoffing retort.

'Leyton – it's not over until the fat lady bites.'

DS Leyton stares rather blankly at Skelgill, wondering what this confused idiom might mean. Skelgill duly enlightens him.

'All big pike are female, Leyton – anything over about eighteen pound.'

DS Leyton takes this information on board with a rather philosophical tilt of his head.

'Whoever bought it, Guv – they might not be all that fussed – say they've got it as a present – could be a son or grandson's birthday, something like that.'

Though DS Leyton is trying to present a sympathetic perspective, this notion only brings a look of consternation to Skelgill's countenance.

'I'd take the Commissioner over some toffee-nosed kid.'

'No danger of that, though, Guv.'

Skelgill folds his arms resignedly.

'It'll be some old buffer – that I'll have to kowtow to for the weekend.'

DS Leyton continues to attempt to put a positive spin on the matter.

'Still – can't do any harm, Guv – impress some geezer in high places.'

Skelgill does not respond. His gaze has wandered to his computer screen – an alert signals an incoming message. He glowers as he scans its contents. After a minute he turns back to his colleague.

'Maybe you're right about the Chief – she's just routed a juicy request through to me.'

'What is it, Guv?'

'I'll forward it – there's an attachment – you can print it and read it on the way down.'

'*Down*, Guv?'

'Haresfell.'

Now it is DS Leyton's turn to appear alarmed.

'The hospital?'

Skelgill glances up impatiently.

'Aye.'

'That's normally out of bounds for the likes of us, Guv.'

Skelgill stares back pensively.

'Manchester crew want us to interview a patient on their behalf – save them the cost of a trip.'

'A *patient*.' DS Leyton says this with a certain trepidation, as though the word is a euphemism for a much more sinister being. He makes an affected shudder. 'Even seeing that place from the train gives me the creeps, Guv.'

Skelgill shrugs indifferently, and rises and reaches for his jacket.

'Look on the bright side, Leyton – I didn't get much of a breakfast this morning – we have to pass Tebay.'

DS Leyton gazes sorrowfully at his rather ample stomach, and then falls in dutifully behind his superior.

3. HARESFELL

With names like Ashworth, Broadmoor and Carstairs, the ABC of Britain's high-security psychiatric hospitals evokes images of austerity, bleakness, chaos – and an uncomfortable sense that each socially impermeable unit is a macrocosm of the depraved and deranged mind, where to gain admission is to become trapped evermore in the living nightmare of stark insanity.

Haresfell in Cumbria shares such qualities: an appellation that hints of Bedlam (albeit an authentic eponym – being built on the lower slopes of Hare's Fell) and an outward appearance that is at once foreboding and forbidding. Not that it is easily seen – although, as DS Leyton has remarked, there is a fleeting view from the West Coast Main Line for those rail passengers who know where to look. To reach it is even more of a challenge, not least since it is unsignposted. (Unkind variations upon, "Out of sight, out of mind," have been suggested.) Skelgill's chosen route takes them off the M6 at Tebay village, and west on the A685 towards Kendal. After maybe five miles he hangs a left onto the narrow lane of Old Scotch Road – the traditional drovers' track from Lancaster to Scotland. Their route is now hemmed in by scudding cloud and chequered black-and-grey stone walls that separate them from rough pasture overgrown with rush and bracken. A couple of miles more finds them cutting back under the motorway and the railway, to pass through the straggling farming hamlet of Hare's Beck Foot, and thence beneath a striking though disused red sandstone viaduct, that once carried the Ingleton Branch Line. Just beyond they come to the River Lune, marking the boundary of the Yorkshire Dales National Park – which by some peculiar administrative oversight lies partially within Cumbria. One other such topographical faux pas, however, was narrowly avoided when the correctional facility was first conceived a century ago; the powers that be were all set to christen it after its waterside location – until someone pointed out that "Lune Mental Hospital" might not have the most auspicious ring to it (although there is a double irony here, in that the etymology of the river has its roots in a Celtic word meaning *clean* or *pure*).

Reaching this natural landmark – which flows south through the county town of Lancaster before its confluence with the Irish Sea – Skelgill promptly parks upon the bridge, effectively blocking the thoroughfare. He steps out of the car, and his sergeant follows with some reluctance.

However, the rain has abated – temporarily, at least – and only a few light drops spot the slick surface that slides beneath them as they lean their elbows upon the parapet. While Skelgill watches the water, DS Leyton's gaze is drawn inexorably to the eastern bank. Above a narrow strip of floodplain, on a raised terrace – half an island created by a great crook in the river – stands the hospital itself. At some distance there is a substantial collection of buildings, their roofs protruding above a grassy horizon. They are mostly of a low construction, largely modern in design, and the arrangement would present the impression of a 1980s-style university campus – if it were not for the security fence. DS Leyton's eyes narrow: though painted green, presumably to blend as best possible with the natural environment, it sends a palpable shiver down his spine.

On closer examination it proves to be not one but three concentric barriers spaced a few yards apart. The outer and inner of these are maybe eight feet tall – and their purpose appears to be to deter any casual approach (from within or without) to the main fence, sandwiched between them in this no-man's land. It is colossal – as high as a house and topped with an anti-climb cage. At regular intervals galvanised pylons support floodlights and CCTV cameras. Perhaps the most disconcerting aspect, however, is that it is more or less see-through. Constructed from slender steel posts and some kind of wire mesh, it facilitates an uninterrupted view into the grounds of the hospital (and, in turn, out into the surrounding countryside).

18

Beyond the perimeter the terrain rises gently. There are no trees or shrubs, just roughly mown grassland – rather like a meadow after the silage has been cut and harvested. Dotted here and there are picnic benches – it seems an extraordinary concept that these could be for the use of inmates, and that a naïve rambler passing along the Dales Way might converse through the transparent barrier with one of Britain's most notorious serial killers (perhaps believing that the person appealing plausibly for a loan of his coil of climbing rope really is just a fellow hillwalker who has got lost taking a short cut).

DS Leyton's expression is one of trepidation as he takes in the scene: all in all it is a depressing sight, the fence that disappears from view, arcing over the rise, embracing the buildings north and south; a miserable backdrop of grey mist and lowering cloud that smothers the desolate hillside beyond.

'Don't much like the look of that, Guv.'

'It's all the rain, Leyton – brings down a load of peat from the fells – knackers the fishing.'

DS Leyton glances at his superior: Skelgill is still gazing intently into the river.

*

'Better not stare, Guv – might upset someone.'

The two officers are being led along a corridor of which the walls are largely glass, recalling an airport, where a corresponding arrangement is employed to segregate passengers 'landside' and 'airside'. There, of course, the similarity ends, for those viewed through the partition, aspiring to departure, will not be taking off anywhere in a hurry. The detectives' transit draws looks ranging from the inquisitive to the suspicious, though DS Leyton's cautionary reaction suggests he detects an underlying hostility. Skelgill evidently harbours no such concerns, and thus his flagrant rubbernecking probably does raise some hackles.

Indeed, as they wait to be conducted through a coded security barrier a woman, perhaps in her thirties, watches them – though her expression is impassive and reveals little of her thoughts.

She is a little plump, with regular features, full lips, and large dark eyes. Most striking is her hair – ginger, and shorn into a tight 1970s suedehead. She faces another female – a slighter blonde with her back to them who has her hair drawn into a tight ponytail – they have drinks on a coffee table and sit upon low modern sofas, though the redhead's pose is stiff and upright. Her unblinking scrutiny causes her companion to turn, subjecting the detectives to an icy assessment before they are shepherded into the next zone.

Skelgill shrugs off his sergeant's warning with a quip from the side of his mouth.

'Couple of women, Leyton – what are they're going to do, scratch our eyes out?'

DS Leyton flinches, as though that would be a small mercy.

'Looks like they might be planning it, Guv.'

The interior of the hospital is clean and bright, with new-looking fixtures and fittings – it has the feel of a well-funded care home, and only subtle clues such as furniture bolted to the floor and framed pictures without glass that hint at precautions unobtrusively taken. They pass an inviting conservatory, afforested with tall pot plants and trailing hanging baskets and lush greenery, its centrepiece a fountain that splashes into an artificial pond; an IT laboratory has the latest screens ranged at workstations around the walls; and a library is patronised by a handful of seemingly assiduous students. There are many people moving about; staff and patients dress in their own clothes, and so the distinction is not necessarily obvious – though the former bear photographic ID badges strung on lanyards around their necks. Skelgill is surreptitiously studying that worn by their chaperone, and he nods to himself as he sees that it has a safety breakaway, and indeed is made from a papery fabric that looks like it would easily rend under strain.

In due course they are shown into a pleasant, airy room, with comfortable seating and large original oil paintings of variable merit adorning the interior walls. A tall man in his mid-fifties rises to greet them; he wears suit trousers and polished black brogues, a matching leather belt with a shiny silver buckle, and an open-necked shirt draped with the regulation ID. He has a large nose with flared nostrils, wide-set greenish eyes beneath crescent brows, a rather broad mouth, and short black hair that has resisted the aging process.

'Inspector, Sergeant – I am Dr Peter Pettigrew – the Consultant Forensic Psychiatrist responsible for the patient you are here to see on behalf of the Greater Manchester police – welcome to Haresfell.'

His frame is a little bowed and stringy, and his manner, though business like, is certainly friendly, indeed kindly, and seems designed to create a good impression without pretence. He is well spoken, though his short Lancastrian vowels suggest a more modest provenance. They exchange handshakes, and he indicates they should be seated – but Skelgill has already drifted to the windows that line the external wall. He presses a palm against the reinforced security glass, and notes the absence of vent lights – but what wins his attention is an area of well-tended allotments immediately outside, where several men are at work with hoes, forks and shovels.

'You are no doubt wondering who they are, Inspector.'

Skelgill turns to face the doctor; they exchange rather shrewd expressions.

'My cabbages are knee-deep in weeds and covered with caterpillars.'

The man grins understandingly. 'We have a full-time horticultural team – it can be very effective occupational therapy.'

'Can anyone garden, sir?'

'Sixty-two of our patients presently have grounds access of some kind – out of a total of one hundred and seventy-four. There are different levels of supervision.'

That the doctor delivers these numbers with such precision seems to impress Skelgill. He nods appreciatively and moves back to take a seat – though as he does so it becomes apparent to both men that some thought has disturbed DS Leyton, for he stares at the 'gardeners' with a look of dismay fixing his features. It is reasonable to conclude that their wielding of the tools has called to mind a particularly gruesome escape involving similar implements that made national news headlines almost two decades ago.

Dr Pettigrew evidently decides not to skirt around the matter.

'Gentlemen, in line with similar institutions, we have a staff-to-patient ratio of over five to one – and as you can imagine the safety of our personnel is the number one criterion in the taking of any such decision.'

Skelgill prefers to dwell upon the current statistic rather than the historic horror.

'Five to one.'

Dr Pettigrew, somewhat apologetically, spreads wide his palms. He has long fingers with neatly manicured nails, and skin that looks untroubled by manual work.

'Since our patients cannot access services in the wider community, we have to provide them. These include many aspects of learning, sports and fitness, craft and design, art and drama, a health centre, a bank, a shop, a library, chaplaincy, dentistry, hairdressing, a dietician – and so on.'

DS Leyton puffs out his cheeks, though he does not remark. Their host, however, remains sympathetic, and his tone is philosophical.

'Such is the cost to an enlightened society of treating the mentally disabled with humanity.'

Skelgill is regarding the doctor in a manner that suggests he has yet to make up his mind how he feels about this burden upon the taxpayer. But his next question is more pragmatic.

'Dr Pettigrew – you said you are a Forensic Psych –'

Skelgill suddenly succumbs to a cough – but if it is affected in lieu of the elusive ending, the doctor is content to fill in the gap without being patronising.

'Psychiatrist – yes, that is correct, Inspector.'

Now Skelgill nods as if the word had never escaped him.

'It was the forensic aspect – what's that about, sir?'

Dr Pettigrew glances patiently from one detective to the other.

'Forensic literally means *belonging to courts of law* – but of course you would know this in your profession.' (DS Leyton nods enthusiastically, if unconvincingly; Skelgill is more circumspect.) 'And so I am charged by the court to carry out its will: to act at the interface between law and psychiatry. In the first instance this can concern competency to stand trial, and subsequently the provision of treatment such as medications and psychotherapy. At a more practical level I oversee the clinical team that cares for each patient – it will typically comprise a ward manager and nurses, a social worker, a psychologist, a psychotherapist, an occupational therapist, and other therapists as needed.'

DS Leyton looks increasingly bewildered as this list lengthens; Skelgill, however, is keen to get down to business.

'Dr Pettigrew – your patient,' (he leans across to glance at the papers that DS Leyton has placed on the table) 'Meredith Bale – what sort of state is she in?'

'To all intents and purposes you will find her completely normal – articulate, calm, endearing even.' The doctor bends forwards, resting his elbows on his knees. 'However, the difficulty with a person who is suffering from psychosis is that they are unable to hold the same view of reality as those around them. In common with many of our patients Meredith's primary diagnosis is one of schizophrenia. She experiences delusional beliefs and paranoia – and we suspect auditory hallucinations, although she is unwilling to be forthcoming in that respect. She insists there is nothing wrong with her.'

Skelgill gestures to the documents. 'You've had a copy of the questions they want us to ask – any problems with those, sir?'

The doctor sits back and folds his hands on his lap. After a moment's delay he shakes his head.

'I do not think so, Inspector. Of course, it is always difficult to predict how a patient will react. Our concern is the rehabilitation pathway – but I do not anticipate anything relating to your inquiries that might disrupt our current progress.'

'To be frank, sir, I'd say we're going through the motions – but these things have to be done.'

'I quite understand, Inspector. I shall call her through.' He rises and stalks over to an intercom unit mounted beside the door. But before he presses the first button some thought must strike him, for he hesitates and inhales to speak once more. 'And, gentlemen – please do not be disconcerted by the fact that she is Britain's most prolific female serial murderer.'

4. PEEL WYKE

It is five to nine and Skelgill is ready for Dr Walker.

He propels his boat into the narrow mouth of Peel Wyke harbour and trails his oars to avoid clashing with the walls. The craft slides smoothly beneath the great concrete lintel that carries the A66 – for motorists affording a momentary glimpse uninterrupted across Bassenthwaite Lake. The tiny inlet, large enough to moor perhaps three boats, lies in a wooded arbour at the end of an overgrown track; rarely patronised, it is an arrangement that suits Skelgill well. And still his car is the only one there.

He steps ashore and secures the painter to a staff gauge that tells him the lake is lapping at its highest summer level for many years. He gives this fact a moment's consideration, and then digs his mobile phone from a breast pocket of his battered Barbour. He consults the weather app; there is a small hope that the rain will ease this afternoon. He returns the handset and adjusts his hat – it has a broad floppy brim that just about keeps the drips from penetrating his upturned collar. His practical if somewhat rustic ensemble is completed by wellingtons rudely cut off at the ankles and threadbare waxed-cotton leggings, of the single-limb type held up by belt straps, rather like a cowboy's chaps.

He glances up as a lorry passes. The trunk road emerges only briefly from the thickly timbered western bank of the lake – perhaps a twenty-yard section that is exposed, an incongruous urban intrusion into the ancient natural environment. As each vehicle makes its unheralded and fleeting passage the sound of tyres upon the wet tarmac comes like the crashing of a wave upon a shingle beach, a sudden abbreviated crescendo, an illusion rendered authentic by the proximity of the lake. However, the Saturday morning traffic is sporadic, and mainly there is silence, the air still and resonant, and just the occasional urgent trill of a wren, or the languid lilt of an off-duty blackbird, half-hearted now that his brood has fledged and his job is done for the time being.

Skelgill notices a new bat-box nailed upon an oak, one of a dozen or so great corrugated pillars that encircle the glade. Craning his neck and squinting into the background brightness of the sky, he screws up his features – as if he doubts that such a flattened structure can accommodate a daddy longlegs, let alone a community of small mammals with twelve-inch wingspans. He rotates on his heel, examining each tree in turn. There is quite a collection of high-rise real estate up there; the bat conservation trust has been busy since his last visit. And then a movement at ground level catches his eye.

Standing like a shadow against a grey trunk, resting with one arm behind her back and clad from head to toe in black outdoor gear, is the figure of a woman, slender and of medium height. Thwarted by constricted pupils, Skelgill blinks several times until his eyes adjust. Her hood is drawn close about her face and she has one hand to her lips, for she is smoking. Is this a guest (or perhaps a member of staff) from the old coaching inn a quarter of a mile down the lane – who has sought out this secluded spot for a sneaky cigarette break? Yet she regards him with a knowing mixture of amusement and insouciance. And in his reaction is there a vague sense of recognition? If so, it is transitory, for he affects to remember something, and sets off with a jerk towards his nut-brown shooting brake. However, he realises he cannot pretend that he has not noticed her, and he glances self-consciously in her direction.

'Morning.'

The woman – in the midst of inhaling – tips her head in a casual gesture of acknowledgement. Skelgill continues purposefully, patting his pockets in a hammed act of searching for his keys.

'Inspector Skelgill?'

Her voice is confident.

Skelgill halts and stares with some alarm.

'Aye?'

'I'm Agnetha Walker.'

A few seconds pass before her identity dawns upon him.

'*Doctor* Walker?'

'That is correct.' She discards the cigarette and pushes off from the tree and approaches him. She smiles, revealing even white teeth. 'But since we are about to spend the weekend together perhaps we ought to move on from Doctor and Inspector?'

Skelgill has his head cocked just slightly, as if he is listening to her accent. (South of England, perhaps? A trace of Teutonic? Certainly her enunciation seems a little stilted.) Then he suddenly registers that he should complete the informal introduction.

'Aye – it's er, Dan.'

The woman extends a hand. Skelgill hesitates – he has only minutes earlier been hooking-up dead baits. He makes as if to wipe his palm on his jacket, but in the nick of time it dawns on him that this would be poor form. In the end he reciprocates, and is distracted for a moment by the surprising warmth of her grip.

'That is a relief.'

'Oh?'

'They told me you were *Daniel* – but since Agnetha generally proves too challenging my friends call me Annie.'

Skelgill is looking puzzled.

'*Danny* and Annie sounds like the precursor to a rhyme, don't you think?'

'Aye – I see where you're coming from.'

For a second his eyes seem to glaze over. Then he starts and his cheeks colour. It is as if his mind has suddenly leapt of its own accord into limerick mode, and has composed a ditty that would embarrass him – if his companion were clairvoyant, that is. She regards him quizzically, and he turns away and resumes his progress towards his car.

'I'll just, er...'

He does not complete his sentence, but ducks beneath the creaking tailgate, and begins to rifle amongst the gear that fills the flatbed. He discards his hat as though it impedes his search.

Then rather surreptitiously he locates a small emergency signal mirror that is strung to a rucksack. Still bending out of sight, he checks his appearance; he bares his teeth, and then rakes the fingers of his free hand through his hair; but otherwise there is not much he can do. He is unshaven and unshowered, having risen well before six to "scout out" Bass Lake (in fact to get in a couple of hours fishing before his day became spoiled) – and anticipating his client to be some elderly male police surgeon, he figured he could dispense with time-consuming ablutions. Now he covers his tracks by exclaiming, "Ah!" as he 'finds' the item for which he has ostensibly been searching. He backs out of the rear of the estate and ostentatiously pockets a lock knife. The woman is waiting patiently.

'Dan – will I need anything?'

Skelgill turns to face her directly. She has given him permission to appraise her. The new-looking outer shell and walking shoes sport expensive brand logos, and are more than a match for the light rain; the gear fits her well, and the jacket is tailored and hints at feminine curves. Her age is rather more difficult to discern. With so little to go on – just the oval of her countenance, pale blue eyes beneath blond brows, and skin that seems unlined – he would be hard pressed to make a better guess than his own thirty-seven years plus or minus five. He senses he has used up his available credit – that he has scrutinised her for long enough – and he begins to chew pensively upon his bottom lip.

'Have you been to the loo?'

The woman grins shrewdly, though her reply is a little cryptic.

'I gather you fishermen have a means to cross that particular bridge.'

Her intonation has a peculiar rhythmical inflexion, rising questioningly at intervals, and Skelgill seems unsure of how to interpret her response. He glances rather disconcertedly out to the lake through the three-quarters picture window of the bridge's plinth and piers. Then he comes up with a suggestion that might explain her lack of urgency.

'Did you walk down from the inn?'

Her sky blue eyes narrow perceptibly.

'Just nearby, yes.'

Skelgill hesitates, and then makes a rather wistful retort.

'They do a good breakfast.'

He shrugs and begins to move towards the water's edge, tentatively holding out an arm to indicate she should accompany him.

'I imagined we would be catching ours.'

Now he reacts with a stiffening of his posture, as if she has thrown down a small challenge.

'It's not out of the question – there's decent trout in here.' Then he simpers rather inanely. 'But I've got plenty of back-up.'

*

'That should do it – I'll drop anchor and then I can put the brolly up for you.'

Skelgill ships his oars and hauls them dripping into the boat; they produce clunks from the hollow sound box of the hull as he stows them to starboard, blades pointing into the bow. He raises the steel anchor and carefully lowers it hand over hand, counting under his breath the depth.

'Thirty-six feet – that's ideal – we're on the edge of a shelf here.'

It has taken the best part of ten minutes' all-out rowing to reach a wooded bay that provides shelter from the north-westerly breeze; a spot where a stream feeds in, bringing interest for hungry fish and in turn the angler. Skelgill has grimaced at each successive stroke, the effort requiring all of his available lung capacity, and a mixture of rain and perspiration streaks his brow. Silent in the stern, Dr Agnetha Walker has trailed a hand in the water, watching him contemplatively, her eyebrows unevenly arched in what might be an innate asymmetry. Now Skelgill reaches past her to erect the fishing umbrella; though she has seemed unperturbed by the light rain, she glances up approvingly as it unfurls.

'Is this the biggest lake in the Lake District?'

Skelgill lowers himself back into a seated position astride the centre thwart. He can't conceal the boyish glee that takes hold of his features.

'It's the *only* lake in the Lake District.'

His companion regards him searchingly.

'I suspect you are teasing me.'

Skelgill begins to untie the rods that are fastened along the port side, their quivering tips protruding over the bow. Unseen by him, a gentle smile plays on the rosy lips of Dr Agnetha Walker. For his part, he begins to intone a series of names.

'Buttermere, Grasmere, Windermere – Crummock Water, Ullswater, Wast Water.'

'And this is Bassenthwaite *Lake*?'

Skelgill glances up sharply – perhaps irked that she has so quickly shot his fox – but his frustration quickly dissipates. Beneath the protective canopy of the umbrella she has drawn back the hood of her jacket and shaken out her hair. Now a striking mane of wavy blonde completely transforms her appearance. Where a moment earlier sat a decidedly asexual nun-like creature – she now presents him with an altogether different proposition. Unpretentiously she leans to one side, enlisting gravity to gather her tresses into a ponytail and secure it with a band from her wrist. If she is aware of the distraction caused, she does not show it, and continues with the thread of the conversation.

'Buttermere and Grasmere – *and* Windermere – but these are also villages, are they not? I have visited them.'

Skelgill shrugs. The local hydronym-toponym duality is a fact he has grown up with and never felt the need to question.

'It's like cricket – a wicket's the stumps and a wicket's the pitch and a wicket's when you get someone out.'

She regards him with a degree of consternation – though it may just be the irregularity in her eyebrows that exaggerates any dissatisfaction.

'English is such an infuriating language – especially in the hands of the English.'

Skelgill is testing the knot that fastens a vicious-looking lure to a wire trace.

'Are you not English?'

'*Inspector* – you mean to say you have not detected my accent – or deduced my origins?'

Though her words are reprimanding, her tone is playful. Skelgill, however, is unable to disguise a hint of self-reproach – perhaps he ought to have taken a little more advance interest in his paying guest. Rather belatedly, he makes a stab at catching up.

'I thought you might be German.'

'Bitte lassen sie wertvolle artikel in ihren wagen.'

'Come again?'

She chuckles throatily.

'There is a sign on the gate post at the entrance to the harbour – it warns drivers in multiple languages not to leave valuable items in their vehicles – except the German, which for some reason says the opposite. It needs *keine*.'

'Aye, well – you know about us and the Germans.'

Under the circumstances this glib remark might be considered something of a faux pas – but Skelgill has blurted it out before engaging his brain. He is fortunate that she quickly lets him off the hook, the amused smile putting in another appearance.

'Well, I am not German – but Swedish. I grew up in Stockholm and came to London to study as a post-graduate.'

The revelation of her nationality causes Skelgill to study her furtively – as if he should revise his opinion of her accordingly.

'Then I married and never went home – my husband was English.'

She narrows her eyes and gazes across the water. Sheltered from the breeze, the surface is an even grey expanse, matt beneath the drizzle. She remains determinedly silent, obliging Skelgill to respond.

'*Was*?'

This question, too, might be considered to have overstepped the mark of just-met decorum, but she is unperturbed. Her tone is matter-of-fact.

'He died – he was a good deal older than I.'

She slides her hands along the tops of her thighs onto her knees. He watches the movement; her nails are quite long and coated in a natural varnish and her fingers ringless.

'If you want to smoke – Annie – feel free.'

She seems a little alarmed by this offer – and Skelgill appears surprised at himself, too, that he has made it.

'Oh, I don't really smoke – only when I'm nervous – or excited.'

She gives him her quizzical look that may mean nothing at all, and then turns back to consider the lake. She holds out an open palm.

'I feel like I could almost walk across there.'

Her demeanour does not hint at any suicidal tendency, but Skelgill's response suggests he might prefer to take no chances.

'There's a life jacket in the compartment behind you.'

She reaches back with one arm and wraps her fingers around the metal shaft of the umbrella.

'I was told I would be in safe hands.'

Skelgill can't help a small involuntary puffing out of his chest. He raises a proficient eyebrow and affects a modest shrug. Then he picks up a rod and fiddles with the reel in an expert sort of way. Secretly he must be itching to know what prior research she has done on him, and with whom.

'I've never lost a passenger yet.' Then he laughs ironically. 'Can't say the same for big pike, though – the females can be slippery customers.'

5. BRUNCH

'We call it a *vulkan vattenkokare* – literally a volcano water boiler!'

Skelgill is looking a tad peeved that Dr Agnetha Walker has stolen his thunder as far as his cooking contraptions are concerned. Not only has she pointed out that his Trangia stove is made in Sweden (where she says it is nicknamed the *stormkök*) but to add insult to injury she recognises his Kelly kettle – it seems that her childhood involved a good deal of wild camping and fishing, and that he does not have exclusive rights to the quirky device. On the plus side, she competently feeds a steady supply of dry kindling into the chimney without burning her fingers, leaving Skelgill – less diligently, it must be said – to fry the Cumberland sausage.

The weather has driven them ashore for an early lunch. Skelgill has quickly rigged up a simple tarpaulin bivvy with its apex roped to the bough of a bankside alder and its converging sides weighted down by mudstone boulders. The rain casts an opaque veil over the scene; the distant wooded bank is just a pale ghost of an image that merges with the sky at five hundred feet, where cloud billows into the corries and combs of the fell. Closer at hand, a stately mute swan sails by, living up to his name, occasionally dipping his elegant neck like an inverted periscope. Skelgill watches appreciatively, and his eyes dart about as the occasional hatching sedge makes a clumsy break for freedom, wrestling its untried wings from the surface film, or a mysterious stream of bubbles suggests some aquatic action is afoot.

'And now – *kokning*!'

With this exclamation of triumph Dr Agnetha Walker lifts the bubbling kettle from its fire base. Skelgill is somewhat hamstrung – he sits on the ground with the stove between his ankles – but it appears she requires no assistance, and with practised aplomb she deftly fills the two enamel mugs he has charged with teabags and milk. Indeed, he can have no complaints; she has taken to roughing it, and is uncomplaining though the shelter is choked with the pungent vapours of wood smoke, methylated spirits and burning fat – an eye-watering concoction that generally has Skelgill as high as honey badger in a beehive.

He has rolls ready buttered on tin plates and he crams them with a couple of juicy lengths of sausage. Then from his rucksack he produces a bottle of ketchup and raises a small cry of approval. With the sole of his boot he pushes the various items of scalding equipment out of harm's way, and the pair settle to enjoy their meal. Skelgill is content upon the shingle, but he has pressed Dr Agnetha Walker to use his jacket as a picnic rug. Now she makes herself comfortable, resting easily with her legs beneath her in side-saddle fashion. She takes a mouthful and nods favourably, and after a moment she swallows and holds up the roll.

'What do you call these?'

'Sausage butties?'

She is already bending for another bite, and now she shakes her head. She covers her lips with a polite hand in order to speak.

'Just the bread part, I mean. When I worked in Leicestershire they were cobs. Now I live in Cheshire they call them baps. At the hospital in Manchester a lot of the staff refer to them as barm cakes.'

Skelgill chews pensively, as though this is another linguistic conundrum that has not hitherto particularly troubled him. After a few moments he shrugs.

'Come to think of it, my old Ma calls them teacakes. But I reckon they're just rolls in the police canteen.'

Nomenclature aside, Skelgill is making short work of his sandwich, and it would be a surprise if he were to stop at one. There is spare sausage in the pan, which he has been ogling covetously. However, as he and his companion munch steadily and gaze across the lake, they both appear to sink into a kind of reverie. And perhaps this hiatus prompts Skelgill to reflect upon their morning thus far. Certainly, his eyes gradually narrow, and his brow becomes increasingly knitted.

From an angling perspective, his hunting instinct has somewhat overridden his chivalrous obligation: that being, for his guest to catch the fish. While she has proved herself adequately capable in the cast-and-retrieve technique required for plugging – fishing with a lure – both of the two bites to date have come to the dead baits. The method here is to cast out and leave the rod resting, keeping a sharp eye on the line and tip for signs of a nibble. In such circumstances, Skelgill is rather like a dog with a rabbit. When the rabbit breaks cover, to expect the dog to remain at heel is patently absurd – and thus it is when a 'take' occurs under Skelgill's nose. Before he can utter the words, "Look, Annie – we've got a bite – pick up the rod and strike when I say," he has picked up the rod, struck, and hooked the fish. Then, rather sheepishly, he has retrospectively offered her the chance to play it – which she has politely declined on the grounds that he who hooks the fish is the true 'owner', and she really ought to catch her own. Predictably, this happening once did not prevent it from occurring again (much to the clandestine entertainment of Dr Agnetha Walker).

In between inadvertently monopolising the action, Skelgill has likewise dominated the conversation. Indeed he has regaled her with his full repertoire of Lake District anecdotes, and conveniently related personal details. These include pointing out that Skiddaw, looming over them but not presently visible, is England's fourth-highest mountain (and that as a youth he set the under-18s fell-running record for a particular route of ascent); and that as a member of the local mountain rescue team, he is also called upon to attend waterborne emergencies, and is four times winner of the Borrowdale Triathlon, which involves swimming the length of Derwentwater (note: not *Lake* Derwentwater) and thus she should have no fear of falling overboard, as she was informed. For good measure he added the peculiar detail that, while Bassenthwaite Lake might *not* be

Lakeland's largest (with reference to her earlier inquiry), it could nevertheless accommodate the entire population of China.

Now, it would be reasonable to suggest that Skelgill's self-absorbed behaviour stems from a wish for self-aggrandisement. Dr Agnetha Walker may consider hypotheses ranging from a lack of inner self-confidence to a certain naïve vanity. However, she seems to prefer to interpret his efforts to impress as a sincere if gauche form of flattery. Indeed, it is true to say that she has provided subtle encouragement, and received his replies with a serene delight. Nonetheless, she is clearly surprised – and amused – when it dawns upon him to ask her a question.

'So – Annie – you live down in Cheshire?'

Gripping the handle of her mug through the cuff of her cagoule, she takes a careful sip of her steaming tea.

'Ah, well – if I'm being honest that makes it sound countrified. A suburb of Greater Manchester, I'm afraid, on the Cheshire side.'

Skelgill nods.

'And you're what – a hospital doctor in the city?'

'Oh, I am not a doctor – at, least not that kind.'

'What other kind is there?'

'My title comes from having a PhD – I am a psychologist.'

Skelgill makes a surprised sound, expressing air between his lips.

'Queer thing – London buses, as the saying goes – you never meet a psychologist, then two come along in the space of a week.'

'How is that?'

'We had to interview an inmate down at Haresfell – the mental hospital. We met this doctor chap there – name of Pettigrew.'

She gives an audible intake of breath.

'Dan – that is where I am working – indeed I report indirectly to Dr Pettigrew.'

'Small world.' Skelgill momentarily seems distracted by some thought. 'What are you doing there – if you live in Cheshire?'

'My role is peripatetic – I roam – I have a six-month assignment to work with some of the patients at Haresfell – my last job in Manchester was at a medium secure unit in Bowdon.' With her free hand she brushes a couple of stray strands of hair from her eyes. 'And, by the way, Peter – that is, Dr Pettigrew – would never forgive me if I did not point out that he is a psychiatrist rather than a psychologist.'

Skelgill looks affectedly dim.

'They sound much the same to me.'

She places her mug in one of the little depressions Skelgill has drilled in the shingle. Then she uses both hands to embellish her explanation.

'To become a psychiatrist one must first qualify as a medical doctor – followed by perhaps nine more years of specialist study. Ultimately one will be concerned with the treatment through drugs and therapy of patients suffering from mental disorders.'

'And you?'

'I read psychology – not medicine – as an undergraduate.'

'But you must have some string of letters after your name.'

She tilts her head on one side in order to look at him.

'I take it you did not attend the recent conference?'

Skelgill pulls a disparaging face.

'That would have been well over my head.'

'Dan, I am sure that is not the case – however, I was one of the speakers. I am a forensic psychologist – my area of expertise is in malingering.'

'Ha!' Skelgill cannot help the ejaculation. 'You should meet my sergeant – Leyton – he's an expert, too!'

She waits patiently while Skelgill has a good chuckle at his own joke.

'So you see, psychology is the study of the relationship between the mind and behaviour – in this context it particularly concerns assessing the risk of reoffending, and the design and implementation of rehabilitation programmes.'

'Where does the malingering come in?'

'Well, to begin with, a plea of insanity is often entered – to avoid a jail sentence.'

Skelgill frowns.

'I can see that – in countries where they still have the death penalty – but what regular criminal would want to be locked up with a bunch of –'

'Loonies?'

She smiles a prim touché.

'You are thinking of *One Flew Over The Cuckoo's Nest*.'

'Aye – that kind of thing.'

She gives a little shrug of her shoulders.

'You might be surprised – although currently I have someone who claims to be in much the same position – rather ironically a former psychiatric nurse who murdered her elderly patients.'

Skelgill's antennae prick up.

'Meredith Bale?'

'That is correct.'

'She's the one me and Leyton went to see – the Manchester cops couldn't bother their backsides driving up, so we got lumbered.'

Dr Agnetha Walker nods slowly. Her preternaturally quizzical eyebrows make her underlying interest hard to gauge.

'She is a fascinating case – not that I ought really discuss my patients.'

Skelgill looks at her a little askance.

'I reckon we're singing off the same hymn sheet, Annie.'

She yields a little, bringing her delicate fingers together into a conciliatory lattice.

'Well, it is true to say there is a good deal of information already in the public domain – the trial attracted a great many news headlines.'

Skelgill picks up a small pebble and flicks it with his thumb into the water's edge.

'She reckons she never did it – that she was framed. By the time we left, Leyton believed her.'

Dr Agnetha Walker smiles archly.

'It would have taken quite a conspiracy – have you studied the statistics?'

Skelgill hunches rather defensively. He had delegated the reading of the background report to DS Leyton, who in turn had complained of car-sickness thanks to Skelgill's erratic driving and an enforced second breakfast from the motorway services. They had arrived for their interview rather poorly informed.

'I remember hearing about it at the time – twenty-odd patients they reckon she killed.'

Dr Agnetha Walker inhales deeply, as if she is steeling herself to recount some unpleasant narrative.

'Over a twelve-month period there were twice as many deaths on her shifts compared to the average. She activated the emergency alarm over fifty times – more than all the other nurses combined. It appears she liked to instigate a crisis and then receive praise for her nursing skills – and in fact she was hard working and highly able.'

'Able – and twenty-odd died?'

'That may have been her intention in such cases. The transcripts of the trial make rather ghoulish reading. It seems that on some occasions she accelerated their demise simply because she wished to finish her shift on time. Records indicated that the high-dependency unit in which she worked had used almost one hundred ampoules of epinephrine not ordered by doctors.'

Skelgill frowns.

'It's adrenaline, right? Same as an *EpiPen*?'

'Except a much larger dose is used to restart a heart.' She pauses reflectively. 'Or stop one.'

'And it's hard to detect?'

'Well – not, actually. But since it is naturally occurring it is likely to go unnoticed at autopsy – and of course an unusually high level in the blood might well have been injected by a doctor or paramedic in an effort to save the patient's life. That is why it is always so conveniently on hand.'

Skelgill stretches and fills a spare roll with plump sausage. He slices it in half with a wicked looking knife and offers the plate. Dr Agnetha Walker smiles but shakes her head. Skelgill adds a daub of ketchup, but then he pauses to speak before taking a bite.

'I'm amazed they didn't get on to her sooner.'

'Her close colleagues had suspected for some time. But there was no proof. She was never caught in the act. And among patients of that age and condition sudden cardiac episodes were normal – it was just the frequency that was not. The administrators did not notice the trends, and she was just considered to be unlucky.'

Skelgill makes a scoffing sound.

'And now she denies all knowledge.'

'She has claimed from the beginning that she was framed by her colleagues because they were jealous of her competence.'

'And what do you reckon, Annie?'

She has full lips, and Skelgill's gaze is drawn to their beauty as she purses them contemplatively.

'Well, you might say it is a game of bluff and double bluff. Normally, I would be dealing with someone who is sane that is pretending otherwise – that is a claim which is quite straightforward to debunk.'

'Really?' Skelgill sounds genuinely surprised.

She nods with conviction.

'You see, people who feign mental illness – they are generally naïve – they have little knowledge of how a sufferer truly behaves. They will perform in tests – such as for memory – according to their own view of the stereotype. Since we have the data from thousands of genuine patients, it quickly becomes apparent that they are making it up as they go along.'

'But Meredith Bale was trained as a psych – '

'A psychiatric nurse – that is true – but she is not simulating such an illness, of course.'

Skelgill nods and tucks into the 'spare' half roll. He washes down a mouthful with the dregs of his tea. Then he reaches for the Kelly kettle and gives it a shake.

'I reckon acting normal is just as tricky.'

Dr Agnetha Walker watches him closely as he makes another mug of tea.

'And what makes you say that?'

Skelgill checks her mug – but it is still almost full.

'I interview plenty of folk who might be lying. I've not got a test for it – but it's usually obvious when they're telling porkies, as my sergeant puts it.'

'And how is it obvious? I think this takes more intuitive skill than you give yourself credit for.'

Skelgill can't conceal his pleasure in response to this compliment; a small swagger seems to take hold of his upper body.

'When folk lie they try too hard.'

He casually flicks another pebble but by dint of bad luck his shot goes awry and it lands with a splash in his mug, drawing an involuntary giggle from his companion. He picks up the mug and defiantly drinks without bothering to remove the stone. She giggles again, amused by his stubbornness.

'You see, Annie – they're so busy thinking how they'd behave if they were acting normal – and then at the same time trying to do it – but that's not humanly possible. It's like patting your head and rubbing your belly.'

Her eyes seem to widen a little.

'But aren't people under great stress when they're being interviewed by the police? They feel guilty even when they are not. And so they behave differently in any event.'

'Aye, maybe – but you get used to that – it's something more subtle that I'm talking about.'

Dr Agnetha Walker places the tips of her fingers together, signalling that she is deliberating from an academic perspective.

'One could argue that Meredith's demonstration of being calm and collected is in fact evidence of her abnormality. It never ceases to surprise me how utterly convincing people with mental disorders can be. For instance, she sometimes claims she has a dossier of evidence stored remotely on the internet that will prove she was the innocent victim of a conspiracy.'

Skelgill turns to look at her.

'Aye – that's what she told us – that she's keeping it back for the right moment.'

Dr Agnetha Walker nods knowingly, the semblance of a smile tugging at the corners of her mouth.

'It is a common ploy – not just by Meredith – you might say an attempt to gain some leverage over one's gaolers.'

Skelgill swallows the last bite of his sandwich.

'Strange thing is, she seemed to know in advance what we'd come to ask her about.'

'As if she had been informed?'

There is a note of alarm in Dr Agnetha Walker's question, but Skelgill shakes his head reassuringly.

'More like she was just expecting it – off her own bat.'

'What sort of thing are we talking about?'

Skelgill shifts his position, stretching out his legs and leaning back to rest on the heels of his hands.

'My guess is Greater Manchester CID are investigating missing drugs – medicines, I mean – from the hospital where she used to work.' He brings an arm around to rub the top of his head in a gesture of frustration. 'You'd think they'd have clamped down since the murders. The questions they wanted us to ask were about loopholes in the ordering and stock control systems.'

'But she was not forthcoming.' Her response is a statement rather than question.

'She said it wasn't her – so why should she know?'

Now Dr Agnetha Walker gives an ironic smile.

'Yet she has some 'explosive' revelation up her sleeve.'

Skelgill shrugs resignedly.

'She said the doctors weren't fully qualified, the nurses were badly supervised, and no one kept proper records because they were understaffed and overworked.'

'That sounds like the standard media criticism of the NHS.'

Skelgill grins ruefully.

'Or substitute doctors-and-nurses for officers-and-constables and you've got the police.'

'It is true that all of the public services are stretched – and with fewer administrators it makes it easier for the maverick operator.'

There is a curious emphasis in her voice as she says the word *maverick* and beneath her scrutiny Skelgill reaches away and begins fussing with a fold of the tarpaulin where rainwater is dripping into the mouth of the shelter. After a few moments he gives it up as a bad job and slumps back with a little tut of annoyance. Then, rather out of the blue, he poses a question.

'Could she have had an accomplice?'

Dr Agnetha Walker's startled brows edge a fraction higher.

'What makes you say that?'

Skelgill shrugs.

'If drugs are still going missing – and she's so definite about being able to blow the gaff.'

There is a silence, but when Skelgill looks at Dr Agnetha Walker for her reaction she is grinning benevolently. He opens his palms to indicate she should elucidate.

'And just what is a *gaff*? I have still not got used to this expression.'

Skelgill seems pleased to demonstrate his superior knowledge.

'Aye, well – what I just said means to give away a secret – but if you asked Leyton he'd tell you it's where someone lives – and if you asked me any other time I'd say I've got one in the boat – a stick with a hook on it – not that I'd ever use it on a fish, mind.'

'Not even a slippery female?'

*

That Skelgill has a fisherman's gaff in his boat – and a nasty piece of work it is, too – does beg the question as to why, but he remains evasive when he exhibits the said item. The fact that it would make a fairly useful (legal) deterrent in the face of unwanted aggression might just have something to do with it, but Dr Agnetha Walker does not press the point. If anything she reacts in a fashion that seems to flatter his machismo – though his focus quickly shifts, for it is clear that playing upon his conscience is the matter of the thirty-pound promise.

The afternoon draws on, however, with few indications that the elusive fish will be forthcoming. Skelgill shifts the boat at regular intervals, trying all of his favoured spots: shelves, inlets, weed beds, submerged shingle banks, wind lanes, and deep channels – but to no avail. Even the dead baits – productive before lunch – are left unchewed. He becomes increasingly tetchy, and finds a succession of excuses (all *external* factors, of course, such as the atmospheric conditions and corresponding state of the water) to explain away the lack of bites.

The only bright light on the horizon is almost literal – imperceptibly by the minute, but gradually by the hour, the weather improves. At some stage Skelgill declares it is no longer raining but 'mizzlin' – a drizzle accompanied by the residual mist of low cloud – and in due course even this dries up. The day is in fact deceptively warm – around the seventy Fahrenheit mark – and Skelgill eventually discards his jacket. He looks mightily relieved to do so, for stiff with age and smeared with layers of roughly applied wax it restricts the actions of rowing and casting. He has explained his choice of traditional outer fabric for its durability – such as when enlisted into service as a picnic rug – and its resistance to hooks; beneath he wears only a shrunken and faded olive green t-shirt that reveals his physique to be more muscular than his lean frame might suggest. The brolly, too, is dismantled, enabling Skelgill's angling companion to cast more freely. Indeed, she demonstrates considerable fortitude of mind and body and continues to fish with unstinting energy and enthusiasm. Like Skelgill she affords herself of the opportunity to make herself more comfortable, and wriggles out of her waterproof trousers and cagoule to reveal a close-fitting ensemble of stretch black yoga pants and a matching purple-and-charcoal tailored zipper top.

However, despite their efforts, it is not until the time has crept into the last hour of their allocated session that some action finally occurs. Skelgill is at the oars, manoeuvring the craft into a small bay when suddenly Dr Agnetha Walker lets out a cry of surprise.

'Herregud!'

Though Skelgill has no idea what she says, the panic in her voice prompts him to spring from his seated position and before he knows it he has lunged to grab her by the hips – ostensibly to prevent her from being dragged over the stern.

There has been a powerful crashing hit on her line, mid-retrieve, and the carbon fibre rod is bent into a crazy arc as she struggles with all her might to hang on. She seems to welcome Skelgill's intervention, and dips her backside against him, so that he is able to hook his right arm about her midriff for a more secure hold.

The unseen fish is giving no quarter, and by the look of the angle of the line, is diving away from the boat. A snap seems inevitable and Skelgill reaches round with his left hand to ease the drag on the reel, but just as he does so the creature changes its tactics, turns abruptly and leaps towards them out of the water. It is a spectacular moment – a mammoth specimen, comfortably above the target figure – indeed a rare sight as it tail-dances over the surface – but a wonder paid for at the cost of losing the fish, for it succeeds in slipping the hook and celebrating with a backflip.

'Look out!'

Skelgill's warning seems in vain, for the lure, suddenly released, comes flying like a lethal missile as the rod springs into shape and the pair of them staggers backwards as one. But in the nick of time – a split second before it hits Dr Agnetha Walker between the eyes (or, worse, *in* an eye) – Skelgill raises his left hand and blocks its trajectory with the flat of his palm.

'Aargh ya b – !'

With this abridged oath he releases his shocked companion and collapses in an ungainly manner onto the centre thwart.

'Oh, no – what is it?'

Dr Agnetha Walker drops her rod and falls to her knees in front of him. Their uncoordinated movements have the boat rocking rather alarmingly, and she has to take hold of the gunwale on either side to steady herself. Skelgill is grimacing and inspecting his hand, home-made pike lure attached.

'I've hooked myself.'

Sure enough, one of the prongs of a treble hook is embedded in the centre of his palm. Dr Agnetha Walker glares with concern, though a certain calm seems to possess her now, as if this minor medical emergency is more akin to her experience.

'It looks painful – it is past the barb – but it is not bleeding badly.'

Skelgill inhales grimly.

'There's a kit in the stern compartment – marked First Aid.'

She turns and kneels on the rear thwart, and leans over to rummage in the storage box. Skelgill, baring his teeth, watches patiently. In their entwined wrestle with the fish he has displaced the waistband of her leggings, and the top of a sleek stretch satin thong is revealed against her pale Scandinavian skin at the base of her curving spine.

'It is heavy.' She faces him holding a rusty box. She places it on the bottom boards between his boots and prises open the lid. 'Oh.'

Skelgill chuckles, despite his discomfort. The tin contains only tools.

'Pass me those pliers, will you?'

She glances up with alarm in her eyes.

'You cannot pull it out – it will tear your flesh.'

He shakes his head, but nonetheless indicates she should give him the tool.

'Plan B – you'll see.'

Reluctantly she obliges. The pliers are a chunky pair, long-nosed with red rubber grips. He takes them in his right hand and tilts his left so that the lure dangles in mid air. Then he slides the open jaws between lure and palm and with a grunt he makes a sudden jerking movement and the lure falls away.

'What happened?'

Skelgill grins – but rather ruefully. He offers his hand so she can see. The lure might be free but half an inch of gleaming silver shaft still protrudes from his palm. He has used the side cutter to snip the hook below the eye. A thick trickle of crimson blood seeps from the entry point.

'Looks a bit tidier, eh?'

She takes hold of his fingers and draws his hand closer.

'I wish at this moment I were the other kind of doctor.'

'Now's your chance.'

'Dan – what on earth do you mean?'

'It's in my left hand – I'm hopeless with my right – I need you to push the point round and out – then the shaft will slip through.'

He juggles the pliers and presents them to her grips first. She hesitates, and stares anxiously at the hook.

'I don't know if I can do it.'

'It's either that or row the mile back.'

Under such sufferance she takes the tool. Apprehensively she gets a grip of the hook. Then she glances about the lake, as if she is having second thoughts. 'I've rowed before. The harbour is hidden in the trees over there, is it not?' As Skelgill scans the distant bank for the exact spot she suddenly plunges with the pliers.

'Aargh!'

She has taken him unawares – and though Skelgill recoils in pain and shock she has done the job – a proficient tweak has the barbed point of the hook now protruding from his palm – carefully he draws it out with his teeth and spits it overboard, then dips his hand into the cooling water.

'I'm sorry – did that hurt?'

'About ten per cent of what it would if we'd pulled it out backwards.'

He wipes his palm on his t-shirt and inspects the wound – now it oozes blood from both exit and entry points like the bite of a vampire bat.

'It requires a dressing.'

'I reckon there's plasters in my car.'

She runs her hands over her hips and the bodice of her zipper top. 'I don't even have a tissue.'

'No worries.' Skelgill takes hold of the frayed hem of his t-shirt and with a sharp wrench tears off a horizontal strip. 'Here we go.' He splits one end and bandages his palm, then holds it out to her.

'Could you just tie that – it'll last while we catch that fish.'

'What do you mean?'

'We've still got three quarters of an hour till six – can't let that one get the better of us.'

She looks alarmed.

'Oh, no – *Daniel* – we must go back – you could get an infection – we have a whole day left for fishing.'

Skelgill regards her suspiciously – though beneath his scowl there is perhaps a hint of relief.

'You've just got the knack of that plugging.'

She smiles modestly.

'That is praise indeed from such an expert angler – but my arms are tired and I feel that a hot bath and relaxation are what I need.'

Skelgill ducks away from her returned compliment and reaches rather laboriously for one oar after the other.

'She who pays the piper.'

'Oh – it is not like that – I have enjoyed myself immensely – so far.'

There is something in her tone that makes Skelgill glance up.

'You're not wishing you'd gone for the spin in the sports car and the posh meal?'

She regards him with what might be a reprimanding expression.

'I suspected an ulterior motive – it was a rather blatant appeal, don't you think?'

Skelgill is leaning into his strokes, apparently none the worse for his hand injury. His breath is beginning to be in short supply, and he has to time his response accordingly.

'I shouldn't – like to say.'

His reply is curiously neutral – when a jibe at DI Smart was on offer. It is as if her analysis has caused him to pull in his own horns. But now she seems amused, and her lips press into a rosebud as she suppresses a smile.

'Besides, you were in higher demand – it brought out my competitive spirit.'

Skelgill appears uncharacteristically discomfited by this notion, and he concentrates upon consolidating his hand and foot positions, as if his disquiet has spread through his limbs. A thoughtful silence descends upon the pair, punctuated by the regular swish and splash of the oars, and Skelgill's rhythmical breathing. Facing him, she leans back with her hands behind her on the stern, emphasising the curves of her breasts beneath the tight fabric of her top. Her eyes seem to glaze over, though with a strange light, her gaze fixed upon Skelgill's midriff – the trim musculature of his stomach exposed by the torn t-shirt at each stroke, his jeans tight around his groin above the tops of his leggings.

'You could have Scandinavian ancestors.'

'Come again?'

Her sudden break from reflection has taken him by surprise.

'If I saw you in the street in Stockholm – I would think you were a local.'

Skelgill seems unsure of how to respond to this observation, and pulls harder at the oars. He raises his eyebrows apologetically, as if he has no breath spare for conversation. However, she is intent upon developing the point.

'I have been swotting up on my local history – the Vikings ruled here once, did they not?'

Skelgill gasps an "Aye" but it seems her question is rhetorical, for she continues.

'This landing place – for instance – *Wyke* – it is the same word in Swedish, except we pronounce it with a "V" and spell it *v-i-k* – and of course the Vikings were so-called for their camps in hidden bays and coves. And certainly your name – it must be from the Old Norse.'

Skelgill frowns and responds disjointedly between gulps of air.

'My old Ma – she swears it's – from the bible.'

Dr Agnetha Walker giggles.

'I do not mean your Christian name!'

Skelgill raises his head in a rather dumb show of acknowledgement, but they have almost come upon the little harbour and he has to crane around to line up the prow with the narrow entrance. As he had done some nine hours earlier, he deftly guides the craft with just sufficient momentum for it to come to a gentle rest against the retaining bank. He grabs hold of a mooring post and then reaches back to hand his passenger to shore. She accepts his assistance, though she is nimble and springs lightly from the boat. As Skelgill turns to busy himself with the painter and oars and fishing gear, she appears in no hurry and drifts across to study a public information sign that details conservation measures being taken to preserve the lake's unique ecosystem. Skelgill calls up to her, though he is preoccupied with detaching a reel from a rod.

'Sorry we never cracked it today, Annie.'

'Oh, don't worry – I have faith in my pheromones – we females are renowned for catching big fish, are we not?'

Skelgill harrumphs indignantly, as though he might be piqued by such profligacy on Mother Nature's part – although perhaps it is just his failure to deliver. He wipes perspiration from his brow with the back of his bandaged hand. The humidity of the afternoon and the stillness of the clearing, combined with his exertions, make for uncomfortably clammy conditions. He is now kneeling in the boat, and she is out of his line of sight. Thus her voice must seem disembodied as it reaches him through the resonant ether.

'You asked if I came from the inn – in fact I have rented a cottage just beyond there, for the duration of my assignment.'

'Aye?' He sounds surprised to hear this so late in the day.

'It is a short walk – but if you would care to give me a lift I can find some antiseptic for your wound.'

Skelgill hesitates; he is critically examining the offending lure with its repair in mind. He scowls as though he is inclined to refuse the offer of her ministrations on the grounds of unnecessary pampering – but perhaps it strikes him that it would be discourteous not to run her home. Before he can reply her voice comes again.

'After all – you saved me from certain injury – perhaps I can repay you with something stereotypically Swedish.'

Skelgill half-rises and turns her way, still frowning doubtfully. She has removed her zipper top to reveal bare shoulders and a tight-fitting white sporty vest, clearly worn braless. She regards him with her interrogative stare and calmly lights up a cigarette.

6. POLICE HQ

'So – how'd it go, Guv – catch the Loch Ness Monster?'
Skelgill, his nose buried in a plastic cup of unsatisfactory machine tea, sniffs grumpily.

'A cold's just about all I caught, Leyton – it hossed it down most of the time.'

DS Leyton looks a little perplexed.

'I thought Sunday was alright, Guv – we took our nippers on the Ullswater steamer – like you've been recommending.'

Skelgill is bleary eyed – unusually for him as an early riser. He cranes around rather stiffly and stares at the map of the Lake District on the wall behind him.

'Aye, well – happen we didn't fish Sunday – the doctor had something come up – we've postponed the second day till maybe next weekend.' He shrugs resignedly. 'See what the weather's like.'

They both gaze out of his office window. Heavy cloud has returned, great looming battalions that marched in overnight and now shed a hail of dark arrows. Rivulets stream down the pane, blurring what little view remains; in miniature, a distant tractor battles the elements. Even for a seasoned local like Skelgill, he looks like he finds it hard to believe this is July. Yet, in a week the English schools will break up, and hardy families from the great conurbations of Birmingham and Leeds will flood into Cumbria undeterred and underprepared.

'Morning.'

The two male heads are turned by the arrival of DS Jones; fresh from her holiday, suntanned in a short skirt and sleeveless top, she breezes into Skelgill's office bearing a tray loaded with frothy cappuccinos (the canteen's proud new offering) and bacon rolls.

Skelgill, rather than seeming pleased to see her – or at very least the breakfast she has thoughtfully procured – regards her with alarm, as if she is an uninvited stranger making some brazen entrance. His brows become severe cowls for eyes that scrutinise her bronzed limbs and the golden highlights in her glossy shoulder-length hair – and though he appears most captivated by her appearance, it is DS Leyton that makes a complimentary observation.

'Cor blimey, Emma – you'd take a tan in a flash photo.'

She is indeed naturally honey-skinned, and fair-haired, but has returned as an enhanced and glowing version of herself. She grins apologetically at her colleague.

'They say it's been much drier down in the south-east.'

She places the tray on Skelgill's desk and retreats with just a mug to her regular seat by the window. Skelgill makes a kind of nod of acknowledgement and half-heartedly forces a simper. DS Jones, however, is clearly perplexed by his guarded reaction – she might wonder if he is seeing her with fresh eyes and is disconcerted by the accentuation of the decade that separates them.

'Morning campers.'

Any further interrogation of DS Jones and her vacation – and how she defied the British weather – is put on hold. Around the door the gaunt face of DI Alec Smart has materialised in the haunting fashion of Alice's Cheshire cat. Indeed, the grinning countenance appears disembodied, until his skinny form slides around the jamb, pressing close against the wall, half cocky, half apprehensive, like a crafty fox entering a well-stocked coop, knowing the limits of the dog's leash.

The 'dog' glowers his disapproval from behind his desk, thus obliging his pack to observe restraint in any greeting, though DI Smart ranks as their senior. The 'fox' casts furtively about the office; inevitably his gaze comes to rest upon DS Jones, whose bare legs – crossed demurely – present easy pickings for his narrowed eyes. However, when he speaks it is clear he directs his remark at Skelgill's rather than DS Jones's recent exploits.

'Surprised to see you in one piece, cock. Word is she had all the top brass eating out of her hand at that dinner.'

He glances slyly at Skelgill and – having thus emasculated him – saunters across to the window and leans against the sill beside DS Jones. Certainly Skelgill seems tongue-tied. His sergeants watch him with differing shades of interest – DS Leyton with an intrigued frown (he realises that DI Smart, for all his repugnance, has dislodged some stone Skelgill would rather remain unturned) – and DS Jones for perhaps more complex reasons.

'Happen I can look after myself, Smart – comes with the territory when you're the chosen one.'

Skelgill seems to think this is a clever comeback, and begins to look pleased with himself – without overtly stating it, he has reminded his adversarial colleague that it was he who was selected in the auction. However, DI Smart shrugs off the retort by simply ignoring it and transferring his attention to an examination of DS Jones's tan, from his elevated position beside her.

'How was Ibiza?' His Mancunian drawl has the word coming out as "Eye-bee-*thoh*." He chuckles salaciously. 'I hear virgins go free on homebound flights.'

DS Jones does not respond initially – as though it does not register that the question is aimed at her. But she notices Skelgill's sudden glower, and looks up at DI Smart with some consternation.

'Sir, I was just –'

But DI Smart waves away her explanation and interjects before she can say any more. Confident now that he has subdued his audience, he steps into the centre of the room.

'Got a nice job for someone – cleared with the Chief, Skel.' He straightens the lapels of his designer jacket and checks the tips of his pointed shoes as if he is posing in some trendy bar. 'Manchester mafia are muscling in on the Cumbrian licensed trade – we need to do a bit of undercover work down there.' He preens himself and glances at Skelgill and then at DS Jones. 'Always best when it's a pukka couple – who look the part – cool, if you know what I mean.' He glances with a sideways sneer at Skelgill, who can't help an involuntary brushing movement of one hand against his own, rather more rustic, attire.

'We're just going through the workload.' Skelgill's expression has progressively blackened during DI Smart's pitch. 'We've been a man down for a week, so I can't see it.'

Smart performs a pirouette and clicks his heels. He moves casually towards the door. Once again he looks at DS Jones but addresses Skelgill.

'Let us know, Skel. Expenses all approved – boutique hotels, top restaurants, swish clubs – got to go to the places this crowd hangs out. I only need a volunteer for a few days.' Then he stares disparagingly at DS Leyton, as though he has only now noticed his presence. 'Can't see you having the dance moves, cock.'

All three are silent as he departs the office – but he leaves the door wide open and his footsteps diminish slowly down the corridor. Then they stop altogether, as though he may be eavesdropping – and then they begin to return. His head reappears around the door.

'Just remembered, Skel – got a joke for you – you can use it to impress your lady shrink – if it's not too late – ha!' He makes a nudge-nudge wink-wink gesture. 'Hear about the prisoner with a stutter who kept absconding? He couldn't finish his sentences!'

He throws back his head and laughs at his own joke. Then the head retracts and the footsteps once more beat a Doppler retreat, more purposefully now. Skelgill emerges from behind his desk to close the door. He makes no comment as he resumes his seat. He raises his bacon roll two-handed and rotates it to assess the most propitious angle of attack. He glances up at DS Leyton as he takes an oversized bite.

'So – what have we got?'

DS Leyton jolts – he is not quite prepared to run through the live cases. More likely he anticipates some fallout from DI Smart's raid upon Skelgill's territory – a show of exasperation or anger – but Skelgill exhibits neither, and prompts him with an expectant jerk of the eyebrows. DS Leyton gathers his papers from the cabinet beside him and scans the top page, blinking and inhaling like a novice best man about to make a wedding speech.

'Er, righto, Guv – well, same old stuff as we were on last week – then a few things what have come up over the weekend.' He glances at DS Jones, who nods to indicate he has her attention. 'Gunpoint robbery yesterday at the petrol station on Scotland Road – poor cashier girl got pistol-whipped – fake weapon – then an off-duty constable recognised the plonkers' getaway van outside a chippy in Carlisle – so they're in custody. Assault at *Tiffany's* nightclub on Saturday night – two suspects still unidentified. Three cars broken into near the railway station – a satnav taken from one of them. Pair of mountain bikes nicked from an unlocked shed along Folly Lane. Industrial unit broken into down Gilwilly Road – nothing reported stolen but an estimated thousand gallons of diesel drained from a storage tank. Toolbox taken from a shed on Salkeld Road. And twenty-six prize pedigree Swaledales rustled from a field along Beacon Edge – farmer reckons they're worth fifty grand.'

DS Leyton is getting a little wheezy as he nears the end of this monologue; he takes a deep breath, and slumps against his seat. Skelgill has listened implacably, with a disinterest that suggests he has heard this story rehashed a thousand times. The sergeant taps his page with his pen – for he has not quite finished – but before he can resume Skelgill makes a pronouncement.

'That's no amateur job – it'd take plenty of dog power, plus shepherding skills.'

DS Leyton waits expectantly, but his superior apparently has nothing to add. After a moment he re-locates his place on his page.

'Last of all, Guv – just phoned in this morning – and here's a coincidence,' (he tips his head on one side to emphasise the happenstance) 'report of some thefts from that mental hospital – Haresfell.'

Skelgill's attention level appears suddenly to heighten. He straightens his spine and folds his arms.

'What kind of thefts – medicines?'

'Nah, Guv – garden tools and what have you – and bulk foodstuffs.'

Skelgill glares at his half-eaten roll as though it has acquired a bad taste. The hiatus provides DS Leyton the opportunity to speculate. He grins cheerfully.

'Sounds like some geezer's stocking up to tunnel out, eh, Guv?'

But Skelgill is not inclined to go along with the jest – rather he appears focused upon the facts of the matter.

'It's going to be a member of staff, Leyton – where would an inmate hide bulk foodstuffs?'

'Dunno, Guv – bury 'em with the tools?' But then he looks perplexed. 'Mind you, how would you bury the shovel?'

Skelgill shakes his head.

'Leyton – if we're ever prisoners of war together remind me not to be on the same escape committee as you.'

'Very good, Guv.'

While DS Leyton takes this banter in good humour, DS Jones has remained silent; she has her eyes fixed interrogatively on Skelgill. And that her woman's intuition has detected some anomaly in his behaviour is perhaps borne out by his next pronouncement. He checks his wristwatch in a business like manner.

'We'll pay them a visit.'

'Really, Guv?' DS Leyton is clearly surprised that Skelgill would prioritise such a trivial matter.

'Can't be too careful with a history like theirs.' However, his explanation does not have an entirely convincing ring to it. He turns to DS Jones and addresses her somewhat brusquely. 'Me and Leyton will go – save messing about – they've got our ID on their system.'

'Sure, Guv.'

She tries to sound upbeat but it is clear she is a little crestfallen that she is the one being left behind.

'Make sure someone follows up all the victims on Leyton's list, in person – then if you're still free have a word with Smart –

tell him I can spare you till the end of the week, but that's his lot.'

DS Jones is nodding determinedly through her disappointment – but as Skelgill drops the bombshell that he is willing to second her into DI Smart's clutches she is unable to conceal a look of alarm.

'But, Guv – you mean – go down to Manchester with him?'

Skelgill's features remain taciturn.

'Jones – you've told me before – you can handle him. If I show a bit of give and take every now and then it'll keep the Chief off my case – next week the grockles arrive and we'll be back to normal. Happen as not we'll need some of Smart's lot.'

She nods and looks down at her notes. DS Leyton seems to sense the tension between his colleagues, and with an ostentatious groan he hauls himself to his feet.

'I'll pull my gear together, Guv – want me to drive this time?'

Skelgill ponders for a second or two.

'Aye – if you promise to take it steady.'

DS Leyton hesitates at the door; he looks back with a frown, as if he is about to remind Skelgill of their last journey. But then he changes tack.

'Guv – what was that all about – DI Smart's gag – the lady shrink?'

Skelgill begins to busy himself for departure, gathering up his phone and wallet and keys before putting them down again. His reply is somewhat offhand.

'He means the doctor who won the auction – she's a criminal psychologist.'

DS Leyton raises his eyebrows, rather exaggerating his interest. Then he flashes a look of parting resignation at DS Jones.

'Meet you in the car park in ten, Guv?'

'Aye.'

DS Jones rises, though she too loiters at the open door, as if she is waiting until her colleague's footsteps fade.

'I tried to call you on Sunday morning, Guv – in case you wanted to catch up on things.'

Skelgill is still fiddling rather aimlessly with his personal possessions.

'Aye – I was on Bass Lake till late on Saturday – the phone ran out of juice – you know what they're like – I must have forgot to charge it.'

7. HARESFELL

'I wouldn't have minded if you'd swapped me for DS Jones, Guv – you know what I'm like about this place. I'd be over the moon to get on the tail of those sheep.'

DS Leyton glances about fretfully. He and Skelgill have been left to wait in an alcove of a larger communal area. There is a small coffee bar and clusters of casual seating arranged around low tables, some of which are occupied, and there is a general background hubbub of quiet conversation, and the continual tread of passers-by on the polished tile floor. Before Skelgill can assuage his sergeant's fears they are interrupted by a short, elderly, rather portly man, with a round face of unremarkable features and thinning mousy hair combed across his pate in the style known as a 'Bobby Charlton'. He wears pinstripe trousers and, beneath a maroon cardigan, a formal shirt with a bow tie. He has bustled into their recess, and halts a little breathlessly facing them.

'I'm sorry to trouble you gentlemen, I think I may have left my identity card here a while earlier – I was sitting where you are, sir.'

He is well spoken – received pronunciation that gives no clue to his provenance – and he holds out an upturned palm to indicate he refers to Skelgill's chair. Both officers rise and turn to examine their seats, and Skelgill kneels to check beneath his – but to no avail.

'Not to worry, it must be in my office – I'm Dr Gerald Bumfrey – Head of Psychiatry?'

He extends a hand to each of the detectives, who announce themselves in their formal capacity. The inflexion in his voice has made a question of his own introduction, and Skelgill nods as though he recognises the significance of the man's name and title. Meanwhile the doctor indicates they should be seated again, and takes the chair opposite. Then he assumes a distinctly conspiratorial manner, bending towards them and lowering his voice.

'I think you'll find you have your work cut out here, officers.'

'In what respect, sir?' It is Skelgill that replies.

'Well, first of all – ' (he checks over his shoulder to make sure nobody can overhear) ' – to get any sense out of a bunch of loonies – it is a perpetual challenge, I can tell you.'

He looks from one detective to the other, and – seeing their consternation at his lack of political correctness – he breaks into a broad smile, revealing two rows of rather uneven teeth.

'Oh, don't worry – even the patients call themselves loonies – they may be bonkers, but they're far from stupid – they know why they are here.'

'I see, sir.'

'But what I really mean, Inspector, is the medication – the doses some of them are on – dulls the senses, plays tricks with the memory – and, of course, that's why the devils are so fat.'

Skelgill seems uncertain as to how he ought to receive this information, and perhaps inadvertently glances sideways at DS Leyton, who folds his arms and frowns defiantly.

'Due to the medication?'

'Eighty-nine per cent were classed as overweight or obese in the last study. One of the side effects of psychiatric medication is to heighten the appetite for sugary foods – it's impossible to get the blighters to eat healthily – and then of course they stock up with junk from the hospital shop.'

There follows a somewhat awkward silence, during which the doctor, grinning rather inanely, looks from one policeman to the other as though he is awaiting some further question. When none is forthcoming he pats his own ample stomach and continues.

'Of course, who isn't partial to the odd iced bun? I know I am – and on the plus side it rules out most of them from using the tunnel.'

Skelgill can evidently sense that DS Leyton is staring at him expectantly. He leans forwards and rests his forearms upon his thighs, and intertwines his fingers.

'The tunnel, sir?'

The doctor mirrors Skelgill's pose. He lowers his voice to a hoarse whisper.

'They think I don't know – they're digging an escape tunnel from inside one of the garden sheds – heading down towards the river – about halfway there, I believe they are.'

Skelgill stares hard at the other man.

'Does anyone else know about this – I mean, Security?'

The doctor sits upright and shrugs unconcernedly.

'Oh, they probably do – but they're all on the take.'

'You mean being bribed, sir? By who?'

'By the *inmates*.' He pauses for a moment, as if he is reconsidering his use of the term. Then he nods decisively. 'We refer to them officially as *patients*, but let's face it, they've been locked up for doing something unprintable – however that doesn't stop them having bank accounts – and what else can they spend their money on?'

'But how would they manage their accounts – and obtain cash?'

'Oh, it's all online these days, Inspector.'

'But, surely there's no unsupervised internet access?'

'Do you have a mobile phone, Inspector?'

Skelgill pats his pockets.

'Aye – but we've had to leave them at the security gate.'

The doctor gives him an old fashioned look

'Inspector – last year there were seventy-three recorded breaches of security – the report was hushed up, of course – can't have HM's Inspectorate getting hold of that sort of information – the Director would tell you it was staff playing the game, trying to get the top management fired – but we all know what's going on.'

He taps the side of his nose with an index finger – but just at this moment there is the patter of hurriedly approaching footsteps.

'Frank! What on earth are you doing here? Your drama class began ten minutes ago.'

The stentorian voice belongs to a matronly woman in her mid thirties; her hospital ID perches conspicuously on an ample bosom and she clutches a clipboard two-handed with plump fingers. With a curious symmetry, the instant she begins to speak the doctor stiffens and then springs to his feet and – without excusing himself or a word of farewell – scuttles cowering past her with a short-striding effeminate gait, and disappears from sight around one wall of the alcove. The woman watches him go, and then turns to address the detectives, her face a picture of exasperation.

'This is one of his favourite tricks – if he notices a visitor he fastens onto them.'

Both officers are momentarily dumbstruck; before either can speak she offers a suggestion.

'Lord Grenville Gretton?'

'I'm sorry?'

'Or was it The Right Honourable Charles Cholmondeley, MP?'

Skelgill slowly raises his head in a gesture of understanding.

'It was Dr Gerald – ?'

'Bumfrey.'

'Aye.'

Shaking her head, the woman lets out a vexed groan and wheels away. She sets off in purposeful pursuit of her charge, making some extravagant note on the clipboard as she goes. It takes several moments before Skelgill and DS Leyton look at one another.

'I thought so.'

DS Leyton glares at his boss.

'Come again, Guv?'

'He never fooled me for a minute – I reckoned we might as well play along.'

DS Leyton's brows unite in disbelief. He folds his arms and stares with dissatisfaction at the coffee table. However, after a short while a notion comes to him and he perks up.

'Think it's true what he said about the tunnel, Guv?'

Skelgill inhales resignedly – as if he has been expecting this question.

'Aye – I've nominated you for the escape committee.'

*

'Officers – the Director is ready to see you now.'

As they rise, DS Leyton blatantly scrutinises the young woman's identity badge – perhaps not wishing to fall for another 'Dr Gerald Bumfrey' ruse so quickly after the first. However, it bears the title 'PA to the Director' – and in due course using a security swipe-card the wearer admits them to an elevator and thence into an airy office suite. Situated on the upper storey of a central tower block, it boasts expansive views on three sides, over much of the grounds, recreational facilities, outbuildings, boundary fence, and the curving valley of the Lune – though the river itself is hidden by the lie of the land. It is a spectacular panorama – albeit blighted by a sliding blanket of grey cloud that draws mist and rain across the landscape and presents its image in little better than green-tinged monochrome. Regardless, Skelgill's instinctive need to know his bearings gets the better of him, and he is diverted from his professional purpose.

'It is quite a vista is it not? I rather feel we torment our patients with the unachievable prospect.'

The voice – rich and throaty with a faint but discernable northern edge to it – is that of a woman, and she rises from behind a large desk to intercept him and offer her hand in greeting. Skelgill turns with a look of surprise – whether this is because, for the second time in almost as many days, his preconceptions of gender have been misplaced, or more specifically is due to the woman's appearance, it is hard to know – but certainly his gaze lingers upon her.

'Don't worry, Inspector – I shall change if we go out onto the shop floor.'

She tilts her head in the direction of an alcove where there is a settee, a wall-mounted mirror and a clothes rail hung with various garments. That she apparently divines his reaction suggests she is accustomed to such attention. She must be in her early forties and, though her looks may be waning, her figure is trim and her attire – a simple ensemble of pencil skirt and white blouse – restrains feminine curves; the skirt is well above the knee and wrapped asymmetrically to reveal angles of the inner thigh, and the blouse could have a button or two more fastened in order to conceal the decorative underwear beneath. She has long glossy raven hair, parted but otherwise untied, and chestnut eyes – a combination that could speak of Mediterranean origins, were it not for a pale milky skin that contrasts starkly with a deep ochre lipstick and striking cat eye make-up. Significant heels raise her to DS Leyton's height, just a few inches short of Skelgill. She introduces herself as Briony Boss – a name that has DS Leyton regarding her suspiciously as he waits his turn to exchange pleasantries. She ushers them to a casual seating area where refreshments are laid out.

'All of the patients in Haresfell present a grave and immediate risk to the public – in spite of their medication and treatment, many are not stable. As you may have observed, our visiting conditions for females preclude dressing in a fashion that could be regarded as sexy – and the same rule applies to our patient-facing staff.'

She uses the word 'sexy' unselfconsciously, and proceeds to dispense the hot drinks and biscuits. That she does not elaborate implies she is satisfied her male visitors have got her gist: while there is a requirement to comply on the 'shop-floor', as she puts it, she sees no reason to compromise in her own private domain. They might speculate on her motives – simply the desire to look the way she wants, or an effective form of power dressing? If it is the latter, it does not extend to her manner, which is casual and friendly, and seems designed to put the detectives at their ease.

'I believe you met our lead psychiatrist?'

Skelgill avails himself of an offered digestive and sits back upon the settee.

'At our interview last week, madam – Dr Pettigrew?'

She smiles, a little coyly.

'Oh, no – I was referring to this morning – Dr Gerald Bumfrey.'

Skelgill compresses his lips ruefully, and glances at DS Leyton, who shuffles uncomfortably in his seat. Perhaps the woman is ribbing them.

'Aye – he seems to be a bit of a conspiracy theorist.'

'The escape tunnel?'

Skelgill nods.

'Staff poisoning patients of whom they disapprove?'

'We didn't exactly get that one, madam.'

She nods and leans forwards a little, inviting him to enlarge. She listens patiently while he regales her with the full list of charges. He is uncharacteristically disciplined in not making a joke of the matter, tempting though it must be – and despite her implied permission. However, he does end his account with a rather offhand reference to "no smoke without fire'. For a split second she bridles at this suggestion – but just as quickly she reins in her reaction. She folds her hands carefully upon her lap and smiles in a knowing way.

'Of course, Inspector, we have called you in – *I* have called you in – and so in a sense there is both smoke and fire.' Her manner is composed; she leans back and crosses one thigh over the other, revealing – viewed from Skelgill's position – the merest glimpse of a stocking top. 'But first I should stress that the definition of a breach of security is very broad indeed. You might imagine a patient being discovered attacking the perimeter fence with a pair of industrial wire-cutters – but a recordable event is a thousand times more likely to be a missing plastic kitchen utensil that has been accidentally discarded with potato peelings.'

The detectives smile in polite unison.

'Naturally, madam.'

'My career has been in hospital administration, Inspector – I have never yet held a post where there was not some shrinkage, as it is commonly called in the retail trade.'

Skelgill nods.

'Staff helping themselves to NHS property?'

66

'Anything from toilet rolls to bedpans.' She shakes her head with an affected disbelief. 'Of course – as you have experienced – here at Haresfell we have an infinitely stricter regime than a regular hospital – although the security procedure is focused upon preventing staff and visitors from accidentally bringing mobile phones or sharp or dangerous objects into the patient areas. But the mere fact that we have a uniformed presence ought to dissuade the casual pilferer. However, I understand it is human nature to be a magpie – and viewed by many as a right of employment rather than a crime against one's fellow taxpayer.'

Skelgill seems to be listening with exaggerated interest. Meanwhile, DS Leyton, who has begun fidgeting in a manner that indicates he has a burning point to make, takes advantage of his superior's silence.

'I had this old uncle – used to work as a toolmaker in one of the big car factories in the seventies – when they were state-owned. He reckoned that's the reason the British motor industry went down the Swanee. Because of all the thieving, know what I mean?' (The other two look a little bemused – but he presses on regardless.) 'I asked him, how bad was it? He replied, put it like this: every day, everybody has something! And the Security daren't touch 'em – the unions had the place in an iron grip. If a guard so much as looked at someone suspiciously on their way out, it'd have been down-tools for a week. They were hiding twelve-volt batteries on slings under their overcoats, spark plugs in cigarette packets, wiper blades down their trouser legs – even windscreens, they used to half inch.'

'Windscreens?' Now Skelgill is intrigued, and is drawn off course by this improbable claim.

'Not up their jumpers, Guv – obviously.' DS Leyton shakes his head enthusiastically. 'Apparently they used to sneak 'em out at lunch break and slide 'em under the fence where it bordered wasteland – then go round and collect 'em after they'd knocked off.'

'*Knocked off*, Sergeant – an apposite term.'

It is possible Briony Boss is humouring him, though beneath the surface twinkle there is in the depths of her eyes a keen appreciation; he has made a relevant point. If Security is complicit in some conspiracy to defraud an employer, then its presence as a deterrent force may be considered token.

'It's bulk foodstuffs and garden tools you've had a problem with, madam?'

DS Leyton poses this question – it seems a natural extension of the practicalities of concealing large objects.

'I don't know the precise detail, Sergeant – I shall hand you over to Eric Blacklock, our Head of Security – but my understanding is that, yes, the missing items include those categories you mention. Apparently an entire shipment of *Marmite* has disappeared.'

She utters this latter phrase with a note of incredulity – which DS Leyton mirrors with an expression of distaste, as though the mere mention of the famous brand name has triggered a wave of post-traumatic nausea. Skelgill, on the other hand, nods in an appreciative sort of way, suggesting he could be tempted to commit such a larceny himself.

8. TEBAY

I' reckon it's all a bit of a storm in a teacup, Guv.'

DS Leyton examines the chunky morsel on the end of his fork, dunks it in ketchup and pops it into his mouth. He nods approvingly as he chews. 'Definitely my favourite, Guv, this Cumbrian sausage.'

'Cumberland.'

'Yeah, sorry, Guv – I keep forgetting that.'

'It's named after a type of pig, not a place.'

'Peppery pig, Guv.'

DS Leyton grins broadly, but Skelgill, lacking his sergeant's brood of small brats, is blind to the allusion and replies in earnest.

'Aye – that's because they make it with pepper – none of that poncey herb malarkey. Plus they chop the meat instead of mincing it so there's something to get your teeth into. Proper sausage.'

DS Leyton nods, though he regards the half-eaten coil on his plate rather forlornly.

'Wish the missus would get some in – except she's back on my case about healthy eating – plus the nippers won't touch anything that looks like part of an animal.'

Skelgill shrugs and attacks an improbably loaded forkful of his midday breakfast. After a minute he washes it down with a gulp of tea and smacks his lips.

'It's what I was expecting. Storm in a teacup.'

That this statement is at odds with Skelgill's original determination to visit Haresfell at the expense of other investigations brings a frown to DS Leyton's features. He was clearly surprised by his superior's decision regarding priorities, and has been doubly perplexed by his behaviour since. However, he knows well enough that to point out this apparent contradiction would not win him any favour.

'Thing is, Guv, it's uncertain whether anything's been stolen – or even hidden. The place is like a rabbit warren – and without a full-scale search you could never be sure.'

'What did you make of Eric Blacklock?'

DS Leyton rubs one side of his head rather absently, holding his knife such that it sticks out like an antenna.

'Seems a decent enough geezer – been there the best part of ten years – in the prison service before that. Old school, like – but he knows his stuff, despite all the new technology.'

'Trust him?'

'I should say so, Guv – and he don't think it's staff what's doing the food pilfering. He says he wouldn't put it past the delivery drivers to pull a fast one – reckons he's got a brother-in-law in the distribution game who says it's a regular dodge – deliver ninety-nine cases, distract the back-door man, get him to sign for a hundred. Driver scores a free case of beans.'

'Or *Marmite*.'

'Or *Marmite*, Guv. Not that I can imagine there's much of a black market in it.'

'There's a black market in everything, Leyton. Though I'm surprised they let trucks in.'

'They have to, Guv – there's a thousand people on the site to feed. Blacklock says they get through a couple of tons of food a day.'

'That's just the inmates.'

DS Leyton grins obediently at Skelgill's rather cruel observation. As one losing the inch war himself, he suffers mixed emotions when it comes to his superior's unsympathetic attitude towards over-indulgence. This is compounded by the fact that Skelgill would give the average racehorse a run for its money in the eating stakes; even now he eyes up his colleague's plate, beginning to assess what leftovers may be forthcoming.

'There's nothing on CCTV, Guv – and they've got cameras all over the joint – so I can't see what the fuss is about. Blacklock reckons the Boss woman is just having a bit of a purge because of the Government cuts. Boss woman – ha!'

Skelgill appears to be only half listening. His eyes follow the aerobatics of hirundines that hawk for hatching flies over the ornamental pond beyond the large plate-glass windows of the service station cafeteria.

'It's taking a liberty, Leyton – getting the police to do the job for your internal Security.' He sounds irked by this prospect.

'I suppose if it improves their figures, Guv – reduces shrinkage, as she calls it.'

Skelgill appears unimpressed.

'It's a sledgehammer to crack a nut.'

DS Leyton suddenly glances up.

'There's a sledgehammer missing, Guv.'

Skelgill stares rather wanly.

'What else?'

'A shovel, a rake and a hoe – polythene sheeting – and some of that string they use to tie up sweet peas.'

Skelgill ponders for a moment.

'Not exactly the stuff of the Great Escape, Leyton.'

DS Leyton shrugs, somewhat defeated.

'Any road, Guv – a shovel or whatever could have fallen into a bush and been forgotten about. Like last week – I found my missing shears in the long grass.'

Skelgill allows himself a heartless grin.

'Bet that wrecked your mower blades.'

'I spotted the shears in the nick of time, Guv – I'd swear I hardly had to cut the lawn once a month when I lived down south.'

Skelgill's gaze drifts again, and he is silent as he watches raindrops dapple the surface of the pond. After a few moments DS Leyton continues with his account.

'Most likely it's a member of staff who's got an allotment. Blacklock suspects someone's been nicking fertiliser and siphoning off the petrol they use for the rotavator.'

At this revelation Skelgill glances sufficiently sharply at his colleague to draw a reaction.

'What, Guv?'

'Fuel and fertiliser, Leyton.' Skelgill screws up his features like a wrinkled soothsayer who sees inauspicious portents. 'Last time I looked in my terrorist handbook they were two out of the three ingredients you need to make a bomb.'

DS Leyton's eyes widen with alarm.

'You serious, Guv?'

Skelgill returns his attention to his plate, and begins to assemble an assortment that includes some of each item of food. It is a tricky challenge, and requires all of his concentration. But when he eventually replies, it seems his words were uttered with ironic intent.

'Like you say, Leyton – without a proper search we can speculate all we like. And if their systems are not watertight, we're just barking at shadows.'

DS Leyton looks somewhat baffled.

'I tried stamping on the shed floors, Guv.'

Skelgill's retort is disparaging.

'Not the tunnel, Leyton.'

DS Leyton's wide mouth breaks into a sheepish grin.

'Nah, Guv – I was thinking you could hide gear under the floorboards – but it all sounded pretty solid. Concrete base, I reckon.'

Skelgill puts down his fork on the table and feels the stubble on his chin with the fingers of his left hand.

'What about any patients who would have access to the gardens and the stores?'

Now DS Leyton shakes his head decisively.

'There's none work in the stores or the staff kitchens. Some of 'em get to cook under supervision in special classrooms – part of their therapy. And in the more relaxed wards they have a kettle and a microwave so's they can make those pot snacks.'

Skelgill nods and returns to address his diminishing supply of food. Indeed they both eat in silence for some minutes, before DS Leyton casually – in fact rather too casually for it to sound natural – poses a tentative, but perfectly fair, question.

'How did you get on, Guv?'

That Skelgill has thus far been debriefing his sergeant is explained by some rather clandestine behaviour on his part that followed their meeting with Briony Boss. (At least, *clandestine* is how it had seemed to DS Leyton). This perspective was subsequently reinforced during their fifteen-minute journey from Haresfell to Tebay, when Skelgill had hijacked the conversation to recount a string of police incidents that had occurred in the vicinity, "before your time, Leyton". Scenically unexceptional, the no-man's land between the two great competing national parks of the Lakes and the Dales (no contest, according to Skelgill) is most notable as the conduit for three significant arteries: the concrete and tarmac of the M6 motorway, the hewn embankments and cuttings of the West Coast Main Line, and – of course – the river valley of the rushing Lune. Accordingly, Skelgill's anecdotes featured high-speed car chases, minor railway disasters and disorganised crime in the shape of salmon poaching. In listening patiently to such fishy tales, DS Leyton quite reasonably suspected avoidance tactics were afoot.

As for what Skelgill was avoiding, having left the company of the Director – on reflection a questionable formality, given the limited overview she was willing to impart to them – they were conducted to a transit area to be handed over to Eric Blacklock. Prior to the Head of Security's arrival, Skelgill had suddenly sprung from his seat and crossed with what had seemed like indecent haste to engage with an attractive blonde woman who had unobtrusively materialised from an elevator. Her identity badge marked her out as a member of staff. Under the critical scrutiny of DS Leyton, they had conferred for a minute or two – during which time the woman, rather bizarrely, appeared for a moment to read Skelgill's palm – before he sauntered back wearing the patently ingenuous expression he reserves for what might be called 'buck-passing' moments.

'Time to divide and conquer, Leyton.' His words had been accompanied by a forced grin. Then he had glanced ostentatiously at his wristwatch. 'Meet you at reception in an hour.'

And, with that, he had returned to the waiting female, who had gazed at him rather admiringly (in DS Leyton's assessment), and spirited him away through a security door. A glowering DS Leyton – thus jilted to wait for the apparently delayed Eric Blacklock – was forming the opinion that Skelgill's meeting with this woman was not a chance encounter. Such a summary abandonment no doubt amplified the sergeant's general anxiety, and heightened his irrational fear of being 'discovered' by those in authority – who inevitably would not believe he was a police officer and detain him at Her Majesty's pleasure.

But now, at last, Skelgill cuts to the chase.

'She's the doctor, Leyton – the one who won the fishing trip.'

DS Leyton nods slowly several times, as if by so doing he buys essential seconds in which to process the implications of Skelgill's statement before being required to reply. Perhaps he revisits DI Smart's probing references to Skelgill's "lady shrink" and his somewhat evasive response.

'So when you said divide and conquer, Guv – ?'

To the extent that he dare, DS Leyton leaves this question hanging – but Skelgill remains phlegmatic.

'On Bass Lake – I mentioned we'd been down to interview Meredith Bale. She's doing some work with her.'

'That's a coincidence, Guv.'

Skelgill shrugs and pulls a face to indicate he thinks it is a small world.

'She offered to give me a tour – if there were cause to come back. Thought I might as well take advantage – bit of an open goal.'

The confirmation that Skelgill must have had this plan in mind from the moment mention was made of Haresfell at their morning meeting – and that he somehow contrived the arrangement – serves only to deepen the expression of suspicion that creases DS Leyton's features. Thus his retort is uncharacteristically belligerent.

'And did you score, Guv?'

He utters this question without drawing upon any of the great well of innuendo the words contain – instead remaining straight-faced and within the strict limits of Skelgill's metaphor. Nonetheless it causes Skelgill to twitch as he fiddles to herd together the last few morsels of his meal. He takes his time to chew, affirmatively tapping his empty fork in the air. However, his answer when it finally comes is less tangible than the signal promises.

'She's not really in the loop as far as the management of the place is concerned – she's temporary – only been there a month. But I got to meet a few of the nurses and lower-grade staff – behind the scenes.'

DS Leyton nods, a little reluctantly.

'So – was that unauthorised, Guv – as far as the Director was concerned?'

Skelgill tilts his head back and drains his mug of tea. Then he shrugs nonchalantly.

'I didn't notice her laying down the law either way, Leyton.'

'I saw that Dr Pettigrew looking at you, Guv.'

DS Leyton's sudden revelation draws a sharp glance from Skelgill.

'What do you mean?'

'Well, Guv – Eric Blacklock was taking me along this corridor, up on the first floor, and ahead of us I spotted the Pettigrew geezer, staring out of a window. When we reached him I realised he was watching you and your lady doctor friend – you were right out across the grounds, a long way off, walking together.' DS Leyton chuckles. 'Funny thing was it looked like the pair of you were out for a sneaky fag, Guv – must have been the condensation in the air, from your breath, like.'

Skelgill chooses not to be diverted by the mischievous suggestion.

'And what about Pettigrew?'

'He only turned towards us at the last second – kind of nodded to Blacklock – went on his way. I don't recall he even eyeballed me, Guv.'

Skelgill purses his lips thoughtfully. It is a few moments before he responds.

'He's her line manager of sorts – he was probably checking she wasn't wandering about with one of the patients.'

DS Leyton rather flinches, as if this comment has reminded him of his own fears of detention. He is about to remark when Skelgill abruptly pushes back his chair, its squeal of protest against the floor tiles attracting the attention of nearby diners.

'Come on, Leyton – just time for a spot of shopping.'

'Shopping, Guv?'

'I want some *Marmite*.'

'What, for your sarnies, Guv?'

Skelgill regards his sergeant with a look of disgust.

'You must be joking, Leyton.'

'But why then, Guv?'

Skelgill shakes his head impatiently.

'It's a lethal bait, Leyton – you smear it on your lures.'

He spins on his heel and sets off at a pace, leaving DS Leyton to paddle in his wake. He calls back over his shoulder.

'You can get a surprise for your wife, Leyton – they stock a decent Cumberland sausage here.'

9. HARE'S BECK FOOT INN

'Evening, sir – nice dog there – what is he, a dwarf Boxer?'

'Bullboxer. Staffie cross.'

'Looks like he might stop a tank.'

Skelgill smiles patiently. He does not trouble to correct the landlord's mistake regarding Cleopatra's gender. He glances around the shabby, low-ceilinged room, where several mainly elderly men are gathered, silent in the gloom, most of them glued to the highlights of a cricket match displayed on an outmoded and flickering screen suspended above the bar. But at a table in the opposite corner, beside a weakly smoking hearth, one man is watching him. He is rather more tidily dressed than the others, and younger, perhaps mid-fifties. As Skelgill meets his gaze he gives a little nod of recognition.

'What'll it be, sir?'

Skelgill turns back to face the barman.

'Chap by the fire – what's he drinking?'

'Arthur? Mild-and-bitter's his usual poison. Though I believe he's had a couple of whiskies.'

Skelgill ponders for a moment, his eyes scanning the limited range of plastic offerings bolted to the counter. No sign of a cask ale.

'I'll take two pints.'

'Certainly, sir – good driver's drink – the mild's only two-point-eight – brings down the average to about three-point-two.'

That the publican divines he has arrived by car is no surprise. Hare's Beck Foot is a tiny hamlet and probably even most locals arrive using the same means. In any event, it is teeming with rain, and Skelgill has entered wearing just jeans and a t-shirt, and apart from a few heavy spots on his shoulders is dry. He waits, an elbow on the bar, while the man pours the beers into glass tankards, enabling Skelgill to carry them one-handed and keep a hold of his dog's lead with the other. As he approaches the corner table a low growl emanates from beneath the blackened settle that runs along what is the front wall of the building. But Cleopatra – at whom this warning is evidently aimed – pays no heed and nonchalantly makes the acquaintance of what Skelgill sees is a Border Terrier, not so long out of puppyhood.

'Sorry to keep you – got held up by a couple of crooks.'

The man grins at Skelgill's turn of phrase.

'Don't look too hard – you might find a few more in here.'

Skelgill raises his eyebrows to acknowledge that he understands the retort is made in jest. He takes a seat upon the settle, perpendicular to the other man. He cocks his head to one side as though he is replaying the sound of the incumbent's voice.

'You a Geordie, Arthur?'

'Don't wind me up, man – I'd rather you thought I were a Jock.'

Skelgill has no particular axe to grind against his Celtic cousins from north of the border, with whom over the generations his family has no doubt interbred (willingly, and perhaps at times unwillingly, on both sides). He seems a little taken aback by the vehemence of this rebuttal.

'I didn't quite catch your accent – I take it you're a Mackem, then?'

'Aye – cheers!'

The man grins, revealing a missing front incisor, and takes a draught of his fresh pint. Skelgill persists with the theme.

'Your surname – Kerr – it's Scots.'

'Sunderland name, man.'

'Aye?' Skelgill sounds doubtful.

'Remember Bobby Kerr?'

Skelgill looks blank. Arthur Kerr obliges with more information.

'1973 FA Cup Final? Captain when we beat the mighty Leeds United. Took 'em doon a peg or two.'

Skelgill might have something of a craggy appearance, but that he patently could not have been born sufficiently long ago does not seem to trouble Arthur Kerr – and to confound his own argument he adds a rider about his more illustrious namesake, Captain Bobby.

'Mind you – he were a Jock.'

Skelgill has no answer to this contrary logic.

'I guess you'd remember England winning the World Cup.'

Whether Skelgill is diplomatically trying to highlight their age gap – or if this is simply a sliver of wishful thinking spoken aloud – it is hard to know, but he says it less as a question and more as a statement.

'Aye – seven I were – watched it in black and white wi' wor kid – lamped him and gave him a shiner when the Jerries took the lead and he said he'd told me they'd win.'

'But they didn't.'

Arthur Kerr shakes his head determinedly, and Skelgill looks despondent, as if he might be thinking that, rather like the Empire, England winning the World Cup is an exclusively historical phenomenon.

'You didn't come to pump us about football.'

'Sorry?'

It appears Skelgill has drifted off into some brown study. Arthur Kerr flicks his dimpled pint glass with the nails of one hand – perhaps an oblique reminder that the beer is in exchange for his confidences. However, Skelgill seems to interpret it as an encouragement to drink. Indeed, he takes a sup and immediately pulls a face of undisguised disapproval. As he is wont to put it, "I can just about stand it cold and fizzy when the sun's cracking the cobbles." But that is not today. However, he battles with his prejudices and restores a more placid expression in order not to offend the sensibilities of those around him.

'We've had some dealings with Haresfell on behalf of the Greater Manchester Police – there's a couple of issues we're investigating – I've been trying to establish who might be a reliable person to ask – off the record.'

Arthur Kerr gives Skelgill a sideways look, and then casts about the bar – though nobody is close enough to eavesdrop, even were their hearing up to it.

'We're not meant to chinwag about what goes on inside – you'll have seen the posters.' He pauses, and then drinks reflectively. 'Then again, you know what it's like when you've had a few pints.'

Skelgill bends forwards and extracts his wallet from his back pocket. He places it on the table.

'I've put forty quid behind the bar. For starters.'

The man raises his pint and drinks again, as though some sense of urgency has now overtaken him. Above the rim of his glass he eyes the wallet; there is a suggestion in Skelgill's words that he will pay for more than beer alone.

'Haway, man – ask all you like.'

Perhaps in order to compose himself, Skelgill takes another somewhat reluctant draught from his dark-looking pint. Now that he is expecting its carbonated bite he swallows with more circumspection.

'You're a nurse.'

Though Skelgill knows this fact, he regards Arthur Kerr as though it is an improbable guess in a game of charades. And, certainly, nurse is not the obvious occupation any stranger entering this dingy rural pub might ascribe, where woodsman, shepherd or gamekeeper seems more likely. And – the potentially misleading gender stereotype aside – the man's appearance offers few clues to his calling. He is short, though stocky and powerfully built. He has long, rather lank hair, drawn back from a receding hairline into a ponytail; teashade glasses perched on a hook nose; and a gold ring in his left ear. His complexion is swarthy, and small beady brown eyes peer from the recess between prominent cheekbones and brow. The jaw is strong, but the lips mean. It is a physiognomy that suggests a Romany provenance, though his get-up is a retro ensemble of black winkle-picker ankle boots, skinny jeans with a plate buckle

80

belt, and a faded denim shirt – more jobbing jazz guitarist than gypsy horse-trader.

'Primary nurse, aye.'

'How does that work?'

'I've got four patients that I'm permanently assigned to – so's I get to know them – "Relational Security" we call it. The other nurses float around according to shifts.' He swallows more beer and tosses his head somewhat scathingly. 'And absenteeism.'

'Is that a problem?'

'Haresfell's got twice the staff sickness of the NHS average.'

Skelgill purses his lips.

'It didn't look so bad – from what I saw – it all seemed quite civilised where I met you, with Dr Walker.'

The man allows himself a quick grin – as if the mention of Dr Agnetha Walker prompts some other line of thought. However, his reply deals with Skelgill's observation.

'Aye – but I work on an Assertive Rehab ward.'

His rising inflexion suggests he expects Skelgill to understand the significance of such an arrangement.

'Who does the asserting?'

Arthur Kerr chuckles and takes a small sip of beer, enough to wet his lips.

'Look, man – all the folk who come in to Haresfell are a danger to the public. Like as not they'll start in a High Dependency Ward. We've got patients in there who are on a Six-Person Unlock. You know what that means?'

'I reckon I can work it out.'

'If they make progress – demonstrate that they *want* to make progress – they can move to Assertive Rehab, get a key to their room, some of their own stuff, more freedom to move about and make drinks – it's the first step on a long road to an RSU – Regional Secure Unit.'

'And after that?'

'Possible release into the community – under supervision.'

'Even murderers?'

'Aye.'

Skelgill drinks silently for a moment.

'What do you think about that, Arthur?'

The man replies without hesitation.

'It means people like me have done a good job – else what's the point of the place? It costs five times as much to keep someone in Haresfell as in prison.'

Skelgill is pensive. It is perhaps intriguing that the man takes this progressive view – he seems an unforgiving character, of working-class origins, and hardly academic – yet he is sympathetic to the pathway society has designated for those deemed to be not just vile offenders but also unfortunate victims.

'So – Meredith Bale – she's one of your patients?'

'Aye, Meredith.'

'And how would you feel about her getting out?'

This time Arthur Kerr has to consider his opinion.

'Can't say I've got to the bottom of her yet – she's been spending a lot of time with your doctor friend lately.'

There is a flash of a probing glance here. And – in Arthur Kerr's use of the attributive adjective "your" – a tangibly provocative suggestion of familiarity. Skelgill might have cause to wonder what signals he has inadvertently given out.

'I gather she claims she's completely sane – that she was framed.'

'Mebbes she was.'

'You think?'

Arthur Kerr shrugs apathetically.

'Who knows – they're a canny lot.'

Skelgill nods and contemplates his drink. Then it suddenly dawns on him that Arthur Kerr did not mean what he had thought. A shadow darkens his features, and he takes temporary refuge in the act of draining his glass. He rises and fetches the refills that have been set ready on the bar by a landlord eager to optimise his profits from the generous stranger's float. Skelgill slides a brimming pint carefully across the table.

'How long have you been at Haresfell?'

'Coming up four years.'

Skelgill nods, as though he feels this is a useful fact.

'Me and my sergeant – we met a patient called Frank – he introduced himself as a psychiatrist.'

The thick circular lenses of Arthur Kerr's spectacles cannot conceal a wary sideways glance.

'Frank Wamphray.'

Skelgill's features take on a sceptical cast.

'That's a river – Wamphray Water – runs into the Annan, up towards Beattock.'

'I wouldn't know. It's definitely his name – despite all his aliases.' He takes a drink with exaggerated care. 'What did Frank have to say?'

Skelgill makes a scoffing sound, as if to indicate there was nothing of importance.

'He sounded like a stuck record about breaches of security.'

Arthur Kerr seems satisfied by this answer.

'Frank-and-a-large-pinch-of-salt – that's what we call him.'

Skelgill nods agreeably, though he presses the point.

'I did notice there were a lot of searches taking place.'

'Aye – that's standard procedure when we move patients from one area to another – they're used to it. If you're an outsider you'd probably think it's a bit over the top.'

'What's the idea – it's not like they're going anywhere?'

Arthur Kerr winks conspiratorially.

'You want to guess what's the biggest problem?' He pauses, and Skelgill turns out his palms to indicate he should continue. 'Self harm. Smuggle a plastic spoon back to their room; sharpen up the edge on a rough surface. Next thing there's blood seeping under the door.'

Skelgill receives this intelligence with a phlegmatic tilting of his head.

'If you're trying to rehabilitate folk – you can't wrap them in cotton wool.'

Arthur Kerr rails somewhat at Skelgill's inapt metaphor.

'It's easy for you to say that – we have to mop up the mess – and get paid a pittance.'

He shakes his head and looks pointedly at Skelgill's plump wallet – although what is not immediately apparent is that it is padded with many weeks' worth of unfiled expenses receipts.

'You lot do alright – Government's got to keep the polliss sweet.'

Skelgill glances ostentatiously at his wristwatch – he perhaps makes the point that he is working now.

'You wouldn't want the hourly rate I'm getting for being here.'

'Ah well man, at least you're enjoying the company.'

It is difficult to discern if this is an ironic comment or not – but Arthur Kerr pats Skelgill on the forearm and simultaneously drains his glass. Skelgill rather snatches at the empty, and withdraws hastily.

While he is standing at the bar a sly-faced character enters with an even meaner-looking Lurcher at his side. The newcomer is hailed by an acquaintance; this diverts him from his path to the counter, but the dog spots Arthur Kerr's young terrier, which has trailed Skelgill from their corner. Without fair warning the malevolent hound lunges at the terrier; heavily outgunned, the poor pup scrambles behind Skelgill's legs. The Lurcher sways from side to side, assessing the best angle of attack. Before Skelgill can do much other than protectively widen his stance, there comes a sudden blur as Cleopatra – living up to her nickname "canine cannonball" – explodes from beneath the settle and sends the bigger dog sprawling across the stone flags. The yelping bully decides it has met its match and slinks back to its owner, who glares at Skelgill. There is, however, some quality about Skelgill in such situations – a presence greater than the confidence of a warrant card in his back pocket – that signals reverse gear is broken (if it were ever fitted as standard). Thus, in due course, the newcomer sensibly blinks first – and turns to vent his ire upon his vanquished dog. Skelgill calmly picks up the drinks and returns to his table.

Arthur Kerr is grinning.

'Police dog?'

Skelgill smiles ruefully.

'Rescue dog, you might say.'

'She came to the rescue there, alreet.'

Skelgill affects a degree of modest pride.

'At risk of trying to sound witty – you might say in our line we look out for the underdog.'

Arthur Kerr raises his glass and then downs almost half of its contents in one.

'There you gan, then – divvent mither yersel wi' us ordinary workers – it's folks wi' power you should have your eye on.'

That his Wearside accent has intensified, Skelgill can read into whatever he likes – it could be the alcohol is loosening his tongue – and perhaps that the incident amongst the dogs has contrived a feeling of comradely bonding.

'The bigger the fish, Arthur, the craftier they come.'

To Skelgill this is a simple truism – you only get to be a thirty-pound pike by relentlessly outsmarting your prey and your competitors. It is a maxim that pertains well beyond the watery reaches of Bassenthwaite Lake. And, though Arthur Kerr is no angler, the sentiment has resonance for him.

'I can see you're a decent copper, man – an' I'm no whistleblower, like – not against me workmates – me own kind.'

Skelgill leans over the table conspiratorially, and lowers his voice.

'Arthur – when you said a minute back "they're a canny lot" – you meant the people in authority – not the patients?'

'Aye.'

'What – such as the courts?'

'Aye – the courts – the hospital administrators, clinicians – even your lot – at the top level, like.' That he adds this rider suggests he has accepted Skelgill on the side of the artisans. 'You must see it yersel, man – it's all about justifying their existence – getting their snouts in the trough.'

Skelgill seems a little surprised by the man's forthright cynicism – after all, in a more modest way he draws his own subsistence from the public purse.

'You reckon that applies to Haresfell?'

Arthur Kerr downs a couple more swallows of beer.

'Course it does, man – look at the section I work in. Pettigrew – you've met him, reet?' (Skelgill nods.) 'He's gathered an entourage like he's royalty. Snaps his fingers – the old pals act – next thing your Dr Walker's on some spurious project – what's the cost of that? Makes him look good, though. Plus there's the eye candy factor. Meanwhile he's lording it in a Jag – big house over at Kendal – flat in Didsbury – holiday property up here – bairns at Sedbergh. And his wife's onto a cushy number – holding acting classes for four times my salary. I mean, what's that about?'

'At the hospital?'

'Aye – she's qualified psychologist, fair enough – but with all the cuts there's no vacancies, so they've cooked up a whole new area of therapy just to accommodate her – they've converted the badminton courts into a drama studio – lighting rigs, costumes, make-up – the lot.'

Skelgill appears distracted, and when he eventually responds his mind seems to have moved on from Arthur Kerr's grievances.

'Aye, but Arthur – it's petty thefts we've been notified about – and that's come down from the Director.' He takes a drink. 'Are you telling me there's something more sinister going on?'

Arthur Kerr shrugs, and for a moment it seems as though he is found wanting; he squirms and hauls up the pup and cradles it in his arms. Skelgill watches with some distaste as the man allows it to lick him around the mouth, hindering any reply he might make.

'Like I said – them at top's playing the system – feathering their own nests – suiting their own devices – you'll won't catch 'em at it though – they're Teflon-coated – anything dodgy and it's hushed up like it never existed.'

Under this hail of clichés and platitudes Skelgill sits back pensively. He reaches down rather absently to give Cleopatra a congratulatory pat – though somewhat belatedly in order for the dog to associate it with her heroics. Abruptly, however, he jerks around, for Arthur Kerr has once more placed a hand on his arm. Now the man's grip is persistent. He dangles his empty tankard and smirks artfully.

'I'll tell yer what, man – why don't we get a bottle of something stronger with your Government fund – my place is five minutes away – and if you have too many bevvies to drive you can always bunk down for the night – I've only got the one bed – but it's a double, like.'

Out of sight beneath the settle, Skelgill's injured left hand has balled into a fist.

10. CROW PARK

Tuesday morning finds Skelgill exercising Cleopatra. He has a half-day and, for once, he has eschewed the lure of Bassenthwaite Lake and opted for this more ubiquitous leisure pursuit. Indeed, rather out of character, he has gone with the flock (in both a metaphorical and literal sense), and wanders thoughtfully, a lone figure amongst a scattered crowd comprising Herdwick sheep, vaguely disoriented tourists, and more purposeful dog walkers like himself.

The location is Keswick. He has parked beside Derwentwater, near the Theatre By The Lake, at the public landing – a locus where customarily he would have a trailer attached to his car, his boat aboard, and hope in his heart. However he appears unconcerned by the self-imposed exile from angling and his gaze, which customarily would be scanning for signs of aquatic life, surveys his more immediate landside environs. The fact that the shorn field accommodates an ovine population as well as several visiting dogs is a local curiosity at odds with received wisdom – which holds that the only canines that ought to be among sheep are working Border Collies, and any others fair game for the shotgun. However, small clusters of Herdwicks graze apparently unperturbed – and undisturbed – and even those dogs that have been unleashed seem disinterested, instead finding their fun down at the shoreline where feral Greylag geese offer more formidable resistance.

That this is not a Skelgill kind of spot is immediately apparent. In his book, any place that draws people wearing ordinary shoes and carrying ice creams is to be avoided. Happily, lesser mortals lack the imagination to open an Ordnance Survey map and find solitude, which is where he will generally be. And, though the view south over Derwentwater is spectacular – if somewhat constricted this morning by hanging cloud and misty drizzle – the human presence taints it for him, rather in the way that if someone had taken a black marker to a Turner and added a few figures of their own to produce a half-baked Lowry. He does, however, halt and pay brief lip service to the panorama that unfolds as he crosses the rising pasture, for the lake as yet is bereft of craft, and its surface alluring, like mercury that has melted into Borrowdale and found its level in the valley; its mirrored surface reflects what peaks are visible: he nods at the distinctive pap of Catbells, just flirting with the cloud base, at fifteen hundred feet.

'Is that you? My dear – how are you, darling?'

Thus Skelgill's observations are short-lived. He turns and is about to reply when he realises the affectionate greeting is directed at Cleopatra, and the speaker has dropped upon one knee to stroke her. The person is swathed against the elements, indeed wears an ankle-length *Driza-Bone* stockman's coat and an accessorised wide-brimmed suede hat, leaving little uncovered for identification purposes. A damp and portly chocolate Labrador noses Skelgill's jacket pocket for treats, though it will be disappointed; the interesting aroma emanates from a polythene bag that recently contained pilchards.

'She is in fine fettle, Daniel – and I never had you down as sufficiently tolerant to make a dog owner – you have proved me wrong.'

Skelgill, though mildly affronted by this barbed compliment, manages to grin affably.

'And how are you, Alice?'

'Justitia! Come away from the gentleman!' The woman rises with an alacrity that belies her years, and gives her dog a sharp tug on its leash. 'She is incorrigible, Daniel.' The woman produces a fistful of small treats, which has both dogs agitating for a dividend.

'May she have one?'

'Aye – no problem. Just count your fingers.'

He regards the woman as she administers kibbles to each of the dogs in turn, making them first sit obediently. She has a strong, clear voice and a manner that conjures the image of a retired headmistress, accustomed to getting her way. She is tall for a female – almost the same height as Skelgill – and her bearing noble. The backs of her hands have a gardener's tan, and beneath the broad brim of the hat the heavily lined skin of her face is weathered likewise; though vital pale blue eyes and regular features testify that she was once something of a beauty, perhaps an ingrained factor that drives her self-confidence.

'You've not lost your touch, Alice.'

She smiles sardonically.

'In the court, Daniel, I rarely encountered such willing subjects, so easily manipulated and so gratefully chastised.' She waves long fingers in the air. 'Midges wait for those who waver.'

She begins to move on and Skelgill, though inured to such low level no-see-um attacks, falls in alongside her, reversing the direction of his so far rather short excursion. He makes a little exclamation of discord.

'You were always a fair Judge, Alice. We knew we'd need our ducks in a row whenever you were sitting.'

She seems pleased by this admission, if a little straightening of her shoulders is anything to go by.

'I don't imagine you were always thrilled by my judgements.'

Skelgill shrugs.

'The law's the law – if you left it up to our lot we'd be building prisons like there's no tomorrow – and think what that would cost the taxpayer.'

'It is certainly an expensive road to go down, both short term and long.'

Skelgill's demeanour seems to take on a rather exaggerated casual air.

'Aye – mind you – I was down at Haresfell recently – now that place burns serious money – they were telling me there's five staff for each of the inmates.'

'Patients, Daniel.'

Skelgill starts – as if this phrase, or its homophone at least, is one with which he has been systematically chastised at some formative age – but then he realises she is correcting his terminology.

'Aye, of course – *patients* – what with you having been on the NHS Board.'

Alice Wright-Fotheringham was formerly a high-flying London barrister, the youngest of her generation to take silk. She had moved to Cumbria upon widowhood, to eke out the autumn years of her career, opting for the 'quiet life' of a County Court Judge. She became well known among the county set, and her profile and reputation led to several commissions such as that to which Skelgill refers. That the conversation has conveniently swung around to the 'coincidence' of Haresfell (not to mention Skelgill's appearance at this dog-walking location popular with certain local regulars) might lead the cynic to suggest that some connivance is afoot.

'It may be a drain on the public purse, Daniel, but I hear the current regime has made significant inroads into superfluous costs – for which I can assume a modicum of credit.'

'How's that, Alice?'

'It was during my term as Chair that the incumbent Director was engaged – there was a sub-committee responsible for the actual recruitment, naturally – but the appointment had to be ratified by the full Board.'

'That'd be Briony Boss. I met her. Not what I was expecting.'

Skelgill's tone seems to cast a question mark – at least sufficiently so for his acquaintance to offer a justification.

'She came with an almost unblemished track record – she had been second in command at Broadmoor, and had managed several metropolitan hospitals in the north-west of England – a very strong administrator, despite no clinical background to speak of.'

Skelgill nods and they continue in silence for a short while before he responds.

'When you say unblemished?'

Alice Wright-Fotheringham tuts at his whippersnapper's impertinence.

'Oh – there was a press report after the appointment – some idle gossip – that she was being transferred to Haresfell because there had been an affair with another member of staff.'

Skelgill makes an "it's the way of the world" gesture with his palms. Alice Wright-Fotheringham continues.

'In any event, by the time she took up the post I believe she was divorced. And now my grapevine informs me that sanity has been restored to an expenses regime that was running amok.' She turns to Skelgill and grins, perhaps a little sourly. 'If you will excuse my somewhat politically incorrect turn of phrase.'

They have reached the sprung kissing gate that admits walkers into the meadow from Lake Road. Skelgill steps to one side and pulls it open, although Cleopatra contrives to tangle with Justitia and he is obliged to bundle the four of them out together less gallantly than he had intended. As they untangle and the two humans each step back from one another, Skelgill jerks a thumb over his shoulder.

'My car's beside the slipway, Alice. I take it you've walked down from home?'

The woman touches the brim of her hat in a sign of affirmation.

'You should come here more often, Daniel – I believe our two pets get along swimmingly.'

Skelgill glances briefly across at the shoreline, as if he interprets this allusion literally. Cleopatra needs little encouragement to take to the water, and he has become concerned that before too long she will produce an untimely dive from his boat.

'Aye – it's a handy spot – do her good to meet other dogs.'

'And you to socialise with long-lost acquaintances.'

There is a glint in the woman's eye as she utters these words. Beneath the shadow of his hat, Skelgill's cheeks seem to assume a pinker hue. He forces a bashful grin and glances rather unnaturally at his watch.

'Aye, well – look after yourself, Alice.'

Cleopatra now finds some interest in the direction of Skelgill's car, and he allows her to pull him around and away; he flashes a resigned expression as though he is unable to restrain her sudden momentum. A mischievous smile creases Alice Wright-Fotheringham's lips. She calls out to him.

'And, Daniel – you could always invite me fishing.'

Skelgill has already extracted his phone from his pocket, and now he makes an instinctive ducking movement and holds up the handset to acknowledge the former QC's incisive parting shot. How does she know about that? However, he continues on his way and, composing himself, dials DS Leyton's mobile number. His sergeant answers promptly.

'Alright, Guv – when you coming in?'

Skelgill checks his wristwatch, properly this time.

'About two, I reckon – listen, Leyton – put a call in to Haresfell – see if we can get an interview with Frank Wamphray – the one who pretended to be the psychiatrist.'

'Righto, Guv – what – the safto, like?'

'As soon as.'

'Wilco.' DS Leyton falls silent, but Skelgill does not offer to sign off; he appears to be consumed by some sudden notion. 'Anything else, Guv?'

'Tell you what, Leyton – I'll assume it's on unless I hear otherwise – save me coming in – I'll meet you down at Tebay instead.' (Now it is DS Leyton who fails to respond – perhaps it is the prospect of yet another superfluous meal that troubles him.) 'Alright, Leyton?'

'Sound as a pound, Guv.'

*

'Cor blimey, Guv – I've been trying to raise you.'

DS Leyton has entered the cafeteria at something of a canter, and is blowing hard. Skelgill carelessly glances at his handset, which is lying on the formica table top beside an empty plate.

'It's gone and put itself on silent – does that all the time.'

DS Leyton pauses for breath, but his alarmed features reveal his state of mind. Skelgill kicks out a chair for him.

'Easy, Leyton – you'll give yourself a coronary.'

At this the poor sergeant looks even more disturbed; his eyes widen and he drops down heavily opposite his boss.

'That's just it, Guv – he's had a coronary.'

'Who?'

'Frank Wamphray – he's dead, Guv – passed away about midday.'

Skelgill digs at his front teeth with the nail of his little finger. Then he glares at his empty plate as though it has been raided and he is about to accuse DS Leyton of the deed.

'Wait there – I'm still hungry.'

When he returns a few minutes later he appears more composed. Whether this is due to the tray he bears with top-up rations, or because he has had time to digest the implications of DS Leyton's news, it is hard to discern. Rather cursorily he pushes a mug of tea and a side plate with a bacon roll before his subordinate.

'Get stuck in.'

He says it as though DS Leyton is in need of reviving. His sergeant is clearly not expecting the gesture.

'Oh, cheers, Guv – what do I owe you?'

'It's buckshee, Leyton – I've got a cousin works here now – staff discount.'

DS Leyton now hesitates and regards the offering with suspicion.

'That's a good discount, Guv.'

'Ask no questions, Leyton – you know me.'

DS Leyton looks like he thinks he probably doesn't, but he nods obediently. Skelgill continues.

'So, what's the griff on Wamphray?'

'I phoned, Guv – like you said.' He takes a gulp of tea and splutters, for Skelgill has procured it close to boiling point. 'They were a bit cagey, Guv – so I got myself put through to the Boss woman.'

'How did she sound?'

'Shocked to hear from us, Guv – as if she was wondering how come we knew he was dead. When she realised I was expecting to see him alive – she kind of relaxed and told me he'd been found in his room, lying on his bed – said he's had a dodgy ticker for a good few years – and what with the lack of exercise and being overweight – it was hardly unexpected.'

Skelgill is feeling the stubble on his chin and staring absently out of the window. His eyes are unmoving, indeed unfocused, and he is blind to the various movements of ducks and gulls and small humans that seem to compete in the shallows over scattered handfuls of bread.

'So I guess that's our trip off, Guv?'

Skelgill swings round, his eyes suddenly flaming.

'On the contrary, Leyton – all the more reason to go.' He swallows the contents of his mug, tilting back his head, and then rises and picks up his roll with a paper napkin. 'Your turn to drive, I believe. Always a handy place to leave a car, this.'

11. HARESFELL

'Is this some kind of formal investigation in relation to Frank Wamphray, Inspector?'

Briony Boss wears a not dissimilar outfit to that of the previous day; though if anything she shows a little more cleavage and an extra half inch of thigh as she reposes, legs crossed, opposite the detectives in the informal meeting area of her office. Skelgill gives a non-committal shake of his hands, rotating them simultaneously in mid air, at chest height. It is an action that draws a brief look of alarm from DS Leyton: could his superior's subconscious have hijacked his movements to reveal his inner desires?

'I wouldn't put it quite like that, madam.' Now Skelgill rocks forwards and clamps his hands onto his knees, as if he actually is trying to exert control over his extremities. 'There were a couple of points we'd omitted to ask your Head of Security,' (DS Leyton frowns at being used as a stooge in this white lie) 'and additionally I considered it might be useful to get the views of a cooperative patient who could perhaps shed some light on the suspected thefts. I was on my way down to Haresfell when I got the news about Mr Wamphray – so I asked Sergeant Leyton to rendezvous here anyway.'

This rather disjointed monologue does not sound especially convincing, though the Director seems to give Skelgill the benefit of any doubt, and patiently.

'Not that he can assist you any longer, Inspector – Frank Wamphray, that is.'

Skelgill sits back and folds his arms. His features have a resigned air, and he throws out his next question like a futile re-cast at the rise of a fish he has missed.

'Were you surprised by his sudden death?'

Briony Boss is composed. Of course, a twenty-year-plus career in the NHS means the passing of souls is a familiar experience, and the detectives know this – she is unlikely to vest her own emotions in the slings and arrows of outpatients' fortunes. Or inpatients', come to that. She looks calmly at Skelgill and makes a small adjustment to the lapels of her blouse.

'Inspector, as I mentioned to Sergeant Leyton, Frank Wamphray had a chronic condition – indeed he had suffered several minor heart attacks during the past few years. With such a medical history, it is rather a matter of when not if.'

'And he couldn't be saved?'

'I understand he was beyond resuscitation when he was discovered.' She watches Skelgill for a moment before she decides it is appropriate to elaborate. 'He was lying on his bed listening to music on headphones. There was no opportunity to summon assistance. I am assured by our doctors that nothing could have been done to circumvent the outcome.'

Skelgill remains pensive for some seconds. Then he seems to accept the situation, and falls back on his reserve.

'I reckon we'll just have a chat about the thefts to a few folk – bit of a random cross-section – see if we can come up with any theories that your internal security haven't considered.'

'Be my guest, Inspector.' She stands and smoothes her skirt over her thighs with a single and rather sensual downwards sweep of her palms. 'I shall put my PA at your disposal to make arrangements – however, do come back to me in person with any problems. I shall be here until late if you wish to have a more intimate discussion.'

*

'And you were first to examine him, sir?'

Dr Peter Pettigrew peers at Skelgill over the top of his reading glasses. He is seated at his desk in a well-appointed office, only marginally less spacious than that of the Director, and situated on the floor below. That Skelgill has reverted to the subject of Frank Wamphray is somewhat at odds with his parting commitment to Briony Boss – but it is with a renewed vigour that he poses the question. Its recipient, on the other hand, the senior psychiatrist, seems just a touch piqued by some insinuation (whether intended by Skelgill, or imagined by him, it is hard to judge which), though only for a split second does his accommodating façade threaten to crack. Then an affable grin exercises his pliable mouth.

'I am a fully qualified doctor – it is a pre-requisite for becoming a psychiatrist.'

Skelgill quickly raises an apologetic palm.

'Aye – of course, sir – that's exactly what I was thinking – you would be the ideal person – in the event that there were any unusual circumstances.'

Dr Pettigrew seems to be forming the opinion that these are policemen and they can't help it – and that he had better humour them.

'I think we can be pretty certain about the cause of death, Inspector. The cardiologist who examined the body is in complete agreement with my initial assessment. The signs of sudden cardiac arrest are highly distinctive.'

Skelgill nods. It is possible he is a little disappointed by this report.

'Were you treating him, sir?'

'I was directly responsible only for his anti-psychotic regime. We have an in-house clinical team that deals with what you might call everyday ailments and illnesses. Although Haresfell is not a medical hospital in the conventional sense, for reasons of security we obviously cannot be shipping patients up to Carlisle or Glasgow, or down to Manchester or Birmingham, every time they require the kind of hospital treatment that is offered to the general public.'

'Hence your cardiologist?'

'That is correct, Inspector. As you will probably have observed, there is something of a chronic obesity issue in institutions such as these – largely a function of the necessary medication – and with it comes an above-average level of coronary problems. We have to be fully equipped to deal with sudden cardiac episodes.'

Skelgill inhales and exhales, and allows his shoulders to droop.

'Seems a bit ironic, sir – to die in hospital – of something else, if you see what I mean.'

'Inspector, even in specialist high-dependency units, where patients are constantly monitored, deaths still occur. It is not always possible to resuscitate a person who has suffered a heart attack.'

'Do you think Frank Wamphray could have been saved?'

The man gives a regretful shrug.

'It is impossible to know, Inspector. By the time he was discovered it was too late – perhaps by thirty minutes.'

Skelgill seems to accept this fact without question.

'Was there anything that could have brought on the heart attack?'

Dr Peter Pettigrew glances briefly at a page of printed notes that lies on top of a file on his desk. Then he gazes again over the narrow spectacles.

'There is nothing that has been reported – his behaviour could be a little erratic – but he had been doing well in Assertive Rehab over the past few months – certainly no incidents that could be described as traumatic, or that might have required some form of physical intervention by staff. And when I saw him on my round this morning he was looking well and in his usual good spirits.'

The psychiatrist has been surprisingly tolerant during this off-agenda questioning, and Skelgill perhaps recognises he ought not push his luck. He turns and looks at DS Leyton, and holds out an introductory palm.

'My sergeant has been coordinating our inquiry into the suspected thefts – raised by your Director.' (DS Leyton looks a little uncomfortable; no doubt wondering with what task Skelgill is going to lumber him.) 'Frank Wamphray – his mental disturbance aside – seemed to have some knowledge of what you might call issues of security – that's why we were proposing to speak with him.' (Dr Pettigrew is nodding, if a little sceptically.) Skelgill consults his wristwatch. 'To make efficient use of our time – I'd like to leave Sergeant Leyton to ask you a few more general questions – while I pop off and interview a couple of other members of staff.'

*

'Pity you had to shoot off last night, man – we had a reet little stoppy-backy in the *Beck Foot.* How was your old ma?'

Skelgill seems to be caught off guard. He looks as though he is about to say, "Old ma?" – but then he remembers the gist of his excuse and nods decisively. 'Aye, she were fine – she just needs a hand with the stairs to get to bed.'

Nurse Arthur Kerr does not appear too interested in Skelgill's reply. Instead he has turned his attention to peeling open the wrapper of a biscuit that Skelgill has purchased, along with tea, from the snack bar in the foyer where previously Frank Wamphray had accosted the two detectives.

'You've not let the grass grow, man – did the penny drop after something I told you?'

Skelgill's features are unnaturally stiff.

'Aye – I have had one or two ideas – along the lines that delivery drivers might see this place as a bit of a soft touch.'

Arthur Kerr dunks the end of his chocolate bar into his mug and then bites off the melted portion. He swills it down with a mouthful of tea and smacks his lips. Then he makes a rather scornful exclamation of breath.

'More likely they're dropping stuff off at certain persons' private addresses.'

Skelgill raises an eyebrow with sufficient emphasis to convey to his companion that he acknowledges his subversive point of view. He leans forwards and lowers his voice.

'I'm surprised there's no hue and cry gone up over Frank Wamphray.'

Arthur Kerr returns Skelgill's inquiring gaze rather indifferently.

'*C'est la vie*, as they say.' Then he picks at a nostril in an unbecoming manner. 'Or, not, as the case may be.'

'Is it unusual for a patient to die?'

'Three or four a year. They get ill just like normal folk. Plus some are knocking on – the longest stay's forty years and counting.'

'What age was Frank Wamphray?'

'Sixty-two.'

'He looked in fair health yesterday.'

Arthur Kerr shrugs, but has nothing to add.

'What happened, Arthur – I take it you were around at the time?'

'I found him, man.'

'Must have been a shock?'

'I thought he were kipping. Sometimes they do after their medication.'

'How does that work?'

Arthur Kerr seems to assume that Skelgill means more than to explain the fact that drugs may cause drowsiness.

'He has – *had* – a regular dose at eleven. He said he'd been feeling a bit sick this morning, so I gave it as an injection – standard procedure – if they yack it up you don't know how much they've actually got in their system. Then you don't want to err on the light side, so you go a bit heavy and you end up knocking 'em out.'

'But that wasn't the case, obviously.'

'He got the pre-measured dose. He went back to his room like he usually does. I called to check on him about twelve – he were a goner.'

'And what about resuscitation?'

Arthur Kerr makes a face, as if his tea has become stewed.

'I called the RRT – rapid response team – but they took one look at him and shook their heads – he'd been dead too long. You've got a maximum of seven minutes – they reckoned it had been at least half an hour.'

Skelgill nods pensively.

'Not long after he went to his room.'

'Mebbes.'

'Could the medication have caused it – some sort of shock to his system?'

Arthur Kerr shrugs somewhat disinterestedly.

'You'd have to ask one of the quacks.'

'Such as Dr Pettigrew?'

'Aye.'

Skelgill pauses for thought. After a few moments he has a new question.

'Where does the medication come from?'

'The dispensary – no two patients are on exactly the same treatment – so they manage all the preparation and storage – and everything's signed out as it's used.'

'By the nurses?'

'Or the patients themselves – some of them are allowed to go directly to the counter and swallow it under observation there.'

Arthur Kerr seems to be getting a bit fed up. He checks the clock on the wall behind Skelgill and fidgets about in his seat.

'There's things I ought to be doing – if there's nothing on the so-called thefts.' He stares rather belligerently at Skelgill. 'As far as Frank Wamphray's concerned – you'd be better off talking to the powers that be.'

Skelgill nods grimly, as though he agrees with this suggestion, and that it indeed corresponds with his intentions. He pulls his rarely used notebook from inside his jacket. He flips it open and glances secretively at a blank page before snapping it closed.

'I've got an interview with Dr Agnetha Walker next. They said you'd be able to contact her on the internal system so I can meet her – my mobile's at Security.'

'Aye – no problem.'

A rather cynical smile threatens to break out across his mean mouth, though he rises and leads the way towards a swipe-card-operated door. Skelgill still has his notebook in his hand, and he waggles it as he waits alongside the nurse.

'I need to leave a message with the Director's PA – if you could take me there first.' (Arthur Kerr raises his eyebrows suspiciously, without looking at Skelgill.) 'For my sergeant, like.'

12. POLICE HQ

'I deduce an early start, Guv.'

DS Leyton, in sharp himself, has poked a speculative head around his superior's open office door. A line of empty plastic cups suggests a good hour-and-a-half of work has passed since Skelgill first arrived at his desk. His face is severe, and he has tired shadows beneath his eyes, though for once he forces a grin through his grumpy exterior.

'Sorry to abandon you last night, Leyton – thought I might as well take the chance of a bit of inside information – and a free lift to my car.' Skelgill taps some instructions into his computer and frowns at the screen. 'Plus it saved you from the temptation of Tebay.'

DS Leyton looks a tad miffed at this suggestion, and with good cause, given that it is his superior who continually insists upon opportunistic café stops. However, he suppresses any urge to point out what would be an unwelcome fact, and instead responds to Skelgill's former point.

'And did you get any, Guv?'

Skelgill shifts his gaze from the monitor to his sergeant's artless countenance. His eyes narrow and he bites on his lower lip before he replies.

'The Chief's agreed to call in the Coroner over the death of Frank Wamphray. They're doing an autopsy this morning.'

'Jeez, Guv.' DS Leyton takes an alarmed step into the office, but then reverses and disappears into the corridor. 'Just a tick, Guv.' He reappears a minute later with two machine teas, and slides one in front of Skelgill before taking his regular seat opposite his boss. 'That's serious, Guv. That's telling the hospital they don't know their own job.'

Skelgill, already drinking, raises his eyebrows unsympathetically.

'Like I say – the Chief's sanctioned it. Seems she's on hobnobbing terms with Briony Boss. Must have squared it.'

DS Leyton, seated, has his broad shoulders hunched and his head pulled in like a tortoise.

'They ain't gonna like it, Guv – that's us off their Christmas card list.'

Skelgill's rebellious expression softens.

'At the end of the day, Leyton, it's no big deal. It won't do them any harm to confirm the cause of death.'

'But, Guv – an autopsy – surely that implies suspicion?'

'Sudden death can be enough justification.'

DS Leyton's expression is dogged, as if he is working up courage in order to ask an awkward question.

'Did you mention to the Chief that Frank Wamphray had told us the staff were trying to poison patients – to get the top people fired?'

Now Skelgill scowls.

'Leyton – you're getting your knickers in a twist. It was Briony Boss that used the word *poisoning* – not Frank Wamphray – he just complained about the medication making them dozy.'

DS Leyton looks perplexed – but he bows to Skelgill's greater vehemence and scratches his head vigorously.

'I could have sworn he said something, Guv – at least, about causing bother for the management.'

'Aye, maybe – but it's one thing destabilising the place by nicking things – topping the patients would be a bit extreme. Even I've ruled that one out.'

DS Leyton appears a little pained – as though he has some vested interest in his theory.

'Thing is, Guv – it's the surest way to stir up a media storm – patients dying because of incompetence – system failure – that kind of stuff.'

Skelgill is shaking his head.

'Chance a murder charge to get your boss sacked, Leyton? It'd be a lot less risky to let an inmate abscond from a nature walk – hit the headlines and no one need die.'

'Until some poor hiker refuses to share his packed lunch, Guv.'

Skelgill appears to wave away this minor complication, but in fact a bluebottle is buzzing him. He watches it fly towards the window and crack against the pane. Surprisingly unstunned, it makes more futile attempts to escape. Skelgill rises and opens the ventilation light and shepherds it out. He stands still for a few moments, perhaps considering the weather. There has been a bright dawn but already high cirrus are creating a haze and heralding the next warm front. DS Leyton clears his throat to speak.

'But you're not ruling out foul play, Guv?'

Skelgill turns to face him, his expression neutral.

'Let's see what the autopsy says.'

But DS Leyton has not yet finished mining his vein of speculation.

'If it were, Guv – it could mean someone didn't want him to spill the beans – that he really knew something.'

Skelgill is not open to being swayed.

'He'd already spoken with us, Leyton – and plenty of folk saw that – it's probably even on camera.'

'They might have asked him what he'd said – found out it wasn't anything too serious yet.' (Now Skelgill has his back to Leyton and is examining his map of the Lake District that has pride of place on the wall behind his desk.) 'He could have threatened to blackmail them.' DS Leyton leans forwards in his chair, grimacing as his belt digs into his midriff. 'Whatever he was – a bit loopy – he wasn't stupid, Guv.'

Skelgill resumes his seat and inspects his cup forlornly. He adds it to his line-up of empties and then begins to insert one inside the other until he has a little tower.

'I'll say one thing, Leyton. It was Arthur Kerr who gave him the injection.' Then he tosses the stack into the waste bin beside his sergeant, causing him to flinch. 'And I did notice that when I first spoke with him about Frank Wamphray he never mentioned he was his primary nurse.'

'Guv – where are you?'

Skelgill lowers his mobile and surveys his surroundings. On the shop wall in front of him is a stirring display of fishing rods, though he appears less moved by the price ticket he twiddles between the fingers of his left hand. With his right, he raises the phone.

'In the library – in Penrith – I wanted to check out some medical point.'

DS Leyton hesitates, then inhales and speaks.

'You might not need to, Guv – the autopsy report's just come through – I've got it on the screen now.'

'What does it say?'

'It was a heart attack, right enough – sudden cardiac arrest caused by an excess of adrenaline in the bloodstream – that's natural ain't it, Guv?'

Skelgill has lowered the handset and is again staring at the array of carbon fibre shafts regimented before his eyes – but now it is clear his thoughts are focused elsewhere. DS Leyton's plaintive squeak comes faintly from his side, like a *Borrower* stranded in his pocket. After a few moments he turns and strides out of the shop, and then remembers he is mid-conversation.

'I'll meet you out the back in five minutes, Leyton – bring us a roll and a drink from the canteen, will you.'

DS Leyton makes a sound like a strangled groan.

'Righto, Guv – where are we going?'

Skelgill looks baffled, and does not reply immediately. Then he realises he must enlighten his sergeant and barks an abrupt "Haresfell" and terminates the call. It takes him just a couple of minutes to stride to his car, parked in a supermarket lot, and the same again to stretch the local speed limits and reach Police HQ, where he drives around to the rear of the building. As he slews to a halt DI Smart and DS Jones emerge from the staff entrance; they appear to be sharing some joke. DS Jones carries a neat designer holdall, which Skelgill recognises as her overnight luggage. They stop a few yards from his car, and he winds down the window. At this moment DS Leyton materialises, brown paper bag in hand, and ambles up to make a little group. DS Jones acknowledges him with a smile, and then turns the same upon Skelgill. DI Smart's countenance, meanwhile, bears more of a gloating sneer.

'You've caught us red-handed, Skel – making a break for the big city.' He throws his thin, bony hands up in a gesture of liberation and gazes heavenwards. 'Civilisation!'

Skelgill cannot prevent a disapproving frown from descending upon his brow. He ignores DI Smart and stares at DS Jones.

'How long are you away for?'

'Just until Friday, Guv.'

Her choice of words, avoiding mention of "two nights", and the way in which she slowly and rather surreptitiously tilts her bag from sight behind her legs, only conspire to highlight the obvious facts. Her smile dissolves beneath the weight of Skelgill's glare, and she glances nervously at DI Smart. He has no such difficulty, and invokes a double-edged jibe.

'Don't fret, Skel – if you're worried about her beauty sleep – I don't intend to keep her out late.'

Again Skelgill declines to give DI Smart more than a cursory glance. He addresses DS Jones.

'Keep your phone switched on – something's just come up on the Haresfell case – I might need you in a hurry.'

DS Jones nods, though with the smallest movement possible, as if she is trying to conceal it from DI Smart beside her. Skelgill revs his engine and rocks the car on the clutch. He indicates with a jerk of the thumb that DS Leyton should climb in. Meanwhile DI Smart is leering disparagingly at the mud-encrusted shooting brake with its mackled modifications.

'Skel, if you're heading south I'll race you to Tebay.' He cackles disparagingly. 'Give you a five-minute start, eh?'

Skelgill flicks a parting glance at DS Jones and screeches away, causing the still-open passenger door to slam and an unbelted DS Leyton to flounder and flail in an effort not to scald himself beneath Skelgill's hot beverage.

'Crikey, Guv – you're not seriously racing him?'

Skelgill is scowling angrily.

'Leyton, I'm not even going down the motorway – but let him think we did – we just need to reach the A6 turn before he sees us.'

DS Leyton nods emphatically. He is sympathetic to his boss's sensibilities when it comes to DI Smart. 'I thought you weren't too fussed about DS Jones doing that Manchester jaunt, Guv – it was her that didn't seem too keen on it.'

Skelgill does not offer an opinion either way, on either of these points of view. Instead he concentrates on the job of getting his car off the A66 and out of sight over the hump of the Eamont bridge.

13. HARESFELL

'The concentration of epinephrine in Frank Wamphray's blood was consistent with a dose injected for the purposes of attempted resuscitation – epinephrine being more colloquially known as adrenaline.'

Dr Peter Pettigrew is holding court in the office of Briony Boss, Director of Haresfell. He sits alongside her, while Skelgill and DS Leyton face them across the coffee table. As he adds this footnote, he turns pointedly to his senior colleague.

'I'm perfectly aware of what epinephrine is, Doctor.'

The Director's prickly response hints at some tension in their relationship. Indeed this is already evident from her body language. She has seated herself well apart from Dr Peter Pettigrew, her legs crossed away and her arms folded. (Today she wears her trademark tailored skirt, while her blouse is a sleeveless affair that is partially see-through.) It must strike the detectives as salient that she refers to the man by his title, when it is clear they have a long-standing working relationship. DS Leyton perhaps recognises this tension, and its potential as an unproductive force in their discussion, and blurts out a typically self-deprecating yet intuitively diplomatic retort.

'Colloquial's alright by me, squire.'

Doctor Peter Pettigrew flashes him a look of surprise – though his own origins are probably quite humble, a growing weight of qualifications has brought a certain formality and sense of decorum upon his shoulders – and he is no doubt unaccustomed to being referred to as 'squire' by a police officer. DS Leyton makes a series of confused hand gestures by way of excusing himself, and this seems to provide the necessary stimulus for the psychiatrist to press on. He adjusts his reading glasses and bends over his notes.

'However – there is no record that any member of staff – let alone the RRT – administered such a dose.' He looks up and glances around briefly. 'Our stocks of epinephrine are one hundred per cent accounted for. There is no obvious indication on Frank Wamphray's body that he received such an injection.' (Skelgill starts, and leans forwards to speak – but the doctor continues.) 'The only puncture mark relates to an injection of anti-psychotic medicine given by the primary nurse at eleven a.m.' (Skelgill now visibly relaxes – this was evidently going to be his point.) 'The syringe was disposed of according to the sharps procedure and had already been collected for destruction – but we have traced the empty vial.' He pauses and licks his rubbery lips. Then he looks around the table, his dark eyebrows coming together like a pair of hairy caterpillars meeting head-on upon a twig. 'We have been able to establish that the vial was contaminated with epinephrine.'

There is silence. Then the Director speaks.

'Contaminated seems to be putting it mildly.'

It is hard to divine Briony Boss's stance – both her voice and features are even, and her hands with fingers interlocked clasp her uppermost knee. Perhaps she sits on the fence that divides alarm from anger until she fully understands the situation: to assume responsibility or assign blame? The outcome no doubt could have serious implications for Dr Peter Pettigrew, but for the time being he plays the role of expert witness, a neutral actor in the drama.

'How could that happen, Doctor?'

This is Skelgill, homing in on the crux.

Dr Peter Pettigrew takes off his spectacles and leans back against the sofa. His manner is unpatronising – and he seems genuinely puzzled as he begins to address the question.

'A central dispensary prepares the patients' prescriptions. Because of the numbers we operate on a system of a small buffer stock, two-to-three days' supply.' He glances briefly at Briony Boss. 'And, by the way, we've quarantined all existing stocks and introduced double-checking until we get to the bottom of this mistake. Then when batches are ready we –'

'Hold on, sir – if you don't mind.' Skelgill has raised a hand. 'You say *mistake* – but if none of your adrenaline is missing – how could this be a mistake?'

Now Dr Peter Pettigrew does for the first time look pained, as though a more sinister alternative is not something he can contemplate – despite the obvious conclusion that can be reached from the very facts he has so far supplied.

'It has to be a mistake, Inspector – it just doesn't make sense otherwise.'

He looks rather imploringly at the detectives, and then at Briony Boss – but the antipathy in her expression does not bode well for him. Skelgill appears more equivocal, and presses on in a logical manner.

'The vial you mention – it was the correct one?'

'It was, yes. Labelled with the intended contents and Frank Wamphray's patient number.'

'So it had the wrong stuff in it.'

'It appears epinephrine – adrenaline – was somehow introduced.'

'By the dispensing chemist?'

The doctor shakes his head decisively.

'Not knowingly – the young lady in question is dismayed – we have sent her home with a colleague.'

Skelgill makes a sweeping gesture with one hand.

'But what I'm saying is, given you've not had patients dropping like flies, it was a single vial that was tampered with – not some whole batch of medicine you've had delivered.'

The doctor nods reluctantly, though the word *tampered* clearly troubles him. Briony Boss is seated directly opposite Skelgill and watches him closely. He continues.

'So, somewhere between the medicine being made up, and the injection being given, it became contaminated. Who else could have had access to it?'

Again Dr Peter Pettigrew glances rather apprehensively at Briony Boss – but her attention remains focused upon Skelgill, and she leaves the psychiatrist to field the question himself.

'It would have been taken to the local dispensary on the ward – we have a team responsible for the secure transfer of medicines about the hospital. There it is stored under locked conditions – both the room itself, which has a kind of service counter, and a secure chiller cabinet. Senior hospital staff like myself have keys, and other medical staff such as nurses are allowed appropriate access during their shifts. There will always be a duty manager with keys, and the duty head of the RRT – in case of an emergency.'

Skelgill looks pointedly at DS Leyton, who suddenly realises he ought to be taking notes, and with a jolt begins to scribble frantically. Skelgill waits for a few moments in order for him to catch up.

'That's beginning to sound like a lot of folk.'

The doctor inhales somewhat heavily.

'In the entire hospital it could be as many as thirty people – but in the vast majority of instances there would be two or more qualified professionals present.'

Skelgill looks doubtingly. Being qualified would not seem to lift suspicion.

'Under normal circumstances, who would handle the vial?'

'Once it was transferred to the ward area, only the local dispenser – and in the case of an injection she would hand it directly to the nursing team. Naturally I have spoken personally to the staff involved, and none of them noticed anything unusual about the packaging – they are of course trained to report the slightest fault and take no risks.'

Skelgill now affects a more casual air.

'Doctor, what are your views about the medicine having been administered by injection instead of the more normal method?'

Both Dr Peter Pettigrew and Briony Boss show some reaction to this question – just small movements, perhaps a nervous twitch in the case of the doctor, and a heightened alertness about the Director's demeanour.

'He would not have died if he had taken it orally.'

There is a moment's silence. It seems the doctor needs to be prompted in order to elaborate.

112

'Why not?'

'Because epinephrine rapidly degrades in the gastro-intestinal tract and is not absorbed at all – it must be injected directly into the bloodstream.'

More silence prevails while the detectives, at least, strive to understand the possible implications of this striking fact. The corollary if Frank Wamphray had not been feeling ill – or at least had not feigned illness – is that he would still be alive.

'Who would know that?'

Skelgill looks like he is hoping for a condensed list of names, but he is to be disappointed.

'All clinical staff from a nurse upwards, Inspector – it is a basic property of the compound – that is why the *EpiPen* injects.'

Skelgill ponders. Then, as he speaks, he looks at each of the senior managers in turn.

'Are you aware of anyone who might have held some sort of grudge against Frank Wamphray?'

They shake their heads in unison, and Dr Peter Pettigrew looks to his superior – but again she seems content to let him answer.

'Frankly – if I may use that term, Inspector – he was probably the most popular patient on the ward – a one-man entertainment committee. It's hard to imagine anyone would wish harm upon him.'

Skelgill nods.

'And the nurse who gave the injection – how has he reacted to what has happened?'

Dr Peter Pettigrew leans forwards and rests his forearms on his thighs. He seems more purposeful now.

'His name is Arthur Kerr – I understand you may have spoken to him as part of your other investigation. He is one of our more experienced nurses – and a tough character – there isn't much he has not had to deal with. He is upset, but I would say he does not want to show it. Naturally he is disturbed that he has unwittingly administered what has proved to be a fatal dose.'

'Unwittingly.' Skelgill says this rather severely – but it is clear to all that he has good reason to make such a remark. 'If you were looking for a culprit, wouldn't he be the first person you'd turn to – from a practical angle?'

The Director remains impassive, but Doctor Peter Pettigrew if anything rows back from this prospect, and sits upright and folds his arms. It seems he is still unwilling to contemplate the idea that there could be a 'culprit' in this incident, let alone point the finger at a particular individual. Rather than agree with Skelgill's hypothesis, he stalls with a question of his own.

'But what makes you say that, Inspector? The medicine was available for the best part of two days – albeit under lock and key.'

Skelgill shrugs rather nonchalantly.

'I'm just going by the fact that the poison – let's call it that, for the sake of argument – as you say, wouldn't have worked unless it was injected. That was an on-the-spot decision – made by Arthur Kerr.'

No one offers to dispute this rationale, so Skelgill continues.

'Unless you discover that all of the vials earmarked for Frank Wamphray are contaminated in the same way – just waiting for the possibility of an injection – doesn't it suggest that the adrenaline was added immediately prior to injection?'

Dr Peter Pettigrew now gives Briony Boss a prolonged look, as if he is waiting for her to sanction this line of reasoning. She briefly returns his gaze and then, without speaking rises to her feet and walks around to her desk, her progress monitored by Skelgill and DS Leyton, who face that way. She leans over and makes a couple of clicks on her computer. Her hair falls in a partial veil, and she draws it one-handed from her heavily made-up eyes. She gazes unblinking at the screen. After a few moments she rises and looks to her audience.

'The preliminary test results are through. There is no trace of contamination in any of the other vials stored for use on Coniston Ward. That is the name of the Assertive Rehab ward on which Frank Wamphray was being treated.'

Skelgill might feel entitled to gloat – given that this information supports his theory. However, he merely glances a little self-importantly at his wristwatch; the time is approaching six p.m.

'We'll have to go through the process of identifying and interviewing everyone who might have had contact with the vial. Sergeant Leyton will get a couple of DCs down to help with that task. Realistically that's going to be tomorrow. We'll also need to see what our own boffins come up with in terms of the scientific aspects. These samples have to be isolated and tested independently.'

Dr Peter Pettigrew is nodding.

'I have the vial securely wrapped and refrigerated. It can be handed over as soon as you require.'

Briony Boss now perches against the edge of her desk, and slides one leg across in front of the other.

'Of course, Inspector – we are entirely at your disposal. Perhaps I can personally show you the dispensaries and the journey the medication would take.'

Skelgill returns her gaze reflectively, but then he directs his attention upon Dr Peter Pettigrew.

'You mentioned you were first to examine the body, sir.' (The doctor nods uneasily.) 'Was it you that certified the death – or did that fall to another doctor?'

'No – or, rather, yes – it was I that signed the certificate.'

Skelgill regards the man evenly.

'We shall need to get a formal account from you, sir – but that can wait.' (The doctor does not appear entirely happy at this prospect, though he nods now in a more coordinated fashion.) 'I'd like Sergeant Leyton to speak with Arthur Kerr right away, while events are still fresh in his mind. I take it he's still on shift?'

Dr Peter Pettigrew appears uncertain – but the Director intervenes.

'We gave him the option to go home early, but he was determined to keep calm and carry on. As Doctor Pettigrew mentioned, he is a seasoned nurse and is capable of knowing his own feelings in such a situation.'

Dr Peter Pettigrew rises – he seems keen to do so. He holds out a hand in the direction of DS Leyton.

'Sergeant, I can take you down – it will save calling for a member of staff to guide you through the various security points.'

DS Leyton glances at Skelgill, who gives him an affirmative nod. DS Leyton falls in with the psychiatrist and Skelgill watches as together they exit Briony Boss's office suite. He is still seated in his original position on the settee, but now his attention is captured by the clink of glasses as the Director moves in beside him bearing a small round tray that she has procured from a cabinet. There is a clear bottle that looks like mineral water, but as she sets it down and sits beside him he sees that it is in fact vodka, and the glasses contain ice cubes.

'It has been quite a day, Inspector – I feel we should take a few moments to relax before I must change my outfit for our little tour.'

'I take it that's not to mask the taste of adrenaline?'

She chuckles throatily.

'You just heard the expert, Inspector, it does no harm ingested orally.'

Skelgill raises a wry eyebrow.

'I reckon I'll take a chance.'

She shuffles a little closer to him.

'I believe you are aware I spoke with your senior officer. It seems you have a reputation for rolling the dice – and thereby achieving results.' She raises her glass and smiles across a bare shoulder. 'And since my PA has left us alone for the evening, I shall require some competent assistance with the buttons of my skirt.'

116

14. THE SIREN

'Guv, I didn't realise you knew that Geordie nurse, Arthur Kerr.'

'Who says I know him?'

'He did, Guv – says he's seen you drinking in his neck of the woods. I told him I reckoned you'd have been fishing – the River Lune, ain't it?'

Skelgill does not answer immediately. He must wonder what is Arthur Kerr's game, dropping hints to DS Leyton that he knows will get back to him. Another bung, perhaps? He glares out of the passenger window of DS Leyton's car. Through light rain and trees he can see glimpses of the river to which his sergeant refers. It is Thursday morning and they are en route to Haresfell. He shakes his head, and then involuntarily bangs a fist on the dashboard, rather like a sleeper who strikes out at an unpleasant image in a dream. DS Leyton visibly starts.

'Guv?'

'Aye – the Lune, aye. Good for sea trout, especially at night on the worm.'

'That'd be it then, Guv.'

Skelgill remains tight-lipped, watching the scenery flash by.

'How was he?'

'The Kerr geezer, Guv?'

'Aye. And he's a Mackem, not a Geordie.'

DS Leyton purses his lips – but evidently opts not to pursue this new question of provenance, the raising of which by Skelgill would appear to contradict his opening denial.

'Well, Guv – you might say, considering he'd not long killed a patient – he was surprisingly chipper. Seemed more annoyed than anything. Reckons he's the fall guy for someone else's cock-up. And then again – he was half triumphant about it, Guv.'

'Triumphant?'

'Like as if to say the hospital deserved this to happen. He ain't his employers' number one fan.'

Skelgill does not appear surprised.

'Don't suppose he had any kind words for Frank Wamphray?'

'He said he'd learned a long time ago not to get emotionally involved with the inmates – patients, I mean. Reckons they're highly manipulative – quick to take advantage.'

Skelgill grimaces.

'Sounds like where I work.'

'Right enough, Guv.'

'What about the contamination of the medicine?'

'Must have been the only thing he didn't have an opinion on, Guv.'

'What, nothing?' Skelgill sounds a little exasperated by this suggestion.

'Dunno, Guv – maybe he does, maybe he doesn't. But he weren't in a hurry to speculate.' DS Leyton shrugs his arms as he threads the car through a series of s-bends. 'I'd say he's a hard case, though – if you'd told me he'd done it, I'd believe you.'

Skelgill becomes pensive for a while.

'How about Pettigrew – did he let anything slip once he was out of the Director's earshot?'

DS Leyton twists his prominent lips and eyebrows into a curious expression of concentration. (This gesture proves rather ironic, given his reply.)

'Know who he reminds me of, Guv?'

'No, Leyton.' Skelgill dislikes any such guessing games. His tone is curt. 'Winston Churchill.'

'Nah, Guv – that there *Mr Bean* geezer, off the telly – well, films or whatever. He's a dead ringer, Guv.'

Skelgill casts a disparaging sideways glance at his sergeant.

'And your point is?'

'Not as daft as he looks, Guv – you could hide a lot of badness behind a face like that – and no one would be the wiser.'

Skelgill is frowning. Whether he disagrees with his sergeant, or this rather naïve assessment has in fact struck some sort of chord, it is impossible to tell.

'Did he say anything specific?'

DS Leyton shakes his head.

'Not really, Guv. At a guess he was relieved to get out of the meeting. I suppose it's his head on the block – as the top medical man, like.'

'Comes with the territory, Leyton.'

'Actually, Guv, he seems a decent bloke to me – offered to get me a scone and a coffee on his account.'

Skelgill appears interested by this revelation.

'Did you take him up on it?'

'Not likely, Guv – what if he's the poisoner?'

Skelgill shakes his head sadly, as if such a fickle concern should not be allowed to get in the way of a free snack. Notwithstanding, he seems to ponder something his sergeant has said, and there is a period of hush as they wind through the lanes south of Tebay village. The route is becoming familiar, and DS Leyton drives skilfully – though a flock of Rough Fells grazing the verge beyond a rise might pose a challenge to his reflexes. Eventually, it is he that breaks the silence.

'Think Frank Wamphray was deliberately targeted, Guv?'

Skelgill sits tight-lipped for a good half a minute. Eventually DS Leyton steals a brief glance across at him.

'You know what, Leyton?' But Skelgill does not wait for a reply. 'They've got Meredith Bale in that hospital – on the same mixed ward as they had Frank Wamphray.'

'That's right, Guv.'

Skelgill delays his next sentence, as if he is choosing his words carefully.

'Remember that report on her, the one the idle Manchester crew sent up – that you were supposed to read?'

DS Leyton begins to protest – but Skelgill silences him with an authoritatively raised palm.

'I know the contents – Dr Walker kindly filled me in on the details.'

DS Leyton's expression grows increasingly concerned.

'What are you saying, Guv?'

Skelgill turns to stare almost savagely at his sergeant, who senses the discontent (if not its justification) and affects to concentrate hard upon the road ahead.

'I'm saying that Frank Wamphray's cause of death matches Meredith Bale's MO – and no one has mentioned the fact. Not a single person – not even as a throwaway remark.'

Skelgill sinks back into his seat, glowering. He folds his arms and another silence descends. Perhaps DS Leyton finds this hiatus uncomfortable – or is simply unable to suppress the machinations of his thoughts – for he produces a somewhat unexpected retort.

'Mr Bean did, Guv – at least, when we first went in, remember? About her being Britain's most prolific serial killer, or something like that?'

Skelgill's features remain stern, though his tone betrays a hint of amusement.

'You better watch what you call him, Leyton – else you'll be saying it to his face next. Then he will come gunning for you with his needle.'

DS Leyton seems disturbed by this prospect, but he gathers his features into a mask of determination and grips the steering wheel more vigorously, wrestling the car into a tight z-bend, where the road narrows and the proximity of the nearside dry stone wall has Skelgill flinching.

'But how could she have done it, Guv?'

Skelgill exhales, perhaps with relief that they have emerged intact from the unforgiving chicane.

'She couldn't.' His reply is decisive. 'Last night, Briony Boss took me from the main dispensary to the ward. The person who filled all the vials on Sunday was a trainee – post-graduate, mind – under the constant supervision of a fully qualified pharmacist. Then a pair of security guys transported the batch to the ward dispensary, taking a route bristling with CCTV. Two staff checked it in and locked it in the cabinet. It was signed out on Tuesday by one of the dispensers and a ward nurse, who handed it to the primary nurse, Arthur Kerr. They were both present when he gave Frank Wamphray the injection in a treatment room off the ward.'

'So, if it weren't some freak accident, Guv – accidental contamination – it must have been tampered with while it was locked up?'

Skelgill seems reluctant to endorse this logical conclusion. Already he has highlighted the difficulty inherent in knowing the medication would not be taken orally by the patient. However, with some reluctance he indicates his acceptance.

'Aye – it's possible.'

'So, Guv – Meredith Bale – if she didn't actually do it – are you thinking she had some hand in it?'

Skelgill seems even more resistant to this proposition.

'Like, how, Leyton?'

DS Leyton clearly has some theory in mind – though he procrastinates with a series of facial contortions.

'When Frank Wamphray was pretending to be the psychiatrist – giving us the low-down on the escape tunnel and whatnot?'

'Aye?' Skelgill sounds like he is anticipating reprise of the ramblings of a certified lunatic.

'He said it's easy enough to bribe a member of staff.'

At this point Skelgill appears to lose interest. He begins craning out of the side window to inspect the sky above the fells. But DS Leyton soldiers on.

'Who's to know if a patient's got a bank account, Guv – especially if it's in a false name? Then with a mobile phone – Bob's your uncle.'

Skelgill is scowling.

'So what? We interrogate all Haresfell staff's bank accounts – in case a juicy bounty payment's made this week? How many are there – eight hundred plus?'

DS Leyton looks a little crestfallen. He shakes his head forlornly.

'Trouble is, Guv – an accomplice would probably have a secret account as well.'

Skelgill casts out a hand, in a gesture of "there you go" – as if his subordinate is now seeing sense. However, DS Leyton's mind is clearly dogged by this notion, and he must unburden at least one more aspect.

'Guv – we know full well that jailbirds pull strings from inside regular prisons – so why should Haresfell be any different? It only takes one bent member of staff – and, like you say, look how many there are to choose from.'

Skelgill's continued scepticism could be construed as unreasonable – given his own clandestine experience with Arthur Kerr. He does not reply – but DS Leyton continues in a manner that attempts to rally his superior's support.

'I mean, Guv – now you point it out – Meredith Bale's MO – the more I think of it – the more it seems like one heck of a coincidence.'

Skelgill remains determinedly pensive. After a while he presses his shoulders back into the passenger seat and stretches out his arms, yawning extravagantly.

'If you ask me, Leyton, what's more of a coincidence is it happening right under our noses.'

He does not elaborate upon this somewhat cryptic statement, and instead closes his eyes. It could be imagined that he is sleeping, but after a few moments – without opening them – he speaks again.

'What time do your DC's arrive?'

'Ten-thirty, Guv. Briony Boss's PA has allocated us an interview room right next to that coffee bar.' He glances at his superior to see if this arrangement meets his approval – and sure enough there appears to be a favourable facial twitch. 'I thought we'd need time to get our feet under the table – get a cuppa.'

'What are you going to tell them?'

Skelgill is still conducting the conversation from behind closed lids. DS Leyton appears disconcerted, having assumed his superior will brief the detective constables. He glances at Skelgill – and seeing his eyes still shut he pulls a distressed face and with one hand picks at the hair on the top of his head, in a passable silent impression of Stan Laurel. When he looks back, however, Skelgill is regarding him quizzically.

'Er – right, Guv – what I thought was – er, CCTV.'

'Aye?' Skelgill's tone hangs heavy with cynicism.

'Yeah, Guv – there's cameras in the lobby area that cover the Coniston Ward dispensary – I figure we could identify everyone who went inside – Tuesday morning – and maybe Monday night – right through the night, even.'

It is hard to tell if DS Leyton is making this up on the hoof – certainly he sounds a little unrehearsed – but it seems to do the trick, and Skelgill's reply suggests the proposal is acceptable.

'We'd need one of their staff, Leyton – our boys are not going to recognise anyone.'

'I thought if we narrowed it down, Guv – noted all the times on the tape – then we can borrow someone for an hour to do all the IDs – someone reliable.' He casts an apprehensive sideways glance at Skelgill. 'I thought you might be able to pull a favour with the Director.'

Skelgill's peeved expression hints at irritation with his sergeant's presumption – rather than an objection to the practicality of the idea. His reply sounds grudging.

'Aye, maybe. What else?'

'Well – like you said yesterday, Guv – get the lads to interview everyone involved in the preparation and transfer of the medicine. And I thought maybe we should talk to Security – Eric Blacklock and his team that operates the x-ray machines and body-scanners – see what they reckon about the drug being smuggled in.'

Skelgill does not respond immediately to this latter suggestion. As a man who likes to know best, he is perhaps a little torn that his sergeant appears to have come up with a sound plan. Thus it must fall to him to act as devil's advocate.

'Leyton – that would be child's play.'

'I know that, Guv – I realise it's just a few drops of liquid in a little plastic bottle – shove it where the sun don't shine – who's going to find that?'

Skelgill, however, finds an objection.

'Leyton – let's just put us off our breakfasts, shall we?'

That they have already patronised Tebay services does not deter Skelgill from making this statement. No doubt he has already incorporated into their schedule a visit to the handily placed coffee bar.

'Sorry, Guv – but you know what I mean – I agree it could be a doddle – but they might just have noticed something – someone acting different to normal – looking nervous or suspicious.'

'Or walking with a limp.'

Though Skelgill says this sardonically his sergeant appreciates that the joke accommodates his hypothesis. He chuckles, and evidently feels sufficiently reassured to pose a significant question of his own.

'Reckon we should interview her, Guv?'

'*Her* being?'

'Meredith Bale, Guv.'

This proposal does provoke a reaction from Skelgill. He draws a sudden breath, and holds it for several seconds before exhaling with a long hiss through his nostrils, like a reformed smoker who has not yet shed the automatous habit.

'She'd love that.'

'How do you mean, Guv?'

'Let's just pretend for a minute she's involved – think how she'd be gloating, watching us floundering around – the fact that we were interviewing her would tell her we hadn't got a shred of evidence to go on.'

DS Leyton ponders this scenario.

'So you think not, eh, Guv?'

Skelgill shakes his head – meaning he concurs with this view.

'But not for that reason.'

Now DS Leyton waits to see if Skelgill will elaborate upon his analysis, but it seems he is keeping whatever cards he might hold close to his chest. (Unless he deems it so obvious to his sergeant that it does not merit explanation.) After a few moments, DS Leyton proffers a supporting observation.

'I suppose the thing is, Guv – if it were her – what's the worst we can do?' He laughs a little hysterically. 'Stick her in a high-security mental hospital?'

'Stop, Leyton!'

DS Leyton does as he is bid, swerving the car onto the verge and grinding to a bumpy halt.

'What is it, Guv?' His eyes are wide and he looks to Skelgill as though he must have experienced a brainwave. But Skelgill is unruffled and appears bemused by his sergeant's agitation.

'The Lune, Leyton.' Skelgill gestures to the bridge ahead of them. 'I want another gander. We're down here so often I may as well get a permit. Especially with sea trout running at the moment.'

DS Leyton grins but fails to conceal a certain degree of exasperation. Dutifully, however, he exits the car and trails his superior to the centre of the bridge. Like on their last stopover the water is high, streaming from the fells and hastening to the coast. Skelgill, as always in these situations, seems immediately entranced. He appears to engage a sixth sense to the exclusion of his other five. The rain has abated, and there is just the hint of drizzle in the air. The temperature is mild, and the conditions not unpleasant. After a minute or two DS Leyton clears his throat as a warning that he wishes to interrupt his superior's contemplation.

'Since it's a river, Guv – why do you call 'em *sea* trout?'

Skelgill, bent over with arms resting upon the parapet, turns sharply to his colleague.

'They're anadromous, Leyton – like salmon. They come into fresh water to breed. Same species as the Brownie otherwise. Bigger, though – we call them *Mort* in Cumbria, you know.'

DS Leyton looks a little flattered that Skelgill has honoured him with this explanation without resorting to his patronising lecturer's tone.

'And do they eat any better, Guv? I always reckon trout taste like spuds you ain't washed properly.'

Skelgill shakes his head stoically.

'Old boy I used to fish with, he had a saying, *"You can tek trout out t'river, but yer kernt tek t'river out of trout."* So you might be disappointed, Leyton.'

DS Leyton puffs out his fleshy jowls and joins Skelgill in gazing into the mesmeric flow of the Lune. It seems not to occur to him that this maxim does not hold good with the salmon, which shares the 'anadromous' habits of the sea trout. However, if there are any such creatures passing beneath them, working their way upstream, today is not the day for fish spotting, since the Lune is coloured by the peat and silt it carries oceanwards, and its sliding surface reflects the impenetrable grey of the skies above.

The detectives watch in silence, lulled by the sensation of false movement, like train travellers captivated by the blur of the embankment, reluctant to prise themselves from their places and collect their bags in preparation for a stop and the stresses it will bring. Until – at least as far as DS Leyton is concerned – the concentration is broken. As a curious sound begins to reach their ears, he raises his head and stares with no little trepidation in the direction of Haresfell's security fence, looming indistinct and ominous in the mist.

'What's that, Guv?'

Skelgill takes no notice for a few moments, detained by the climax of some scene in his daydream. But the unearthly noise winds up in volume – almost literally so – for it is the yowl of a klaxon – indeed of several such devices that must be set apart so that they create an unsynchronised stereophonic effect. The initial start-up wail settles into a rhythmical two-tone signal, like an ambulance or fire engine without any Doppler effect, although many times more powerful.

'Sounds like the war, Guv.'

Skelgill pushes himself upright from his position bent over the water. He looks displeased by the interruption.

'It's the weekly test – I've heard it before – we did a mountain rescue exercise down here a couple of years back.'

'It's one heck of a racket, Guv – how long does it last?'

Skelgill pulls a knowledgeable face, though the seasoned observer might suspect some improvisation coming on.

'Two minutes like it is now, the escape alarm – then they sound the all-clear – a continuous tone, for another two minutes.' He looks at his wristwatch. 'Come on, Leyton, no point getting our lugs panned in by this racket.'

They retreat to DS Leyton's car. He seems unnerved by the siren, and is in no hurry to drive the last stretch – a loop behind a ridge of high ground that defeats any view of Haresfell until the last moment when they swing around and the main gates come into sight.

'Cor blimey, Guv.'

The apprehensive note in DS Leyton's exclamation owes itself to the vision that greets them. Whereas a single operator normally mans the outer barrier, now a dozen black-clad security staff mill about the gatehouse, dressed for action like paramilitaries in shin-high boots and bulging anti-stab vests. They are called in by a senior officer and form a huddle ready for briefing.

DS Leyton noses the car up against the barrier and lowers the passenger window. Immediately the two detectives are hit by the intense sound that fills the air – still blaring out, a good ten minutes after starting up, is the sinister two-tone escape alarm.

15. ESCAPE

'He is called Harry Krille.'

There is no need for Briony Boss to elaborate. It might have been over thirty years ago that this name hit the headlines – when Skelgill and DS Leyton were running around in short trousers – but its mention still sends a chill down the spine of every police officer in Great Britain, and that of a good many citizens besides. Harry Krille was a ruthless murderer, and whilst on the run three policemen were among his victims. There is a period of each-to-their-own-thoughts, until Skelgill breaks what is in danger of becoming a deafening silence.

'He must be pushing sixty.'

'Fifty-seven. He was incarcerated at the age of twenty-six.'

'How long has he been at Haresfell?'

The Director glances across her desk at the detectives, their faces alert. Her own expression is uncharacteristically strained – perhaps exaggerated because her hair is tied back and she wears little of her usual mascara or lipstick, and a tailored pinstripe jacket that together with her skirt makes a severe two-piece. It is as if she has arrived at work accustomed to completing her toilet here, and has now been denied the opportunity.

'He was committed initially to prison – Frankland – but his behaviour began to deteriorate and eventually he was moved to Broadmoor. About two-and-a-half years ago his doctors felt our regime might be more suitable and he was transferred here. It was a low-key procedure – which is why you may not have picked up the news of it. There has been significant progress – within a year he was able to graduate from a High Dependency unit into Assertive Rehab – Bassenthwaite Ward.'

Skelgill grimaces on hearing this unwelcome association – though the Director can only assume that his reaction concerns the notorious patient in question.

'What sort of condition is he in?'

'Do you mean physically?'

Skelgill nods.

'Extremely fit for his age – I understand he has been a regular patron of the gym – and of course since his promotion to a more progressive regime he has applied himself enthusiastically to our horticultural therapy.'

Skelgill shakes his head ruefully – and Briony Boss is forced to raise her palms in a gesture of supplication – for they have been informed that the patient has absconded during this very activity.

'When was it noticed he was missing?'

The Director glances at a lined pad decorated with hastily scribbled notes.

'The four patients gardening were due back on their wards at ten a.m. Harry Krille had asked the supervising therapist if he could return his tools to the storage shed a few minutes before the others, because he had injured an ankle whilst digging and was in some discomfort. There is a bench where they can drink their flask of tea if the weather is poor. The therapist agreed and observed Harry Krille enter the shed. A minute later one of the other patients suffered a seizure and fell to the ground. The therapist went to his aid and radioed for medical assistance. But in the few moments his attention was distracted it seems Harry Krille slipped away. When he went to check inside the shed it was empty.'

'Were the tools there?'

Again she consults her notes.

'Yes. I am advised there is nothing obviously missing – at least, not from today.'

Skelgill looks at his watch and cross-references it against a clock on the wall. The time is now ten twenty-five.

'So this was maybe half an hour ago?'

'That is correct.'

'And when was Harry Krille last seen?'

'As I have described – by the horticultural therapist.'

'Nothing on CCTV?'

She shakes her head.

'The allotments are not covered. CCTV is concentrated upon entrances and exits – the bottlenecks where people must inevitably pass.'

'And the fence.' Skelgill voices this as a statement of fact.

The Director folds her hands upon her lap, her expression showing signs of discomfort.

'The fence is almost five miles long. Our budgets do not extend to such measures. We had security consultants conduct a risk analysis and their report identified the most likely points of attempted escape – and these are monitored continuously.'

Skelgill's thoughts might hark back to his conversation with Alice Wright-Fotheringham, who eulogised the incumbent cost-cutting regime at Haresfell. But he is not a man to dwell upon bolts and stable doors, preferring instead to focus his energies upon the fast-disappearing horse.

'Is he not most likely to be hiding within the hospital grounds?'

'We have a full-scale lockdown, and a systematic search is taking place. It is a procedure we rehearse every quarter.'

'But nothing yet.' Again a statement from Skelgill.

She indicates to a two-way radio resting in a charging unit on her desk.

'I would be informed immediately.'

Skelgill nods.

'And what about... let's call it a stowaway situation – or even a hijack?'

Once more she shakes her head.

'No vehicles passed out of the gates in the time between Harry Krille's disappearance and the alarm being raised. We are talking of only about five minutes. In any event, the entrance is on the north-east side, and the allotments on the south-west. The distance would seem prohibitive.'

Skelgill rises from his chair and strides purposefully to the windows that overlook the grounds. Below him are the allotments, quite an extensive area, a patchwork dotted with sheds and small outbuildings and greenhouses, and various paths that link them and divide the plots. Beyond, open grassland –

recently mown and striped with ragged lines of damp and yellowing cuttings – rolls downhill towards the River Lune, its progress of course interrupted by the triple barrier of the perimeter. He stands in silence staring out, arms at his sides, his head motionless. Without turning he speaks.

'He was a survival fanatic.'

Briony Boss is midway through taking a sip from a coffee in a takeaway cup. She swallows and clears her throat.

'More of a *fantasist*, Inspector – going by the reports.' She reaches out and lays her manicured fingers upon a slim folder. 'I have a copy of his file for you.'

Skelgill glances around, and looks at DS Leyton, who understands he is to take possession of the documents. He accepts them from the Director with a polite nod. Skelgill returns to the desk, but instead of resuming his seat he stands behind it as though he has other plans.

'Was he still into that sort of thing?'

'Only to the extent that it figured amongst his permitted reading.' She flutters her eyelashes in the rather coy manner that she seems to have reserved for several of her interactions with Skelgill. 'It is generally regarded to be therapeutic to allow patients to explore their interests – provided such are considered harmless to themselves and others.'

Skelgill responds with a correspondingly deferential bow of his head.

'As we arrived – there was a security team setting out.'

'They are first checking the perimeter for any breach or signs of escape. Then there is an established sequence of searching likely routes leading away from the hospital. Local communities have been informed – there is only really Hare's Beck Foot – and a handful of farms. And of course the recognised procedure for mobilisation of your own force's resources was immediately activated.'

Skelgill does not appear particularly appeased by this explanation, wide-ranging though it may sound. He knows, for instance, that the immediate police involvement is limited to a handful of local officers and motorised units, and that their capabilities will be stretched like a spider's gossamer across a web of empty lanes linking isolated farms and hamlets – infrequent patrols that would be easily evaded. With a backwards tilt of his head he indicates the position he has just vacated at the window.

'I'd like to take a look at the fence – straightaway.'

There seems to be a flash of disapproval in Briony Boss's dark eyes. Perhaps she reads into the request a criticism of the hospital's own security operation. However, she reaches for the telephone on her desk.

'I shall see if Eric Blacklock might spare somebody to take you out.'

Skelgill nods, though now his expression suggests he means business – there will be no 'might' about it. With a second jerk of the head he indicates to DS Leyton that he should rise.

*

'But, Guv – how could anyone climb that – without a ladder?'

'Exactly, Leyton.'

While DS Leyton cranes his neck and grimaces fearfully at the top of the towering central security fence, Skelgill is looking back impatiently towards the direction of the hospital. From their lowered elevation, only the very tops of the taller buildings are visible, though he can see the windows of the Director's office, opaque as they reflect the grey morning light. Then a figure comes into sight over the grassy horizon, hurrying down the meadow, carrying a bright blue bundle two-handed like a rugby ball. Skelgill now joins with his sergeant's skywards gaze.

'He went over here. Pound to a penny.'

'What makes you so sure, Guv?'

'Two reasons, Leyton.' Skelgill stares imperiously at the barrier. 'For a start it's the lowest point, almost in the flood plain – virtually hidden from view by the lie of the land – apart from those top-floor offices.'

This latter aspect seems to give him pause for thought, and he falls silent for a moment.

'What else, Guv?'

132

Skelgill snaps out of his musing and stares with surprise at his sergeant.

'I could see a clear line of tracks in the loose grass cuttings, leading directly down from the allotments.'

'Cor blimey, Guv – how did you spot that?'

Skelgill responds to DS Leyton's wonderment with a rather disparaging glare – as though it would have been both a failure of common sense and a dereliction of duty to do otherwise. But now the runner arrives panting. He is a junior member of the security staff, assigned to chaperone the detectives, and returns from an errand briefed by Skelgill. He stops just short and addresses Skelgill with fresh-faced enthusiasm.

'From the stores, sir – the quartermaster says they're exactly the same as they've been using for gardening.'

Skelgill relieves him of the bundle – it proves to be a hefty reel of shrink-wrapped synthetic blue twine. Its label reads, *"7200 feet – tensile strength 297 lbs"*. Then from a pocket the man produces and hands over a pair of gardening secateurs.

Skelgill drops the reel on the ground, and slits open the film with one blade of the pruners. Swiftly he strips out a score of arm spans of twine and cuts the length free, and then proceeds to snip off a dozen pieces of perhaps thirty inches each. Next, working with a bewildering hand-speed he ties the shorter lengths to the longer as DS Leyton and the security officer watch with amazement and – in DS Leyton's case – a certain proprietorial pride.

'He's in the mountain rescue.'

'These are dropper knots, Leyton.'

That Skelgill somewhat unreasonably punctures his sergeant's bubble is to some extent mitigated by the fact that neither onlooker comprehends his meaning: the knots owe themselves not to rock climbing but to fly fishing. Indeed, DS Leyton seems about to lavish further praise – but Skelgill rises to his feet, hauling the line into a loose hank.

'Time me, Leyton.'

'Come again, Guv?'

Skelgill is clad in a marginally more respectable version of the Barbour jacket that he employs for angling. He sheds this and marches towards the inner, eight-foot fence. He calls over his shoulder.

'Start your watch.'

Matador-fashion he casts his coat onto the top of the fence, and tosses the hank of twine and the secateurs right over. Then he takes a couple of paces back and springs at the barrier, grabbing the rim through the dense waxed cotton to protect his fingers from the sharp cut ends that project like the jagged dorsal fin of a perch. With a grunt he swings his feet up, and his legs and body follow and he lands – far from perfectly, but the turf is forgiving. Ignoring the admiring sounds that emanate from his audience, on all fours he scrambles to gather his accessories. He fastens the secateurs to one end of the line, and then eyes the main security fence that now looms some thirty feet above him. The anti-climb cage curls inwards from the ridge, but Skelgill takes aim and, left-handed, slings the secateurs, blades open, high into the air. They come clattering down onto the top of the cage and immediately he begins to draw them back with the line. It only takes a second or two for the handles to jam in the wire lattice of the structure, and the line becomes taut. Now Skelgill takes a few seconds to separate out what is in fact a double strand – and suddenly it becomes clear what he is doing – he has made a rudimentary rope ladder. He hitches a foot into the first rung, tests that the twine bears his weight, and begins to ascend. However, when he reaches a height of about ten feet it becomes apparent that there are no more rungs.

'Stop the clock!'

'Righto, Guv – just over a minute.'

Skelgill now concentrates on getting safely to the ground. He abandons the dangling line and levers himself roughly back over the inner fence. It takes him a couple of standing jumps to free his jacket, and then he strolls casually to join the watching pair. As he pulls on his coat he reaches out and lays a paternal hand upon the shoulder of the young security officer.

'Better radio for your gaffer.' He indicates with a jerk of his thumb towards the fence. 'Get his mob down here pronto. And a tracker dog if they've got one.'

The young man nods willingly and reaches for the two-way radio clipped into his belt. As he steps aside to make the call, Skelgill turns to DS Leyton.

'Take, what – three minutes to get right over there?' He runs the fingers of both hands through his hair to restore some semblance of order, and wipes perspiration from his face. 'Even if you were seen on camera, fair bet you'd be away before the guards got here.'

*

'Can't help thinking we tempted fate, Guv – talking about bad publicity and folk escaping.' DS Leyton is generous in his use of the word *we*. 'He could have been climbing over while we were leaning on that bridge, Guv. We might even have seen him – if we hadn't been spotting fish.'

'Who was spotting fish?'

DS Leyton shifts his chair backwards an inch or two in the face of his superior's rather aggressive rebuttal. He opts not to contest the point.

'You hit the nail on the head with that rope business, Guv.'

This admiring apportionment of credit seems to placate Skelgill. DS Leyton refers to the discovery by the search team of a rope ladder – fashioned from the same blue twine – concealed beneath a beached riverside log, close to Skelgill's predicted point of egress. That it had been woven with more care and detail, Skelgill has speculated that the stolen rope was smuggled by Harry Krille to his room, perhaps wound around his waist. Now Skelgill bends over his beaker of hospital coffee, an unappetising facsimile of a cappuccino. He stabs at the froth with a teaspoon in an effort to locate liquid beneath.

'Not sure it's got us anywhere, Leyton.'

DS Leyton furrows his brow, a little disappointed by this pessimistic analysis.

'I reckon he went into the river, Guv – to cover his tracks.'

'Leyton – if he knows what he's doing – and quite likely he does,' (Skelgill places a hand on the manila file provided by Briony Boss) 'He's laid a false trail – to get us thinking exactly like you.'

DS Leyton looks like he is wondering if this is a slight, but Skelgill continues before he can frame a question to test his hypothesis.

'He'll want to stay dry – they were wearing waterproofs for gardening, so he's got decent kit. Make it look like you went one way – go the other. Along the shingle, in the shallows – head for the nearest road – there's so few cars you can hear them coming and hop over a wall.'

'I thought these survival enthusiasts were obsessed with hiding, Guv – right under your nose and you don't even know it. Smother themselves in bear urine to put off the dogs.'

Skelgill tuts scathingly.

'Leyton – I know maths isn't your strong suit,' (DS Leyton looks both perplexed and offended – but Skelgill continues) 'And mine neither,' (this brings a little moderation to the offended aspect) 'But let me tell you a little rule of thumb we use in mountain rescue. It's why you want people who get lost to stay put – and not try to find their way home.'

DS Leyton nods reluctantly.

'Sure, Guv.'

'Fifty – two hundred – four-fifty – eight hundred.'

The sergeant remains baffled.

'Come again, Guv?'

'How fast does a person walk, Leyton?'

DS Leyton looks rather panicked by this question, and he stares wildly at Skelgill while his mind wrestles with the conundrum.

'Thinking of going down the shops with the missus, Guv – maybe two miles an hour? Less on the way back with all the bags.'

Skelgill manufactures a wry grin.

'Very good, Leyton. But someone who's fit and wants to get a shift on could probably manage four miles an hour.'

'Right, Guv.'

Skelgill has several unopened packets of sugar beside his mug. He picks one up and carefully tears off a corner. Then he pours the sugar onto the table top, drawing it out into a little line.

'So, you start walking – how far have you gone in an hour?'

'Four miles, Guv.' DS Leyton looks pleased with himself.

Now Skelgill makes several more equivalent lines, all radiating from the same origin.

'So how many square miles would we have to search if someone's gone four miles and we don't know the direction?'

DS Leyton's joy is short lived.

'You've got me now, Guv. I dunno. Eight?'

Skelgill looks at him suspiciously.

'It's the formula for the area of a circle, Leyton – it comes out at about fifty square miles.'

'Cor blimey, Guv – that's a lot of land.'

Skelgill raises an eyebrow, as if to suggest his sergeant's awe is premature. He opens another packet of sugar and extends the original line.

'What do you think that fifty becomes after another hour?'

'A ton, Guv – a hundred, obviously.'

Now Skelgill has a self-satisfied smirk forming across his lips.

'Two hundred, Leyton.'

'Jeez, Guv!'

Skelgill extends the line of sugar twice more.

'Three hours – and it's four hundred and fifty. Four hours – eight hundred square miles.'

The diagram threatens to bleed off the edge of the table, but it appears Skelgill feels he has made his point. DS Leyton is nodding.

'See what you mean, Guv – slip the net and keep going.'

'Exactly.'

'Mind you, Guv – me, I'd never manage four miles an hour.'

Skelgill snorts at his sergeant's candour.

'True, Leyton – but Harry Krille might. And that's why we need a sighting – or at least a sign.'

'Or some intelligence, Guv.'

'That's ruled us out, then, Leyton.'

DS Leyton grins.

'Nah, Guv – what I mean is – if we had some information – say he's got an old auntie we don't know about – lives in the area – he'd maybe make for her gaff, cool his heels there.'

Skelgill becomes silent, and his eyes fall upon Harry Krille's file. He opens the cover and flicks cursorily through what must be a good hundred pages of dense type. He glances up at DS Leyton, who raises his heavy brows in a resigned show of solidarity. It is clear they are both thinking the same thing – roughly speaking: why did Skelgill send DS Jones packing to Manchester?

However, providence may be about to come to their rescue – if only indirectly, and in the form of Briony Boss's personal assistant. She approaches their table – frowning at the sight of the two detectives hunched over lines of scattered white powder.

'Ah, er... Inspector – there is a telephone call for you – I can have it transferred to the duty room just over there.' She indicates a glass-fronted office where several staff stare into monitors. 'It is a Sergeant Jones – she says it is urgent.'

Skelgill glances at DS Leyton and then nods to the woman. He rises and follows and she swipes him through the electronic door. She offers to clear out the staff, but Skelgill says it will not be necessary. She picks up a handset and locates the call.

'Transferring you now, Sergeant.'

She passes the handset to Skelgill and bows away.

'Jones – where are you?'

'Guv – er, at the hotel – just getting ready to go out – for a coffee.' DS Jones sounds unprepared for Skelgill's interrogation, when perhaps "Good morning" or "How are you?" might reasonably be expected – but this is Skelgill, and par for the course. Accordingly, she gets straight to the point. 'I've been following the Haresfell case on the internal feed, Guv – in case you called me in. I just read about Harry Krille.'

'Aye?'

'I don't know if it's been mentioned, Guv – even if anyone would make the connection?'

She falls silent, as if all of a sudden she has lost confidence.

'Spit it out, Jones.'

After a moment she resumes; there is excitement in her tone and her delivery becomes stilted and breathless.

'The first time I heard of Harry Krille, Guv – it wasn't about the murders back in the eighties – it was a more of a gossip story in a magazine about three years ago – a nurse had been writing to him – you know the kind of thing – they call it hybristophilia – the Bonnie and Clyde Syndrome – apparently she was talking about wanting to marry him. I've just searched for the article online. I'll forward the link.'

Skelgill suppresses a yawn. He could be a casual stroller on a beach, supremely confident, unwilling to acknowledge that sunbathers are staring past him in horror of some impending event – when the great breaker of news crashes over him.

'Guv, the nurse was Meredith Bale.'

16. DIRECTOR'S OFFICE

'**D**id Meredith Bale continue to write to Harry Krille after her arrest?'

Skelgill poses this question to a somewhat anxious looking Dr Peter Pettigrew. Along with Briony Boss and DS Leyton, they are once again assembled around the coffee table.

'Not to my knowledge, Inspector.'

'What are the odds of them both ending up here?' Skelgill's tone carries some implied doubt about the conduct of the process.

'It is not so unlikely, Inspector. Of the four similar institutions in Britain, along with Haresfell only Rampton accommodates women. Irrespective of the fact that Harry Krille's transfer from Broadmoor was complete, the probability of any female offender being committed here was high. But they have been entirely segregated.'

'Is that strictly true, Doctor?' This sharp question comes, perhaps surprisingly, from the Director.

Dr Peter Pettigrew shuffles his papers.

'Harry Krille was promoted to Bassenthwaite Ward less than a year ago – his therapeutic regime has been carefully managed.'

Briony Boss regards him with a steely gaze.

'But he has never shown any propensity to be a danger to women – what about group therapies – has there not been some overlap in the time since?'

The doctor appears uncharacteristically flustered.

'I shall have to check in more detail – I do not have the information at my fingertips – this is all so sudden.' He looks at the detectives a little pleadingly. 'But certainly from a day-to-day living perspective, I can assure you they would not come into

140

contact – each ward comprises a maximum of twelve patients, carefully chosen and monitored for compatibility.'

'Did you even know about Meredith Bale having a fancy for Harry Krille?'

All eyes suddenly alight upon DS Leyton – including those of a bemused Skelgill – who is apparently not expecting his sergeant to interpose this challenging question. Rather like the little boy in the tale of the Emperor's Clothes, watching from the wings he has perceived a blatant flaw. Certainly Dr Peter Pettigrew wavers in his response.

'Well, of course – we have detailed background reports on Meredith Bale –'

'Doctor – you were Chair of the forensic panel that assessed her mental condition – you saw her committed to hospital instead of prison. You are considered the leading authority in the North West – if not the entire country – the psychiatric hospital in which she offended falls within your visiting ambit.'

Whatever her motives, it is clear that Briony Boss is in no mood to make an alliance with her leading specialist. He is obliged to mount a defence by falling back upon firmer ground.

'The emphasis at the time was focused upon her criminal behaviour – the terrible series of murders, and those many associated deaths that were suspected but could not be verified – and Meredith Bale's outright denial that she had any involvement, despite the overwhelming statistical evidence.' He grips his left wrist with his right hand, and makes a jerking movement that seems to shoot through his whole body, as if he is suppressing the emotions of such an affront to his professionalism. 'Those were the parameters within which the panel was charged to make a judgement – our work was based upon extensive psychiatric assessments – not the hyperbole of the gutter press, acting upon the unsubstantiated claims of an anonymous whistleblower.'

This is about as hot under the collar that the detectives have witnessed the normally affable Dr Peter Pettigrew become. Plainly he is unhappy that any responsibility for the current predicament – however tenuous the connection – should be attached to him. Indeed, along precisely these lines, he lays down something of a challenge.

'In any event,' he looks directly at Skelgill, 'I do not see the relevance of Meredith Bale to the matter at hand – the absconding of Harry Krille.'

Skelgill shifts in his seat, as if he is stiff from sitting too long in one position. He makes a face that may reflect this discomfort – or it might be a poorly disguised sentiment, that he does not expect mere civilians to understand the ways of the police.

'We have to consider all possible lines of inquiry, sir. If we can understand what prompted Harry Krille to escape – why he's done it, what he thinks he can achieve – it gives us a far better chance of apprehending him before he does any damage.'

Skelgill's choice of words appears to strike a chord with Briony Boss, for she fixes him with a look of alarm. He elaborates – and highlights a concern that cannot be far from her thoughts.

'And if we're talking about media hype – I understand the gardening therapy and all that – but the press will have a field day if they get hold of the wrong end of the stick – a multiple killer who's been handed the means to escape.'

A grim silence settles upon the group; DS Leyton, however, seems resolved to capitalise upon his earlier mischief.

'Think he's got an improvised bomb, Guv? The missing fuel and fertilizer? What if he's made a detonator in electronics class?'

For a second time the sergeant wins the attention of the audience. Were it not for Skelgill's extravagant expression of dismay, an onlooker might suspect some choreography is at play. Is this innocently controversial remark a ploy to prise out an unguarded reaction? Certainly Skelgill is watching the hospital professionals with a good degree of concentration. However, he moves to defuse the growing discord. He throws out his hands in a rather Gallic gesture of unconcern.

'Look – in practice he couldn't have taken all that much with him. Say he had a bag of gear hidden – it had to be small enough to carry on his back, over the fence. It's just as likely he took nothing at all.'

Briony Boss, nonetheless, is agitated. Though she maintains a composed demeanour, she bites her fleshy lower lip and smears lipstick onto her teeth. Since their earlier meeting she has restored her make up to its usual complement – perhaps in anticipation of the press conference scheduled in an hour's time, at one p.m. Clearly, it is with this event in mind that she frames her response.

'We should be very careful not to speculate upon unknowns, Inspector – we do not need to alarm the public unnecessarily.'

At this, Skelgill and DS Leyton exchange brief glances – to the effect that what more disturbing news can there be than Harry Krille is at large? However, Skelgill seems inclined to ease her concern – perhaps the plaintive note in her voice wins his sympathy – and, having raised the spectre of adverse publicity in the first place, he continues in a reassuring tone.

'Just give them the facts. I suggest Dr Pettigrew explains that Harry Krille has undergone successful therapy – that the escape is probably just a moment of opportunism – that he'll realise it serves him no purpose in being on the run – and he'll probably seek a way to turn himself in.' He looks directly at Briony Boss. 'Don't make a big deal of the actual break-out – this is a police matter now – the public will only care about Harry Krille being caught. And you'll have the Chief riding shotgun – that's usually enough to send most hacks scuttling for cover.'

But Briony Boss still sounds uneasy.

'Are you not attending, Inspector?'

'You must be joking – I've a got a killer to catch.'

*

'I'm still starving, Leyton – fancy a cake or something?'

'I'm stuffed, Guv.' DS Leyton leans back in his seat and pats his ample paunch. 'Though I can't say I'm in any hurry to get back to that place.'

The detectives have driven up to Tebay for lunch. An "out-of-earshot meeting", as Skelgill has put it – although his colleague likely harbours suspicions that it is to make doubly sure he cannot be drafted into the press conference.

'Won't cost you, Leyton – gift horse and all that.'

'I'll pass, Guv – if it's all the same – you go ahead.'

Skelgill seems to be disheartened by his sergeant's lack of enthusiasm, and makes no move to rise. It is possible he was hoping his colleague would do the running.

'Aye – give me a minute.'

DS Leyton folds his knife and fork carefully onto his plate. Despite Skelgill's protestations of hunger, for once he has not scavenged the portion of Cumberland sausage that has defeated his subordinate.

'Think there *is* a connection, Guv – between Meredith Bale and Harry Krille's escape?'

Though Skelgill's contorted features are suggestive of some speculation on his part, he makes no reply.

'Thing is, Guv – she keeps popping up – like a flippin' jack-in-the-box.'

Skelgill has his elbows on the table and his arms folded. He makes an indifferent shrug.

'I'd put it down to chance, Leyton.'

DS Leyton produces something of a sigh.

'Right enough, Guv – my old uncle, the bookie – he used to say there was no skill in a winning streak – only in knowing when to call it a day.'

Skelgill stares pensively at his empty plate.

'Unless you know what you're doing in the first place.'

'Not many punters like that, Guv.'

Skelgill raises a quizzical eyebrow.

'Not like us, eh, Leyton?'

DS Leyton grins rather lopsidedly, as if he is not sure whether this is an ironic statement or an indication that Skelgill does indeed have some method in mind. Now Skelgill leans back and stretches his arms above his head. He casts about the cafeteria, which is filling up with tired-looking tourists, predominantly middle-aged couples who have perhaps set out early from southern climes, running the gauntlet of England's overcrowded motorways that skirt the suburbs of London, Birmingham and Manchester. Their reward is a plate of fish and chips, a treat that marks their arrival in the Lakes, with only winding lanes to navigate henceforth – unless the Scottish Highlands is their destination, in which case this 'northern' outpost may represent only the halfway point.

'Leyton – when we go back – there's a few folk we need to see.'

DS Leyton immediately recognises this offhand form of 'we' as that which Skelgill employs to mean 'you'. Thus his response is somewhat guarded.

'Guv?'

'Interview the horticultural therapist – any indications that Krille had this planned. Looks like he swiped the twine well in advance – check again with Security – what's the worst he might have with him? Then the patient who took ill – see if there was collusion between him and Krille. There'll need to be a doctor present – afterwards get an opinion on whether the seizure was faked.'

DS Leyton is nodding, though his brows are knitted.

'What about Meredith Bale – this malarkey with the letters, Guv? Hadn't we better find out what's been going on between her and Harry Krille?'

Skelgill is now leaning sideways to look past his sergeant and through the window beyond. His reply is rather too casual.

'Don't worry, Leyton – I'll take care of that one.'

'Right, Guv.'

There pass a few moments of silence, while Skelgill assesses the weather, or the birds, or whatever it is he is looking at – if there is anything at all. DS Leyton picks up the conversation.

'What do you reckon about Harry Krille, Guv – about what he's going to do?'

Skelgill consults his wristwatch. The time is now after one p.m. On foot, Harry Krille might be twelve miles from Haresfell. By car, he could be swinging from boughs in

Sherwood Forest, skimming stones on the bonnie banks of Loch Lomond, or composing limericks aboard a ferry bound for Ireland.

'Think about it. If he had an accomplice on the outside, he could be anywhere – in a safe house. But he's no gangster – he was a loner when he did his murder spree – and by all accounts he's a loner still. And if he's smart he'd know an accomplice would be the weak link – we'd pick up on it somewhere and track him down. If he wanted to get shifting, he'd need to have stolen or hijacked a car. I reckon we'd have heard about that by now. Okay – it's possible to take someone hostage – make them drive you to their home – but you don't know what you're getting into – risk of the alarm being raised by a neighbour or a relative. If he's planned it – and he's had enough years to think about it – he'd want to do it on his terms – work to his strengths – what he feels comfortable with. He's fit and he knows about survival in the countryside. Plus we're bang in the middle of England's biggest wilderness. It's midsummer. There's maximum cover for concealment – crops in the ground, fruit on trees, burgers in the bins. It's not cold – a bit of bracken's enough to keep you warm at night – and no one ever died of thirst in the Lakes. No need to make a fire to cook or keep warm at night. If I went and hid, Leyton, you wouldn't find me for months.'

DS Leyton seems entranced by Skelgill's informed soliloquy – indeed he sits open-mouthed for several moments before he responds. He clamps his lips closed in a rather frog-like manner. Then a thought strikes him.

'What about Frank Wamphray, Guv?'

'What about him?'

'What if he were ready to spill the beans on Harry Krille?'

There is a long silence as Skelgill apparently considers this notion. But when he replies he seems to have dismissed the idea. He folds his arms and releases the breath he has been holding while concentrating.

'I can't see it, Leyton.'

'Even by accident, Guv – Frank Wamphray just mouthing off about escapes and all that, like he did to us – gets too close for comfort.'

'Krille would need to hear of it, Leyton – and then arrange for what – the injection?' Skelgill shakes his head determinedly. 'It's not feasible.'

But DS Leyton seems buoyed by his idea. He tilts his head and taps the side of his nose.

'Wheels within wheels, Guv.'

Skelgill grins resignedly at his irrepressible colleague.

'Look, Leyton – keep your DCs on the job – fine – but don't go giving them any ideas – else we'll have some crackpot plot out of a detective story played back to us before we know it.'

DS Leyton nods, satisfied that his superior has at least paid lip service to his suggestion. However, now he too reveals some concern, as shadows of doubt cloud his expression.

'Thing is, Guv – we're gonna be stretched – there ain't many officers to go round right now – and them with young 'uns at school are starting to take their summer holidays.'

Skelgill nods grimly. He shows no inclination to acknowledge that DS Leyton himself falls into this category.

'At least the problem of finding manpower for the search falls to uniform, Leyton.' He inhales and slowly exhales. 'Not that I hold out much hope on that front.'

Again discussion wanes as they each ponder their own perspectives upon this conundrum. While DS Leyton rather glumly twiddles his thumbs, Skelgill's attention is attracted to his right, whence unfamiliar voices reach his ears. Perhaps it is the lilting southern American accent – two handsome boys aged about nine and twelve – or maybe the attractive sun-kissed mom that draws his gaze. There is no sign of a father, and the threesome has engaged in conversation with an elderly British couple at the next table. The younger boy is holding court, the seniors inclining their heads with benevolent interest.

'And when I was five Springer broke my thumb because I was being annoying.'

Springer chips in:

'You were.'

The younger sibling grins widely.

'I'm pretty sure I deserved it.'

The old couple nod admiringly, as if the tale has been one of success in sport or exams. Skelgill, still watching, rises and his movement attracts the eye of the mom, who responds with an inviting smile. Skelgill grins, and shrugs rather ruefully as he turns for the exit.

'Let's roll, Leyton – I need to buy a map of Cumbria from the shop – mine are all at home.' He pats his pockets as they weave between tables towards the mall. 'Come to think of it, so's my wallet.'

17. THE YAT

'Such an atmospheric pub – so steeped in history.'
Skelgill looks about as though this is something that has not previously occurred to him. Having intercepted Dr Agnetha Walker near the M6 motorway junction for Penrith and the A66 – the midpoint of her route home from Haresfell – he has driven her protesting to *The Yat* at Gatewath, just a couple of miles thence. Now they find seats in the crowded, beamed bar room, at a small round table beside the hearth. An early evening fire crackles merrily as it explores a lattice of freshly laid logs. Burnished brasses and polished horseshoes are nailed along the soot-blackened oak lintel.

'Aye – happen it is – old coaching inn – dates from the sixteen hundreds.'

Skelgill, rather uncharacteristically, does not seem inclined to take the credit for this small aspect of his local heritage; instead he appears somewhat distracted – and perhaps his companion's next remark touches upon his preoccupation.

'I think we are attracting some interest.'

The landlady, a striking tanned blonde wearing a revealing bodice top, has now materialised and is scrutinising them quizzically. Skelgill raises a hand in acknowledgement, and her expression softens to a smile. She calls out through the chatter that she will bring a menu – *my darlin'* – but Skelgill points to the specials board, as if to indicate it will suffice. She inclines her head and yields to the presence of a leering drinker who dangles an empty jug, and tantalises his thirst by hauling pruriently on a handpump. Skelgill averts his gaze.

'You must be well used to that, Annie.'

In this ambiguous reply, Skelgill wraps a compliment with what might be a more pragmatic reference to her day job. She seems content to interpret it as the former, and indeed turns the tables with a teasing jibe of her own.

'Dan – I sense competition for your attention.'

Skelgill again glances towards the bar – and sure enough the landlady has an eye in their direction. He shrugs and shifts his chair so that he cannot so easily be diverted.

'When folk know you're in the police, they're always curious about what you're up to.'

Dr Agnetha Walker responds with a small knowing grin, as though she does not entirely accept this explanation as valid under the circumstances. However, she folds her delicate fingers around her drink – a suitably slimline vodka and tonic – and assumes a business like manner.

'And what *are* you up to this evening, Inspector?'

Her tone implies an inclination to subvert whatever are his good intentions. But Skelgill does not play along. He sits back and cradles his pint, and it takes him a moment to formulate a reply.

'I thought we might fix a date to finish the pike expedition – this weekend, maybe – but you must be feeling I'm like a bit of a Jonah.'

'What on earth do you mean?'

Skelgill takes a sip of his beer and grimaces as if it is bitter – which it is, by its trades description.

'Every time I come near Haresfell there's a new calamity. This morning me and my oppo Leyton were standing by the river – Harry Krille must have climbed the fence – right under our noses.'

'But that is not your responsibility.' Dr Agnetha Walker appears troubled by Skelgill's assumption of blame. 'That is a matter for Security.'

Skelgill tests the clarity of his pint against the burgeoning fire.

'We must look a bit dim – flapping about trying to make a connection out of a coincidence.'

Dr Agnetha Walker regards him evenly.

'But how is Harry Krille connected – to anything?'

Skelgill puts down his glass and leans forwards on his elbows, his shoulders hunched. Pointedly he turns his head to and fro, but no one appears to be eavesdropping – patrons at adjacent tables are engrossed in their own conversations, and a healthy banter around the servery lays down a blanket of background noise. He makes a face like a contestant speculating an answer to a question master.

'Meredith Bale?'

Now his companion's naturally startled brows seem to edge a millimetre or two higher.

'But how?'

Skelgill does not reply immediately. Perhaps he hopes she will elaborate of her own volition – but in the end her professional patience wins out and he continues.

'She had this obsession – before she was arrested – she was writing to him.'

There is the faintest tightening of Dr Agnetha Walker's fingers around the glass that perhaps suggests this notion creates some impression – though her features offer no corroboration.

'I know this, of course.'

'What do you think about it?'

'I have touched upon the subject with her – not recently, you understand – she is reluctant to talk and I have to tread carefully in order not to send her into her shell. She could perceive it as something that undermines her claim to sanity.'

Skelgill gives a roll of his eyes.

'It's not exactly normal, is it?'

Dr Agnetha Walker appears to contest this statement. She gives a shake of her head and then methodically brushes away a strand of blond hair that falls across a cheek.

'You would be surprised how common. It even has a name – hybristophilia.'

'Aye, aye – Bonnie and Clyde syndrome, eh?'

She fixes him with her cool blue eyes.

'Some females have a strong sexual attraction to men they perceive as extreme alpha males.'

That she stops dead at this – her gaze defiant – seems to rattle Skelgill. He appears uncertain of exactly what kind of response is appropriate. There is a momentary stand off – but any tension is defused by the arrival of a young waiter bearing a pad, pencil poised. He is spotty faced and barely looks old enough to be in a public house. Skelgill seems relieved and gives him a hearty slap on the shoulder. He turns to Dr Agnetha Walker and recommends the special – a local variation on the Barnsley chop – she demurs and there is a small hiatus while they debate sides and sharing. When the waiter bows away Skelgill finds a firmer footing.

'I know you've not been there long – but is it possible that Meredith Bale and Harry Krille have met – face to face, like?'

She reacts to his inquiry with a slow puckering of her full lips, as though she is about to apply some gloss – or is imagining a kiss.

'There is a detailed management plan for each patient. Among other things it is to ensure that certain individuals avoid one another – even when they are being moved around the site. It is the case with all such hospitals, but for Haresfell perhaps more important because it is mixed sex. I do not know what is specified for each of these two – but I would suspect it is to maintain segregation. Unless –'

'Unless what, Annie?'

That she has paused for thought heightens Skelgill's interest. Her expression, however, carries no hint of controversy.

'Well – if there were some experiment – if it were considered beneficial for them to interact under controlled circumstances.'

'What – like a date?'

'Oh, no – no – but perhaps in some group therapy – a drama class, for example.'

'Who would suggest that?'

'It could be any of the therapists – even a nurse – there are regular team reviews of each patient's progress. But it would have to be sanctioned by the Director.'

Skelgill nods. Then he slowly combs the fingers of one hand through his hair, as though he is teasing out a thought from his memory bank.

'Do you know if Harry Krille was writing back to her?'

Her answer comes without hesitation.

'I believe not – although he indicated he was willing to receive correspondence.' She produces an ironic smile. 'However, I doubt Meredith Bale were the sole member of his – how shall I put it? – appreciation society.'

Skelgill rubs his chin – and suddenly appears disturbed by the discovery of a swathe of unshaven stubble. He casts the hand to one side, as if self-consciously trying to draw away his companion's attention.

'Happen the date didn't go too well – so he legged it.'

Dr Agnetha Walker reacts as though she is considering the merits of this idea, despite Skelgill's patently flippant intent. She ponders for a moment and then reaches to lay a hand on his wrist.

'Inspector, what do *you* think is his motive?'

He frowns – this time the use of his title must seem strange, because her tone is entirely serious. Or perhaps it is the suggestion that he should possess some psychological intuition – when she is the expert in this regard. He pulls back and folds his arms.

'Does he need one?'

'But surely you must have some theory? What if you were in his shoes? Consider the situation – would you think of the fishes?'

Skelgill shrugs his shoulders, seemingly reluctant to speculate. But after a few moments his eyes become glazed, and in due course he offers an insight of sorts.

'If I'd been cooped up all those years – and they let me out gardening – with that view of the fells across the Lune – I'd want to start walking – imagine the fence wasn't there – keep walking right out of sight.'

'And then what would you do?'

Skelgill looks a little alarmed – as though control of his faculties has been restored, having been hijacked without his consent. At first he does not respond, but Dr Agnetha Walker's insistent gaze provides him with little other choice.

'I'd live off my wits – wait until the search was scaled down.'

'Could you do that – live off your wits?'

Skelgill nods, though his eyes narrow suspiciously.

'Easy enough this time of year.'

'But wouldn't you be seen – by a member of the public?'

Skelgill shrugs.

'Live in plain sight.'

'What does that mean?'

'So long as you camped where there's good cover – all you'd need is a bivvy to keep dry. Near a beck – there's no shortage of them. When I had to move – I'd act like a hillwalker. There's thousands of folk treading the hill paths – no shepherd's going to look at you twice. In this weather – keep your hood zipped up – who's going to recognise you? It's not like he's wearing striped pyjamas.'

'I suppose that was once the argument for an institutional uniform.'

'By all accounts he was well kitted out – no need to steal something off a washing line or from a shop that would draw attention.'

Now Dr Agnetha Walker nods pensively.

'Do you suspect there is something connected to Meredith Bale that could give you a clue to his movements?'

Skelgill appears uneasy – although his brooding expression may reflect some frustration that she has brought him full circle to his original question. He casts about the room, perhaps sidetracked by the prospect of their food arriving, assessing the progress of deliveries to other diners.

'I like to keep an open mind.' He scoffs. 'It's what my boss calls drawing a blank.'

Dr Agnetha Walker smiles compassionately.

'I am sure I heard you are one of the top detectives.'

Skelgill is unprepared for this accolade, and in the flickering firelight his cheekbones reveal a flush of rouge. He makes a scornful face – it must be plain that his progress on matters related to Haresfell is pedestrian verging upon stationary.

'Would she tell you, Annie – Meredith Bale? Since you're working with her – winning her confidence?'

'She is very clever. Manipulative. She only confides what she wants you to know.'

'How did she react to what happened to Frank Wamphray?' Skelgill again looks around in search of their meals, as if the answer to his question comes a poor second among his priorities.

'Of course – the patients have not been informed about the nature of his death – of any suspicions. But – '

Her checking herself has an immediate impact.

'But what? Are you saying there has been a reaction?'

Now Dr Agnetha Walker seems to backtrack – she shifts in her seat and her trim figure takes on a rather more formal demeanour.

'As you just intimated, it is never good practice to approach an inquiry with a prior interpretation in mind.'

Skelgill narrows his eyes.

'Depends what you know, doesn't it?'

Dr Agnetha Walker remains guarded.

'Naturally – being aware of Meredith Bale's history – one might be predisposed to read some sort of association into her response.'

'So you did ask her?'

'Oh, no – not directly – just about how she felt – she was friendly with Frank Wamphray and it was reasonable to sympathise.'

'And was she upset?'

'Dan, she is a psychopath.'

This blunt declaration causes Skelgill to halt in the midst of forming his next question. He releases the breath and then inhales anew.

'And, so?'

'She was certainly not upset – but I felt I detected a little sense of triumph – that she *wanted* me to detect. It was the merest hint – and that is why I say one should not easily be drawn to conclusions.'

Skelgill does not respond to this analysis. But it is clear his mind is running through some scenario or other. After a few moments' silence he leans forwards and clasps his hands around his almost empty pint glass.

'Annie – I might need your help – a bit of inside information.'

'Are you talking about Meredith Bale?'

'Aye, maybe – but also a couple of the characters that work at Haresfell.'

Dr Agnetha Walker raises her glass and sips demurely, her expression unrevealing.

'You appreciate that could place me in a compromising position?'

Skelgill makes a face of 'so be it' and pushes back his chair.

'Then I'd better get you another one of those – drink up, lass.'

Automatically she does as he bids, though there is too much in her glass to swallow in one go. Skelgill begins to step away towards the bar.

'But – my car is at Penrith.'

Skelgill smirks offhandedly.

'Don't worry – if you need a room I'm well connected.'

He strides away and quickly wins the willing attention of the landlady. Dr Agnetha Walker watches with some satisfaction and casually tosses off the last of her vodka.

*

'Jones.'

'Guv?'

'Where are you?'

'Guv? I can hardly hear for the echo – it sounds like you're in a toilet.'

'Aye – well, you know the signal can be crap up here.'

'It might be me, Guv – can you just wait while I move?' She gives Skelgill no choice, and there is a muted silence before her voice comes back on the line. 'How's that?'

'Fine my end – I can hear traffic. Were you in a club?'

'You're still breaking up, Guv.'

Skelgill takes the handset momentarily from his ear and checks the screen. He has maximum bars.

'Jones – I need to be quick.'

'Sure, Guv.' She appears to hear this statement perfectly well.

'When you told me about Meredith Bale writing to Krille – you said you've got a contact in the NHS for Greater Manchester.'

'In human resources, aha?'

'Can she do some sleuthing?'

'It's a *he*, Guv.'

'Right. Whatever. Write down these names.'

'Sorry, Guv? You went again.'

But now Skelgill is disturbed by the sound of a door opening nearby.

'Jones – I'll send you a text – alright?'

He waits, but there is no reply – it seems the line has dropped off. He glares at his mobile before pocketing it angrily. With one boot he kicks down the toilet lid and pulls the flush. As he bangs his way out of the cubicle and makes swiftly for the exit, the balding, bespectacled middle-aged gent standing at the rank of urinals glances disapprovingly over his shoulder; the man in a hurry has not washed his hands.

*

At around one a.m. on what is now Friday morning, a long brown shooting brake exits the M6 motorway and approaches Tebay services. At this hour there are many empty parking spaces near the entrance to the concourse, but the car stops some fifty yards short, beside a marked picnic area. Cloaked in darkness and backed by rather foreboding woodland, by day it is a pleasant grassy spot, a leafy oasis where birdsong and the gurgle of a stream provide respite for the traveller seeking a breath of fresh air. There are several trestle benches, a couple of waste bins, and – thoughtfully provided – a stone drinking trough for dogs. The only hint of authority is a sign that warns their owners will be fined if they do not clean up after them.

From the driver's side a man climbs out. Rangy in profile and a couple of inches above average height, he seems to be dressed for the weather. What little ambient neon filters through the drizzle reveals him to be wearing some kind of outdoor jacket, and a wide-brimmed hat. He turns up his collar, and in the act of closing the door he ducks towards the car and speaks loudly in a thick London accent.

'Stay there, girl – I'll be back in a mo.'

He leaves the vehicle unlocked, and strides purposefully to the main services building. Although the shops in the small mall will be closed, light emanating from large plate glass windows reveals the cafeteria to be operating, albeit that part of the seating area is roped off. An observer would see him join a queue of lorry drivers at the fast food counter, and turn in due course bearing a tray laden with a stack of assorted cartons. Unlike the truckers, however, who squeeze into seats at individual tables and tuck into their midnight feasts, the man with the hat veers away and half a minute later emerges into the cool of the night, backing out against the manual swing doors.

He returns along the narrow footway that links the floodlit building to the shadowy picnic area. He places the tray upon a table adjacent to his car, and then reaches to open the passenger door. That his companion requires this assistance is explained when out tumbles a medium-sized dog, of mainly dark markings, and uncertain breed – but certainly some sturdy variety. After a short gambol about the sward, the creature tilts at its master, who is in the act of placing upon the damp ground what might be the opened carton of a cheeseburger.

'There you go, girl – get yer 'ampsteads round that.'

The animal requires no second invitation, pausing between bites only to confirm that this human treat really is intended to be a dog's dinner. The man, meanwhile, munches with greater circumspection, punctuating his eating with various other Cockney exhortations to his pet. That he is pacing himself would appear sensible, going by the stack of foodstuffs he has purchased. Indeed, after a few minutes more it appears he is defeated – he has bitten off more than he can chew – and even the dog is unenthusiastic when offered a second portion. The man wipes his mouth on his sleeve and rises to his feet. He stretches his arms behind his head. Then he gives a sharp whistle and calls out.

'Let's roll, girl – Jockland 'ere we come.'

And with that he abandons the unfinished meal, sees the dog into the passenger seat, rounds to the driver's side, clambers in still wearing his coat and hat, and starts the engine. There is an ostentatious revving before the car pulls away, and when it does it sets off at speed, crossing diagonally the hatch of empty parking spaces to join the marked exit lane. But when it disappears from sight – as viewed from the picnic zone – it swerves into the petrol forecourt, slides between the pumps, hangs a left around the kiosk and loops back to the rear of the main services building. Here it draws to a halt. The driver emerges and is immediately admitted through a fire door by a member of staff.

As the crow flies, Tebay is just eight miles from Haresfell.

18. THE BIVVY

'**R**eckon we can trust that dog, Guv?'

Skelgill purses his lips.

'Aye.'

But DS Leyton glowers broodingly beneath his dark brows. The two detectives stand side by side in thick woodland, the leaf mulch damp underfoot and silent to the tread. Twenty yards away within a taped-off section a dog-handler is putting a Working Cocker through its paces. It seems the dog has detected its target, for the handler makes a thumbs-up sign in their direction.

'I always think – with dogs, Guv – if they don't want to bite you, they want to please.' DS Leyton hunches his shoulders against drips from the canopy that find the back of his neck. 'Just like I was reading about the Queen in the paper.'

'What?'

'Yeah, Guv – people were writing in with stories of meeting the Queen. This woman says when she was a nipper the Queen visited their school, and she asks what's your name little girl? She replies Elizabeth and the Queen's eyes light up and she says that's a lovely name – that's my name, too.'

Skelgill is looking askance at his sergeant.

'Leyton – what's this got to do with the dog?'

'Thing is, Guv – the little girl – her name was Daphne.'

Skelgill rolls his eyes.

'I think we can take it the dog's not so crafty, Leyton.' Skelgill turns on his heel and begins to clamber up a rocky bank draped with a cascade of bright green ferns. 'Come on, there's nothing to see here.'

*

'Cheers, Leyton – what do I owe you?'

Skelgill pats his pockets, but before he can plead his usual absence of funds his sergeant pre-empts him.

'It's on me, Guv – I won a monkey on the National Lottery last night.'

Skelgill glances from his sergeant to the breakfast plate that has been placed before him. He scowls rather ungenerously.

'Since when did they start offering exotic pets as prizes?'

'Very funny, Guv – five hundred nicker.'

Skelgill can't conceal a look of envy.

'You jammy git, Leyton – I've never won a penny.'

DS Leyton puts on a sympathetic air.

'You just gotta keep at it, Guv.'

Skelgill shakes his head. He is already tucking into his first mouthful.

'Did it the first week. Didn't get a single number. Total waste of money.'

DS Leyton's features show a flash of exasperation – but then he becomes rather more reserved in his manner. Tentatively he picks up his knife and fork, and pauses with the implements held in mid air.

'Thought I better take the missus out tonight, Guv – seeing as we can afford the danger money for the babysitter.'

Skelgill continues to eat. He inclines his head in a gesture of assent. He understands that his subordinate is putting in an early bid to finish work on schedule – rather than at 'Skelgill o'clock', which can bear no relation whatsoever to contracted hours.

'Should be fine, Leyton – provided there's not a sighting of Krille. I'm taking Dr Walker fishing this afternoon, anyway.'

'On a Friday, Guv?'

Now Skelgill glares indignantly across the table.

'It's work, Leyton.'

'Right, Guv.'

DS Leyton discerns this is not a point to contest. Skelgill, however, evidently feels obliged to elaborate.

'For a start – I did that charity auction to please the Chief. She can't complain when I see it through.' He stabs irritably at a

161

sausage. 'Second – I've asked Dr Walker to do a bit of digging for me – and I don't mean for worms, Leyton.'

DS Leyton nods encouragingly.

'About Haresfell, Guv?'

'Aye.'

Skelgill returns his attention to his plate. DS Leyton is left to speculate upon his superior's machinations.

'There ought to be someone in there who knows what Harry Krille's up to, Guv – even if they don't realise it themself.'

Skelgill gives his sergeant something of a one-eyed look, but he continues to eat. DS Leyton gesticulates over his shoulder.

'And what was he doing here, Guv – hiding in those bushes?'

'Think about it, Leyton – what's this place good for?'

'Fry-ups, chips, burgers – I mean if I'd been cooped up all those years, Guv.' But now DS Leyton tails off. 'Thing is – we had a uniformed officer on duty all day at the entrance – and CCTV recording through the night.'

Skelgill points past his sergeant with his knife, as though he is taking aim for a demonstration of his prowess.

'Look out there, Leyton – what do you see?'

DS Leyton first flinches and then grunts as he heaves his bulk around to stare through the plate glass windows. After a few moments he replies hopefully.

'Rain, Guv?'

Skelgill tuts.

'In the lorry park, Leyton.'

'Oh, right you are, Guv – ruddy great artics.' He pauses for a moment before the corollary of this suggestion becomes clear. 'You reckon he's hitched a lift?'

Skelgill scowls.

'Not hitched, Leyton – but how difficult is it to stow away?'

DS Leyton begins to nod.

'Not very, Guv – going by all that malarkey at Calais.'

'That's exactly where he could be by now.'

DS Leyton suddenly looks vaguely amused.

'Make a change for someone to go the other way, Guv. What chance the French catch him and send him back?'

Skelgill forces a grin to acknowledge his subordinate's attempt at irony.

'He's choosing to keep a low profile, Leyton. Think of all the holiday cottages he could have broken into – farm buildings – garden sheds. Instead he's made a bivvy in a wood.'

'Reckon that explains the polythene sheeting that went missing, Guv?'

Skelgill nods.

'That and a length of twine – all you'd need to rig up a decent shelter. And clear polythene's nigh on invisible. Lightweight. Easy to pack.'

'PC Dodd reckoned there was a burger carton hidden under a rock, Guv. Think he got it from here?'

Skelgill shakes his head.

'Scavenged from the bins, Leyton – that picnic area.'

DS Leyton appears doubtful about this idea.

'Thing is, Guv, weather we've been having – can't imagine anyone using that spot yesterday.'

Skelgill looks up grimly.

'Folk with dogs, Leyton – can't bring them inside.'

The mention of such must transport DS Leyton's thoughts back to the tracker dog – and its inspection of what might have been a transient overnight camp.

'Suppose he'd know how to make the best of it, Guv – what with all those survival guides in his room.'

'What guides?'

'I put it in my email, Guv.'

'I didn't get any email.'

'I sent it last night, Guv – close of play – report on all the findings about Frank Wamphray – and Harry Krille's escape.'

Skelgill looks blank. He pulls his mobile phone from his jacket pocket and glowers at it accusingly.

'This thing's worse than useless, Leyton – anyway, my password's expired – I don't know what it is with these techy guys.'

DS Leyton reaches stoically for his own handset. He places it on the table beside his plate and adjusts its position for his focal length.

'No worries, Guv – I'll give you the lowdown.'

Skelgill raises an affirmative eyebrow over the rim of his mug.

'Staring with Frank Wamphray, Guv – first off – funny thing this – you'd never guess what his job was before he was committed.'

Skelgill looks irked. He is unwilling to play his sergeant's little game.

'Archbishop of York.'

'What!' DS Leyton throws up his hands in surprise. 'How d'you know that, Guv?'

Skelgill for a moment looks nonplussed. He holds his knife and fork against the table so their ends point vertically. DS Leyton breaks into a smile.

'Nah – you're right, Guv – he was a spook – worked for the Security Services.'

Skelgill glowers.

'Leyton – are you sure you didn't get that from beyond the grave?'

'Straight up, Guv – our boys have been through his records – he was in Berlin at the time the Wall came down. Makes you wonder – if that's why someone was wary of him – knowing he was no mug on the eavesdropping front.'

'Aye, well – something filled his head with conspiracy theories.'

DS Leyton swipes at the screen of his phone.

'There ain't much new in the handling of the medicine, Guv. We've spoken to everyone who touched it in the normal course of events – right from the bulk deliveries they get in from the NHS distribution centre to it being signed out from the dispensary that serves Coniston Ward. The conclusion is it couldn't have been accidentally contaminated – else there'd be other samples the same. Then all the correct protocols were followed, and no one can understand how it could have been tampered with – other than while it was being stored ready for signing out.'

'Or Arthur Kerr made a switch.'

DS Leyton nods enthusiastically.

'I know, Guv – only trouble is, he'd need to have done it under the nose of the ward nurse – and she's an old stager – right stickler – I don't reckon you'd get much past her.'

'Unless they were in cahoots.'

Now DS Leyton scowls rather dejectedly.

'If I'm honest, Guv, I can't see it – she's raging that she's being linked to a deadly mistake – when all she did was sign out a dose of medicine.'

Skelgill appears unmoved by this little scenario; perhaps unreasonably he glares at his subordinate, who senses his discontent and moves quickly on with his report.

'Parking the nurses, Guv – there's the CCTV analysis of the dispensary – what a palaver that was. In the end we roped in the security officer who processes all the photos for staff passes. So far she's identified ninety per cent of the people who went in and out.'

Skelgill looks alarmed.

'Only ninety per cent?'

'In the evening the lights are dimmed, Guv – and if you've got two or three folk going in or out together the camera doesn't always get a clear shot. Truth be told, it's set up for the access doors – that's what their security policy's all about – monitoring movements from one restricted zone to another.'

Skelgill nods reluctantly.

'So who did we identify?'

'It's quite a list, Guv – that place is like Clapham Junction.' DS Leyton makes a clicking sound with his tongue as he scrolls down his page. 'Thing is, they've got a kettle in there for staff use, plus the central computer terminal to check and update the patients' medical records. There's doctors, nurses, therapists, security, cleaners – about thirty folk all told – in the twenty-four hours before Frank Wamphray's death. We're working our way through them – course there's some we've interviewed already –

the Boss woman, Dr Pettigrew, your acquaintance Dr Walker, Eric Blacklock – and Arthur Kerr.'

DS Leyton pauses to look up at his superior's reaction. Skelgill is staring at the palm of one hand.

'What news of fingerprints on the vial?'

DS Leyton pulls a rather despondent face.

'I put in a call to the lab while I was driving down, Guv. They're having trouble separating them out – what with it being so small and the prints overlapping. They reckon there might be two or three sets – maybe more.'

'We need that, Leyton.'

'I'll chase 'em up, Guv.'

Skelgill gives a confirmatory twitch of the head.

'What else?'

'The geezer with the seizure, Guv.'

Now Skelgill's eyes narrow suspiciously. His sergeant is in a mischievous mood this morning – not unreasonably given his lottery bonanza – and a pun can be expected to follow this little rhyme. However, DS Leyton continues with a straight face.

'Might be something there, Guv – might not. They wouldn't let me interview him – even with a doctor present. He's taken a depressive bout and won't speak to nobody – not even his psychiatrist.' DS Leyton scratches his head as if to emphasize his puzzlement. 'Now is that covering up – or is it pukka? Whatever – they've put him on extra medication to keep him calmed down – so they reckon there's no point in questioning him – even if he would answer we couldn't rely on what he says 'cause of the drugs.'

Skelgill is pensive.

'What did the shrink think?'

'It was Pettigrew, Guv – they put me onto him. Seems he's got overall access to the medical records – knows all the patients. He didn't attend to the chap who had the fit but he pulled up the report on his computer. Turns out he does have previous.' (DS Leyton squints at the screen of his phone and reads falteringly.) 'Non-epileptic paroxysmal disorder, that's it – not regular – not even in the last twelve months – but often enough to make the attack in the allotment plausible. The doctor who was on call, his report says the patient had regained consciousness by the time he got there – what with them being right out in the grounds – so he couldn't verify absolutely that it was a genuine fit. The horticultural therapist is only trained in basic first aid – so if the geezer was malingering he probably wouldn't be able to tell.'

Skelgill has the countenance befitting one receiving a string of unsatisfactory answers.

'What did he say about the escape?'

'More or less as we've already heard, Guv. Harry Krille turned his ankle digging. He'd been limping around for about twenty minutes and asked permission to rest in the shed. The others were finishing up – hoeing weeds between rows – and the next thing this one's keeled over frothing at the mouth, flattened a load of runner beans.'

'And how about collusion with Krille?'

DS Leyton begins to nod but then quickly shakes his head lest he should give the wrong impression.

'Says Krille was aloof, Guv – he weren't pally with any of the rest – didn't join in the banter – just got on with the gardening.' DS Leyton licks his lips; his mouth is becoming dry and he takes a hasty sip from his mug. 'Says he was really obsessive about it – had his own patch that he wouldn't let anyone else touch – considered he was the only one doing it proper, like.'

Skelgill nods and inhales quietly.

'What's he in for – the one who had the fit?'

DS Leyton flashes a warning glance at his boss.

'You don't want to know, Guv.' Now he wipes his upper lip, as if a film of perspiration has suddenly appeared. 'He's from Shetland – no connection to Krille – I had that checked out.'

Skelgill reluctantly accepts this advice; for a moment there is perhaps in his eyes a flicker of sympathy for his sergeant.

'How about the missing gear – what did the horticultural therapist have to say about that?'

DS Leyton consults his handset once more.

'He reckons there was no obvious pattern – there's other practitioners leading groups doing gardening – and with stuff like rope and polythene being on flippin' great rolls it's hard to tell even if anything has disappeared. He says the odd tool occasionally doesn't get checked back in – stuff genuinely gets dropped in the undergrowth or buried – then they find it again another day. He says the main focus is always to make sure nothing dangerous gets taken back inside the hospital – they have to be searched every time.' DS Leyton looks up from his notes. 'Thing is, Guv – face it – give 'em gardening as an activity – you've got no choice but to let 'em have the proper kit.'

'What's Security's position?'

'Blacklock made a fair point, Guv – if some voice in your head is telling you to whack the geezer next to you with a shovel because he's the devil incarnate – why would you hide the shovel?'

Skelgill is finishing his last mouthful and he makes a resigned shrug; it is a fatalistic perspective. DS Leyton waits for a moment and then grins with evident satisfaction.

'They're red-faced about the escape, Guv – especially since you showed how easy it was.'

Skelgill looks unconcerned.

'I don't reckon he took much with him, Leyton. A small rucksack would be handy – but there's no indication he got hold of one. If I were Harry Krille I'd want a knife – axe, hacksaw, maybe.'

'Most likely he's got a pair of those secateurs like you used, Guv.'

Skelgill nods.

'Aye, maybe – they're no good for sharpening – but they cut the twine and you could trim stakes for a bivvy.'

'Maybe we'd better put out an alert for anyone who wakes up to find their roses have been pruned in the night, Guv.'

19. BASS LAKE

Skelgill is huddled on the wooded west bank of Bassenthwaite Lake. He has beached his boat and climbed some twenty feet back from the water's edge, up a steep bank. The view from within his makeshift shelter is framed by an uneven rectangle, and comprises half lake, half ground. The water is grey and uninviting; the forest floor is carpeted in orange pine needles, with protruding boulders that are covered in moss. A scattering of woodland plants add a touch of green – trailing fronds of bramble, curving foxglove stems, and clusters of enchanter's nightshade – but the dense canopy has not encouraged lush growth. There are such things as 'bothy bags' – portable nylon shelters that protect the hillwalker or rambler from inclement weather. But why would Skelgill pay the inflated price for such an item when a camouflage motorbike cover and a pair of extending aluminium rod-rests do the job? He is ensconced amongst the unfolding roots of a Norway spruce, his back against the trunk. However, from the knees down his legs protrude from the elasticated opening and glisten with rain. The top of his head is pressed against the material and he is forced to crouch rather awkwardly to see out over the silvery surface. The backdrop is shrouded in mist, any detail diminishing as dusk advances. Sporadically he drinks tea from the lid of a flask, picks his nose, and flicks fir cones down the bank – but from within the cramped confines of his camp he is unable to get the required leverage to reach the shoreline. Persistent heavy rain – forecast to continue throughout the night and well into tomorrow – is intercepted by dense coniferous foliage above, but plump secondary drops gather and fall and crackle about his ears, and drips stream out of focus close before his eyes.

There are no other sounds to speak of. The conditions are calm, and what few birds may sing at this late stage in the breeding season have already called it a day. There is an indistinct hum of traffic from the distant A66, but the air thick with moisture muffles its passage across the water. It is perhaps no surprise, then, that Skelgill starts when the unruly tone of his mobile breaches the peace.

He wrestles to retrieve his handset from the breast pocket of his outdoor jacket; the confined refuge has now become an obstructive layer that threatens to defeat his efforts before the call diverts to messenger. His features reveal some hopeful anticipation – but this changes to a look of consternation as he recognises the caller's number.

'Leyton – it's after eight.'

'Sorry to disturb your expedition, Guv, but –'

His sergeant sounds breathless. There are background noises of shrill voices: children resisting admonishment. Then the clunk of a door cuts the decibels.

'What it is, Guv – you'd better get yourself down to Haresfell – there's been an incident.'

'What kind of incident?'

'Dr Pettigrew's wife, Guv – the psychologist that runs the drama classes – she's been attacked – assailant unknown.' DS Leyton clears his throat. 'It's not looking good, Guv.'

'Right.'

Skelgill stares across Bassenthwaite Lake into the indefinable middle distance. It takes a prompt from his sergeant to break his concentration.

'What do you want to do, Guv?'

'Is it just her – Mrs Pettigrew?'

'Far as I know, Guv.'

'Where are you?'

'At home, Guv – when I got the call I had to drop the missus back from the restaurant.'

'I'll meet you at Threlkeld. Park up by the inn – next to the bus stop. Give me twenty-five minutes.'

'Righto, Guv.' DS Leyton clears his throat. 'Er... what will you tell Dr Walker?'

'She's not with me.'

'Oh – I thought you'd still be fishing.'

'She couldn't make it, Leyton – something came up at the hospital and she had to stay this afternoon.'

'I see, Guv.'

DS Leyton's tone suggests he is calculating that his boss took off fishing anyway. However, he might also reflect that it did enable him to finish work on time – albeit he has now been obliged to abandon his celebratory meal. It seems unlikely that Skelgill will acknowledge his sacrifice.

*

'I thought this morning, Guv – at least the Chief would have something positive to tell the press – the discovery that Harry Krille had been around Tebay.' DS Leyton shakes his head and turns out his fleshy bottom lip. 'But this is going to be a setback.'

Skelgill, disregarding the motorway speed limit, squints into the headlamps of oncoming traffic. His features are gaunt, cast into sharp contrast by each surge of light; indeed he looks haggard as he hunches over the steering wheel. His reply is somewhat oblique.

'What are we supposed to do, Leyton?'

A few moments' silence ensues, while DS Leyton makes a series of supportive shrugs and indeterminate noises of exasperation. Then Skelgill continues.

'All this bother, Leyton – it's coming from within their four walls – it's their house that's not in order – now we're taking the rap.'

DS Leyton glances surreptitiously at Skelgill, as if unsure of his motivation. Perhaps his boss has received a message from on high that he has not shared – along the lines that enough is enough, and that it falls to Skelgill to put a stop to it. Or else.

'There's been half-a-dozen reported sightings of Krille, Guv – nearest one in the blacksmith's at Gretna Green – furthest on the prom at Torquay. All of them too far apart to have been the same person. The geezer in Gretna turned out to be a German tourist.'

171

Skelgill shakes his head dismissively.

'I doubt any of them were Harry Krille.'

'Probably not, Guv.'

'Most likely he's within a few miles of Tebay, Leyton.' (Again DS Leyton looks sharply at his superior, as if he suspects some insider knowledge.) 'Or in a bar full of dancing girls on the Champs-Élysées.'

Now DS Leyton sighs.

'That's the Moulin Rouge, ain't it, Guv?'

Skelgill shrugs.

'It's all the same to me, Leyton.'

DS Leyton ponders for a moment – but it would appear that France is not his strong suit either, and he reverts to the local angle.

'I called back in at Tebay yesterday afternoon, Guv. The DC that was checking their CCTV footage had finished and had a few clips to show me.'

'And?'

'Nothing much, Guv – a couple of odd characters – ha!' He chortles. 'One geezer looked a bit like you – came in after midnight for a big carryout – couldn't really see him for his hat. But no danger of it being Harry Krille – according to the description he's no more than five-seven.'

'Aye, well – I've got that common look, Leyton – if they were after me there'd be hundreds of sightings all over the country.'

DS Leyton frowns doubtfully; he would be entitled to disagree with Skelgill's assessment, for there is something about his boss that most certainly makes him stand out from the crowd – although perhaps that is more about his rebellious nature than his physical appearance.

'Still, look on the bright side, Guv – he don't seem bent on any harm – it's not like he's gone on the rampage.'

'Aye, well – give him a chance, Leyton – he's only been out thirty-six hours. Maybe he's saving it up for the weekend.'

DS Leyton makes a face like he is evaluating this wisdom. But then another thought strikes him.

'That reminds me, Guv – I got a message from George on the front desk – DS Jones was trying to get in touch with you.'

'Aye?'

Skelgill's indifference is unconvincing.

'Seems DI Smart's wangled it with the Chief that they stay down in Manchester. The surveillance is getting results, and Smart reckons it's going to kick off on Saturday night – whatever *it* is.'

Skelgill remains silent. He stares pensively as headlights flash relentlessly into his narrowed eyes. Unblinking, he resists their interrogative glare like a prisoner determined not to yield.

'Looks like we're on our on own then, Leyton.'

*

'It is worse than we thought, Inspector.'

'How can it be worse?' The innocent note of inquiry in Skelgill's voice could almost be a front for sarcasm.

Briony Boss carefully adjusts her hair – clearly a displacement activity. She has applied extra layers of make up – fortifying her façade – and with dark shadows for eyes, she has a gothic look in the low light of her office, lit just by an *Anglepoise* lamp. From the Haresfell side she is the sole representative; Skelgill and DS Leyton sit broodingly across her desk.

'Dr Helen Pettigrew's identity pass is missing – Meredith Bale appears to have absconded — we suspect her of the attack.'

Skelgill mutters to himself.

'Bonnie and Clyde.'

'I'm sorry, Inspector?' (He has hissed the words under his breath.)

'Nothing, madam – carry on.'

'Eric Blacklock is reviewing the CCTV – I am expecting him any moment. We are undertaking a search – just in case she is still on the premises.'

Skelgill gets up and walks across to the windows. He digs his hands into his pockets and peers out in the direction of the allotments and the Lune valley. This cannot however be an exercise in surveillance, for the grounds are shrouded in darkness, and the cold halogen floodlights that illuminate the perimeter fence blind sight of anything beyond. He presses his forehead gently against the cool pane. It takes a few moments before he comes to some sort of conclusion and returns to his seat.

'You'd better start with Mrs Pettigrew.'

Briony Boss nods despondently.

'Dr – Helen – she has severe head injuries – perhaps caused by blows from a hammer – she has been taken to the intensive care unit at Cumberland Infirmary.'

'What about her husband?'

'He has been alerted – he should be at Helen's bedside by now.'

'He wasn't here when it happened?'

Briony Boss shakes her head.

'He had worked a normal shift – he swiped his card out at just after six-thirty. We think the attack took place at least an hour later.'

'They live in Kendal.' Skelgill states this as a fact, though he does not reveal his source, Arthur Kerr, the well-informed nurse begrudging of the privileged lifestyle of the Pettigrew family.

'That is correct, Inspector – their teenagers board at Sedbergh – so for the time being they are in good hands.'

Skelgill nods.

'What were the circumstances?'

The Director begins to reply, but her mouth is dry and she reaches for a water glass close at hand. There is the clink of ice as she drinks.

'She was discovered unconscious by a cleaner – she had lost a lot of blood but thankfully we were able to mobilise effective medical care within minutes – such that her condition was at least stabilised.'

Skelgill screws up his features like someone expecting a loud noise.

'I suppose it would be too much to ask for there to be CCTV in the drama studio?'

174

'I am afraid so, Inspector.'

'Why was she working late?'

'Her company is putting on a performance in August – *Romeo and Juliet* – they have a regular slot for rehearsal after the evening meal every Friday.'

'And Meredith Bale – she's in the group?'

'I understand she plays Juliet.'

Briony Boss forces an ironic smile, though Skelgill remains grim faced. The Director continues.

'The class ended at seven-thirty. Helen Pettigrew had called Coniston Ward to say that Meredith Bale would be returning later – that she would contact Security when they had finished. They must have been doing some extra rehearsal, one to one.'

Skelgill inhales, as if to raise a question – but at this moment the telephone rings. Briony Boss answers and listens intently. Though she is already tense it is news that further unsettles her, for she stiffens and her grip on the handset tightens.

'Are you certain?'

She listens again and then terminates the call without a word. The two detectives regard her like starved wolves. She clears her throat and takes another sip of her drink. When she looks up the whites of her eyes seem enlarged with disbelief.

'That was the gatehouse. They say that Dr Helen Pettigrew left with Dr Agnetha Walker at just before eight. Dr Walker was driving.'

'Jeez!'

It is DS Leyton's exclamation that expresses their collectively incredulity. And now the trio sit like actors who have simultaneously dried. Skelgill is first to find his tongue – he speaks tersely through clenched jaws, as if he is wrestling to control his emotions.

'Leyton – go down to the gatehouse – I want chapter and verse – get the registration number of Dr Walker's car – it's a red Volvo – put out an emergency alert. Move it.'

'Right, Guv.'

DS Leyton hauls himself to his feet and bustles towards the door – however, Briony Boss holds up a palm.

'Sergeant – you will need someone to escort you.'

But at this moment the door opens – the Head of Security has arrived with a uniformed subordinate. A brief exchange establishes that the latter will chaperone DS Leyton, and the couple make a hasty departure. Skelgill is introduced to Eric Blacklock. He is an imposing figure – albeit in his early sixties – about Skelgill's height but of a much heavier build. There are the ponderous movements and measured speech of an archetypal English village police constable; a strong chin and grey hair cropped close to a broad head – though beady blue eyes suggest a shrewd brain operates within the uncomplicated exterior. He asks Briony Boss if he may take control of her computer. She yields up her seat, and she and Skelgill cluster around. Eric Blacklock methodically dons a pair of reading glasses, and with sturdy fingers making slow and deliberate taps of the keyboard he logs in. Then he directs the mouse and after half a minute more makes a final click and sits back.

'Watch. This is them leaving through the staff foyer.'

The picture is grainy – a jerky sequence of monochrome stills that shows two rather shadowy figures advancing together, first entering the area, then crossing in close company, almost arm in arm, and swiping themselves out of the exit. Skelgill leans forwards, staring keenly. The leading person is clearly Dr Agnetha Walker – her slim form combined with her long wavy blonde hair is quite unmistakeable. The second woman is taller – a bigger physique altogether; and dark hair spills in coils from the hood of her coat, which has already been raised in anticipation of the rain that awaits them. They appear to exchange no words, although their movements are purposeful. Dr Agnetha Walker glances back anxiously as she passes through the door, but her companion pushes up behind her and she is obliged to move on. Eric Blacklock clears his throat.

'We'll have other footage – I'll need more time to isolate it – but this proves they went out to the car park. To come back in, they'd have to pass through our main Security check – and they obviously haven't done that.' He looks pointedly at the Director, and then to Skelgill. 'We'd have better than this – but the new system that was to be installed was cancelled.'

Briony Boss has been breathing audibly through her nose, at a rate that reveals an elevated pulse. She flashes a dark look at Eric Blacklock, but then she sighs and inhales again. She addresses Skelgill.

'That is not Dr Helen Pettigrew – it goes without saying.'

Eric Blacklock cranes around to stare at her with a curious expression. Clearly he knows the impossibility that it could be the badly injured psychologist – but there is something that perplexes him.

'She doesn't look like Meredith Bale, either.'

Skelgill is supporting himself with his hands on the edge of the desk. He pushes off and transfers his fists to the small of his back. He grits his teeth as he flexes his troublesome spine.

'What kind of wig does Juliet wear?'

Briony Boss's dark eyes flicker in the gloom.

'You are right, Inspector – they have an extensive collection of costumes – and wigs, of course.'

Eric Blacklock swivels around in the Director's chair. He folds his arms stubbornly.

'Why would Dr Walker lead Meredith Bale out of the hospital?'

Involuntarily, Briony Boss backs away. It appears that the idea is abhorrent – and that she is struggling to find an explanation. Then Skelgill supplies one.

'It didn't look like she had much choice, to me.'

This seems to be a straw she is willing to cling to. Now she holds out both hands in hope.

'What do you mean, Inspector?'

Skelgill inclines his head in the direction of the computer terminal.

'I'd say – from the way that Meredith Bale was sticking close to Dr Walker – she had a concealed weapon beneath that coat.'

Eric Blacklock begins to protest, but the Director overrules him with a curt interruption.

'Their movements were not natural. That is plain.'

Skelgill digs his hands into his pockets and takes a turn around the carpet.

'How could Dr Agnetha Walker have become caught up in this?'

Briony Boss takes a couple of paces towards him, as if she senses firmer ground in his vicinity. Indeed she places a tentative hand upon his sleeve.

'Inspector – she has use of a consulting room – it is right beside the drama studio – it was the gymnasium manager's office prior to the conversion.'

Skelgill nods, but he remains silent, encouraging the Director to continue with her speculation.

'She could have heard a noise – a cry of distress – and gone to investigate.' She draws the fingers of both hands slowly through her hair, as though she is tracing the imagery that percolates through her mind. 'Meredith Bale must have intimidated her – perhaps, as you say, with the weapon she used to attack Dr Helen Pettigrew.'

Skelgill joins the fingers of both hands and pulls them down onto the top of his head. It is as if he is unconsciously mirroring the Director's action.

'Why wouldn't she run away, raise the alarm?'

Briony Boss looks pained.

'Inspector – it is not so easy to run anywhere in a place like this – it is designed to prevent exactly that eventuality – to contain patients who might wish to avoid their nurses' ministrations. As you have experienced, there are security doors restricting almost every area.' She shakes her head so that her hair falls back into place. 'And, of course, having Dr Walker to accompany her made her exit appear more convincing – should they have been seen by another member of staff, or been followed on the camera system.'

Skelgill rubs his eyes and then clasps his hands together in a gesture of union.

'I take it they're acquainted – Dr Agnetha Walker and Dr Helen Pettigrew?'

Briony Boss nods.

178

'I understand they get on well – Dr Walker has been a dinner guest on several occasions – what with her living away from home – and working on a project supervised by Dr Peter Pettigrew. It would not be unusual for them to depart together.'

Skelgill nods slowly as he files away this piece of information.

'And you're sure about Dr Peter Pettigrew having left a good hour earlier?'

Now the Director turns back to Eric Blacklock. He seems rather reluctant to supply the answer. His response is accordingly gruff.

'The computer says so. We'll be able to confirm with CCTV. And the duty officer at the gatehouse.'

At this last suggestion Skelgill's eyes narrow doubtingly. It is a reasonable reaction given that the employee in question has already misidentified one Dr Pettigrew. However, he addresses Briony Boss.

'If we could get that confirmation – along with a list of movements in the vicinity of the drama studio between the class ending and the time that Meredith Bale and Dr Walker were recorded leaving.'

'Of course, Inspector.'

At this, Eric Blacklock rises laboriously and with a glance at each of them begins to make his way towards the door. It seems he does not intend to receive an order in front of Skelgill.

'Might take me an hour or so. The technology's slow.'

He departs without further explanation or leave-taking. It is plain that he is reluctant to shoulder any blame for his area of responsibility, when his superior's budget cuts can be scapegoated. As soon as the door closes behind him a somewhat despondent Briony Boss crosses the room.

'Excuse me one moment, Inspector.'

She bears her glass and opening a cabinet recharges it – and then repeats the operation with a matching tumbler. She carries them slowly to where Skelgill is engrossed at her desk – he is replaying the video on her computer, frame by frame to get the best shot of Dr Agnetha Walker's final strained backwards glance into the foyer. Certainly the psychologist appears alarmed – her eyebrows raised searchingly – but he has seen this expression several times in person, and knows it is not so straightforward as face value might suggest.

'These violent delights have violent ends.'

He is jolted from his preoccupation by these melodramatic words. Briony Boss is upon him, proffering a glass – there is the rattle of ice – a hand that trembles – and tears of black mascara that stream down her cheeks – her breathing comes in heavy gasps and she sways alarmingly. Skelgill springs to his feet and grabs at both tumblers simultaneously. Relieved of the burden she collapses against him – wraps her arms around his torso – and buries her head into his shoulder.

*

'This is becoming our second office, Guv.'

Skelgill shrugs.

'Could do worse, Leyton – the food's better than HQ – and at Haresfell there's always a minder lurking.'

'Suppose they've got no choice about that, Guv. Can't trust us not to get blagged by another fantasist like Frank Wamphray.'

Skelgill now scowls disagreeably.

'Pot and kettle, Leyton.'

DS Leyton nods, his nose buried in his mug. They have drinks only – both opting for coffees in recognition of the lateness of the hour and their need for alertness. He wipes away chocolaty froth from his lips with the back of his hand.

'That Volvo's disappeared into thin air, Guv. That's them – and Harry Krille.'

Now Skelgill nods grimly. He casts about the motorway cafeteria, and then thumps clenched fists onto the table in frustration.

'It's like being padded-up, Leyton – waiting to go in to bat – it's a killer.'

'I thought you were a bowler, Guv.'

Skelgill folds his arms and leans towards his colleague.

'Aye – but you still have to bat, Leyton – especially when your team's in trouble. Makes it worse.'

DS Leyton nods appreciatively.

'Got a game tomorrow, Guv?'

'You must be kidding – it was cancelled Tuesday. There's ducks on the square – and I'm not talking about the scoreboard.'

DS Leyton grins at his superior's sardonic joke. But lacking a witty retort, he remains silent, and they both sink into reverie. It may be they reflect on the decimation wrought upon the English cricket season by the climate, but if – more responsibly – the whereabouts of the Haresfell fugitives occupies their thoughts then Skelgill's simile is apposite: there is little they can do but metaphorically twirl their bats in anticipation of a breakthrough. DS Leyton, judging by the various expressions that tangle his brows, begins to wrestle with some deeply perplexing scenario, and one that plainly troubles him. After a couple of minutes the construct surfaces sufficiently for him to air his concern.

'Guv – do you reckon Harry Krille's got a hostage?'

'What makes you say that?'

'Well – it beats me why your Dr Walker didn't put up more of a fight – or even scream out to the geezer in the gatehouse. If he'd have just kept the barrier down they couldn't have gone anywhere.'

'So where does Krille come in?'

'Well, Guv – imagine if Meredith Bale says to you, my pal Crazy Harry's got your kid – so you'd better do as I tell you – then you'd probably obey.'

'She doesn't have kids – or relatives in Britain – she's from Sweden.'

A flicker of suspicion disturbs DS Leyton's features; is Skelgill sufficiently acquainted with Dr Agnetha Walker to know such facts?

'Or maybe a friend, Guv – some connection, anyway.'

Skelgill remains doubtful.

'I can't see it, Leyton – it's too complicated.'

DS Leyton seems determined to find some chink in Skelgill's opposition.

'Well – how about if she's got something on her, then?'

'Like what?'

'I dunno, Guv – she was a nurse, wasn't she? What if she knows Dr Walker committed some misdemeanour and has evidence to prove it?'

'Blackmail.' Skelgill's weary tone implies his resistance remains intact.

'Could be, Guv.'

Again they become subdued – until DS Leyton has another idea.

'Or bribery, Guv.'

'What?'

DS Leyton taps the side of his nose with a stout index finger.

'Remember what Frank Wamphray said, Guv – about how patients are bribing staff – we discussed it before – all it would take is access to a bank account.'

Skelgill frowns testily.

'Leyton – I can see a nurse smuggling in a packet of baccy – but Agnetha Walker conspiring in a murder? Come off it, man.'

DS Leyton's patience is beginning to wear thin, as his suggestions are successively dismissed. This sentiment is surely exacerbated by the fact that he is keeping his boss company late on a Friday night, while the latter makes scant effort to provide theories of his own. Suddenly he lets loose an expletive, one approximately rhyming with duck's wake (and no connection to cricket, or waterfowl) – a minor outburst that attracts the wary eye of a young woman waiting to serve behind the hot food counter. Skelgill glances anxiously towards her, and waves a reassuring hand; perhaps she is the cousin, the insider whom he would not wish to distress.

'Steady on, Leyton – it's only a job at the end of the day.'

DS Leyton is sufficiently perplexed by this statement to forget his anger. He gazes at Skelgill with some amazement – the sentiment does not ring true with Skelgill's irrational dedication to catching criminals, with little regard for his own personal safety, comfort or gain. Perhaps there is some aspect of his superior's make up that he has not fully understood.

'Look, Leyton – your guess is as good as mine – fair enough.'

The sergeant is not one to harbour grudges, and he probably knows this is about as near to an apology that Skelgill is ever likely to stoop. He nods amenably, and Skelgill continues.

'I'm just going by the facts. Meredith Bale's a big hulking serial killer – Agnetha Walker's a seven-stone slip of a lass who looks terrified in that video footage.'

DS Leyton purses his lips thoughtfully.

'I'd put her at more than seven stone, Guv.'

Skelgill shakes his head resolutely, but does not elaborate upon the basis for his confidence.

'Nobody can tell how a person will react in that situation – she might be a trained criminal psychologist, but if she walked in on Meredith Bale battering Dr Helen Pettigrew's brains in with a claw hammer – who knows what switches it would flick?'

'She's not dead, anyway, Guv.'

'Come again?'

'You said accessory to murder, Guv – the hospital report says she's critical but stable.'

'Aye, well – let's hope they're right about the stable.'

DS Leyton nods sympathetically.

'That's some brass neck of Meredith Bale, Guv – knocking the woman on the head and getting herself escorted out of there.'

'What did the duty officer at the gatehouse say?'

DS Leyton pulls the sort of face that precedes the relaying of unfortunate news.

'He knows he's dropped a clanger, Guv – reckons he's in for the chop.' DS Leyton absently rubs his crown with one hand. 'I feel sorry for the poor geezer. Familiar car pulls up – it's sheeting with rain – driver just lowers the window a couple of inches – he recognises her – she tells him she's giving a colleague a lift – why shouldn't he believe her? It's dark and he can't see properly into the car for all the raindrops and whatnot – but it looks enough like Dr Helen Pettigrew – why would he think for a minute she's an imposter? It's not his job to vet members of staff – that's why they've got the electronic ID system.'

Skelgill is nodding pensively.

'Eric Blacklock was complaining about the lack of investment in security – he was laying the blame at the Director's door.'

'She always seems a bit cagey to me, Guv.' He pauses for thought. 'Or if not cagey – distracted about something.'

Skelgill looks away, and it takes him a few seconds to compose a rejoinder.

'She's got plenty on her plate, Leyton.'

Perhaps his use of this idiom triggers a subliminal reaction, for he stares longingly towards the self-serve food counter. A trio of truckers has traipsed in, their boots clicking on the tiled floor, and they begin loading plates with the all-day breakfast. DS Leyton, on the other hand, following Skelgill's line of sight, seems to be reminded of the possibility of Harry Krille stowing away aboard a lorry.

'Wonder how far they've all got, Guv?'

Skelgill does not reply, but instead delves into his jacket, which is draped on the back of his chair. He pulls out his recently acquired map of Cumbria (paid for by DS Leyton) and begins to leaf through its folds in the practised manner of a seasoned hillwalker, efficiently finding a location without the requirement to spread the entire sheet. He stops to scrutinise some point – albeit stretching at arm's length, and not without a good deal of squinting – before he grunts to himself and returns the map whence it came.

'The further they travel the more likely they'll get spotted. The longer we go without a sighting – of any of them – the more I'd be inclined to think they've gone to ground closer to home.'

'We've got a watch on all of the relevant properties, Guv. The Pettigrew's house in Kendal. Dr Walker's cottage near Bassenthwaite. Plus her place down in Didsbury and Meredith Bale's mother's gaff in Wythenshawe. Fact is, Manchester's their old stamping ground – all three of them at one time or another, Harry Krille included – though that's going back some.'

Skelgill is resting his chin on the bridge of his interlocked fingers, elbows upon the table. He closes his eyes for a few moments – and perhaps this is an act borne out of tiredness rather than cogitation. When he does not respond, DS Leyton continues, but not before he too succumbs to a debilitating yawn.

'What should we do, Guv?'

Skelgill glances at his watch – the hour is well on its way to midnight.

'Get a break, Leyton. Hope something comes up over the weekend.'

DS Leyton ought to be relieved to hear this – though his gaze is fixed upon a series of marks that he has noticed on Skelgill's check-patterned shirt, smears of ochre and black that streak his shoulder and breast. After a few moments he starts and looks directly at his superior.

'It's hard lines on your Doctor Walker, Guv. If she hadn't stood you up – she'd be safely tucked in bed right now.'

20. CENTRAL MANCHESTER

'**O**h, no – you gave me such a fright!' DS Jones has one hand over her heart and with the other reaches to brace her spread fingers on Skelgill's chest. 'I didn't see you.'

He has ambushed her in a communal restroom, slinking from a WC as she experiments with complimentary perfume that is ranged around a great central washing fountain, itself crowned by life-sized bronze figurines of a strapping merman and his lithe siren partner, entwined in a somewhat improbable X-rated embrace. There are also bottles of men's cologne, and unisex creams and balms that draw a disapproving scowl from Skelgill. The lighting is subdued, and a low base beat permeates the sticky scented air. The walls and doors – in fact all of the surfaces – are lined with tinted mirrored steel that creates a curious voyeuristic effect, as though the room has been designed with exhibitionism in mind. He glances about uneasily.

'You haven't seen me.'

'Yes – no, Guv – I mean – I wasn't expecting you.'

'Your phone's been off since this afternoon.'

'It's on charge in my room.'

Skelgill regards her suspiciously. She wears just a figure-hugging mini-dress in metallic blue PVC that zips at the front from top to bottom; its glistening shine highlights her contours and its immodest cut showcases a good proportion of what endows them.

'I notice you're blending in.'

'I *am*, Guv – this is nothing – you should see the crowd that arrives after midnight.'

A note of self-consciousness is evident in her voice, but to her rescue into the atrium totter two brunettes on skyscraper heels, clad in what for all the world might be skimpy beachwear. They are drunk (and still drinking) and pay no heed to DS Jones and Skelgill. Instead they clatter into a single cubicle and begin to take selfies in situ, the door wide open and the pair of them perched on the toilet, a tangle of unruly hair and spread-eagled spray-tanned limbs and raised glasses, wrapped in hysterical laughter. Skelgill wrenches his gaze away from the spectacle.

'What is this place?'

'It's a boutique hotel.'

'Seems more like the worst kind of Mediterranean resort.'

'It's the hippest night spot in Manchester, Guv.'

'It that any better?'

DS Jones glances apprehensively towards the door as more females arrive, arm in arm and almost tripping over the stream of tipsy giggles and chatter that precedes them.

'I oughtn't be long, Guv – Al – DI Smart will come looking for me – he says he's worried that our cover's been blown.'

Skelgill casts an eye over her outfit – it is difficult to tell if this is disapproval or in fact the converse – but either way there is certainly something proprietorial in his manner.

'I need to talk to you.'

DS Jones again glances away – although now it is to avoid his penetrating stare.

'It's tricky, Guv – it's only just getting lively here – and it goes on until the early hours.'

'It won't take long.'

'But what shall I say?'

Skelgill shrugs.

'Think of something that'll confuse him – tell him it's a woman thing.'

DS Jones returns her gaze to meet his. Her features are torn – and she looks ready to remind him it was he that consigned her to the clutches of DI Alec Smart – but then she seems to make up her mind. She nods and from her glittering purse extracts a key on an ornate metal fob sculpted into a shapely mermaid. She presents it to him tail first.

'I'm already using that one, Guv.'

Skelgill can't hide his consternation. But before he can protest she swivels on her stilettos and glides easily away, like a catwalk model reflected from all angles in a dozen mirrors. A pair of young guys with trendy haircuts and get-ups to match appear in the doorway, and for a moment they bar her path. Skelgill stiffens as he watches – but she is not fazed and takes them on with a defiant stare – they step aside and form a little guard of honour, bowing to her superior power of attraction, unable to control hungry eyes that steal a glimpse of her alluring form. She passes from sight and they exchange a nod and a wink – as if the gauntlet has been thrown at their feet – then they notice Skelgill, and drift past him, amused smirks turning up the corners of their mouths as they appraise his less-than-fashionable attire.

'Same old chat-up line, cock?'

'Or maybe it's the great smell of *Brut*?'

These quips – barbed though they are – are delivered good naturedly, but nonetheless elicit only a malevolent glare from Skelgill. His brooding, coiled presence suddenly becomes threatening. Unnerved, the jokers shrug ostentatiously, affecting offence at his deficiency of humour, and split into separate cubicles. Skelgill looks like he is ready to take out his frustration on some vaguely deserving object – but an upwards glance at the dome camera quells his urge. He pockets the key and stalks away. A moment later he sidles back, and snatches up one of the brightly coloured bottles of cologne.

*

'Where did you sleep, Guv?'

'In my motor.'

'You could have stayed in my room – the hotel wouldn't have noticed.'

188

Skelgill flexes his vertebrae, as if to emphasise the discomfort of his self-imposed ordeal: the flatbed of his car, parked on the roof of a towering 24-hour multi-storey that had him waking to a view of grim urban incongruity and a dawn chorus of the all-pervasive strained hum of the city.

'I didn't want to be an inconvenience at four in the morning.'

DS Jones shifts from one foot to the other.

'I'll get you another coffee, Guv?'

'Aye – why not.'

She unhitches a chic shoulder bag and drapes it over the back of the chair opposite Skelgill.

'Double shot?'

He nods.

'Where's Smart?'

Again she looks a little uneasy.

'He doesn't seem to surface until about midday, Guv – he says if we're working so late we should get the mornings off.'

Skelgill makes a disparaging face.

'Make sure you claim all your overtime.'

She grins and heads for the counter. The ubiquitous chain coffee shop is located in what to Skelgill is a depressingly concrete part of the city centre. As a largely uninhabited district, it relies upon shoppers and students to give it colour, but neither group is much in evidence this time on a Sunday morning. For once, however, it is not raining. When DS Jones returns with their drinks she seems surprisingly bright eyed, and altogether a different proposition than twelve hours earlier – now in trainers, jeans and sweatshirt, and stripped of her vampish make up and revealing outfit, she could be an eager student meeting a lecturer to review progress on her dissertation; indeed she produces a pad and pen, and several loose pages of handwritten notes.

'Cheers.'

She seems surprised by his word of thanks.

'You're welcome.'

Skelgill, however, does not stand any further on ceremony.

'So he's got back to you?'

DS Jones nods in a qualified manner.

'He couldn't find everything you wanted, Guv – he's been into his office again this morning – he'd already made some progress on what you previously asked for.' She looks at Skelgill and bites at one side of her lower lip. 'I don't know how helpful it's going to be, though. Whether it will take you anywhere.'

'What am I doing in Manchester? I'm on the road to nowhere. *Anywhere* is just fine.'

'I feel like it's the sort of information you could obtain by just asking them.'

'Maybe I don't want to ask.'

DS Jones is stymied for a moment as she tries to work out the significance of his cryptic retort. She opts, however, for an uncomplicated question.

'Any news this morning, Guv?'

'Bale and Krille have gone to ground. No idea if they've linked up.'

'What about Dr Walker?'

Something in DS Jones's voice causes him to glance sharply at her. An interrogative note beyond the professional question, perhaps?

'No word.'

His response is terse and now DS Jones looks down at her notes.

'It must be worrying, Guv?'

'How?' Skelgill uses the Scottish *how*, that really means *why*.'

'Oh – DI Smart – he said you and she were... that you'd been taking her fishing.'

Skelgill is irked.

'You can ignore Smart. He's jealous because she turned down a ride in his poncey car. I *had* to take her fishing. The Chief's publicity stunt.'

DS Jones regards Skelgill warily, as if she suspects him of massaging the facts.

'He seems to be well informed, Guv – he's never off the phone – it's the way he operates – he encourages gossip and rumour, inside and outside of the force.'

Skelgill shrugs casually.

'So what does he know about Annie Walker?'

DS Jones seems to react to his use of this diminutive for the doctor's Christian name. It is a few seconds before she answers.

'Nothing really, Guv – not of substance, at least.'

'What then?'

'Oh – he said the word going round at the forensic conference – she was one of the speakers – that she has a bit of a reputation for getting what she wants.'

Skelgill growls irritably.

'She's got ability – that's what narks people like Smart and his cronies.'

He glances away as he says this, and he does not observe DS Jones's raising of her eyebrows. There is a look in her eye that tells some womanly curiosity is as yet unsatisfied. However, her response errs on the side of diplomacy.

'She's well qualified, Guv.'

Now DS Jones reaches for her notes – though she fans herself and gives a little sigh – and then she lets the pages drop and takes hold of the hem of her sweatshirt. Certainly the air in the coffee shop is warm and stifling. With crossed arms she peels back the thick cotton garment, pausing to manoeuvre it past her earrings. Beneath she wears just a sleeveless white vest and – as is evident when the fabric of the latter tightens against her torso – no bra.

There is something of a hiatus as she emerges from the tangle and shakes out her hair. Skelgill is looking unsettled, and there is colour in his cheeks. He suddenly coughs and seeks relief from his coffee, but the milk has been scalded and it is too hot, even for him. DS Jones smiles demurely; she re-gathers her papers and sorts through them, pulling one sheet to the fore – it is a table of sorts; names written along one axis and dates down the other, seven years up to the present in chronological order. She rotates the page so that Skelgill can see better, and then she moves around to take the chair perpendicular to him.

'I drew this chart, Guv.'

He is nodding approvingly – in its graphic simplicity it panders to his aversion to the written word.

'I thought it made sense to start with Meredith Bale.' She points to the top left corner with a neatly manicured nail that still bears a metallic blue reminder of last night. 'Her original degree is in biomedical sciences – she went into nursing and qualified as a mental health nurse five-and-a-half years ago. That's when she got a post at the NHS psychiatric hospital – Altrincham Vale – where her known offending took place.' (Skelgill nods – he is vaguely familiar with this affluent town-cum-suburb of Manchester.) 'She worked there until two years ago – when she was arrested. It was another six months before she was found guilty and committed to Haresfell.'

Skelgill nods.

'Harry Krille was in Broadmoor from before the turn of the century up until two-and-a-half years ago, when he was moved to Haresfell.'

'A year before Meredith Bale.'

'That's right, Guv. There's nothing in the NHS records about the letters she wrote to him, but I can't imagine they continued after she was arrested.'

'Leyton's supposed to have a DC looking into the court files.' Skelgill grimaces with frustration. 'There's been a suggestion it was one-way traffic – that Krille had quite a fan club.'

DS Jones sits back in her chair and looks at Skelgill earnestly.

'Guv – is there actually any evidence to indicate that Harry Krille and Meredith Bale acted in concert – that they coordinated their escape?'

Skelgill immediately shakes his head, as if this prospect is very much top of mind.

'Nope.'

'So it could be a coincidence?'

'As likely as not.'

DS Jones becomes increasingly pensive; she turns to one side and sweeps back her gold-streaked fair hair with one hand. After a few moments she reverts to the chart, and lightly taps the page with spread fingers, as though they are halfway to being lost, and it is all they have to go on, a flimsy road map.

'If there was any collusion, Guv – between either Bale or Krille and someone who was treating or managing them – then these dates do reveal a history that might be relevant – at least for several of the names you wanted checked out.'

Skelgill takes a wary sip of his coffee and finds it has cooled sufficiently to follow up with a more substantial gulp.   He swallows and licks his lips.

'Fire away then, lass.'

DS Jones begins to trace a nail across the top of the page, and stops at the third column.

'The Director of Haresfell, Briony Boss.' She glances briefly at Skelgill, but his features remain impassive. 'She was second in charge at Broadmoor until five years ago – so her time there would have overlapped with Harry Krille being a patient. She had worked her way up through the administrative ranks after starting her career in nursing. From Broadmoor she went on to manage two regular NHS hospitals in Greater Manchester – both jobs were considered promotions, and required urgent troubleshooting, so she must have been successful. Then she was appointed to the number one position at Haresfell two-and-a-half years ago.'

'Same time as Harry Krille arrived.'

DS Jones nods – though neither detective appears to attach any significance to this particular conjunction. DS Jones moves on to the next column.

'Dr Peter Pettigrew. He has been based at Haresfell for over eight years.   He seems to be a highly regarded forensic psychiatrist. He sits on various NHS steering committees and advisory boards, such as for public appointments, and he also has a roving teaching and consulting role, mainly in psychiatric hospitals. He is a prominent advisor to the courts – considered to be the leading authority in the North West.'

Skelgill is scowling – this is not fresh news.

'Aye, that's come up – he was in charge of the panel that sent Meredith Bale to mental hospital instead of prison.'

DS Jones again nods.

'His wife, Dr Helen Pettigrew, her background has been mainly academic – most latterly she was at Lancaster University lecturing in psychology. It looks like she took a career break to have children, and then started back part-time. Obviously the NHS doesn't have records of this – solely what's filed on her CV. Then she got the post at Haresfell – six months ago.'

Skelgill raises his eyebrows to indicate her bad luck – falling victim in so short a time.

'Dr Agnetha Walker.' Now DS Jones hesitates – it seems she anticipates an interjection from Skelgill; she has pronounced Agnetha in the authentic Scandinavian style, with the silent 'g' and the hard 't', and it must surely strike a chord with Skelgill – although there is something in her demeanour that suggests she is testing the name upon herself. 'She's a psychologist employed by the NHS – it seems to be quite a specialist role and involves assignments in various locations, on a patient-basis rather than being attached to a specific hospital. She also sits on advisory panels – largely for court work. She was based around the East Midlands until about three years ago, and then transferred to Greater Manchester – until this latest project in Cumbria. It appears because of the isolation of Haresfell she has worked there exclusively since the move in May.'

DS Jones falls silent, but her closing intonation suggests that this particular résumé is not yet complete. She watches for Skelgill's reaction, but when nothing is forthcoming she continues. A more solemn note takes possession of her voice.

'The psychiatric unit in which Meredith Bale worked at Altrincham Vale – it falls within the list of hospitals in Dr Walker's remit.'

Now Skelgill is scowling.

'So what?'

DS Jones indicates a section of the chart with a movement to and fro of an index finger.

'There's a period of about a year in which their paths could have crossed.'

'But she's outside the management hierarchy – she doesn't have anything to do with nurses. She works directly with patients.'

DS Jones evidently senses a rise in tension.

'Sure, Guv – and the same possible connection applies, by the way, to Dr Peter Pettigrew – his teaching and consultancy portfolio includes Altrincham Vale.'

Now a flicker of uncertainty crosses Skelgill's countenance – DS Jones detects his grudging interest.

'The point is, Guv – there *are* overlaps – we don't know what might have happened during these times – but there could be reasons why Dr Walker and Dr Pettigrew, through his wife – have been targeted now by Meredith Bale. If the woman's crazy, like they say – even a misplaced word could have got them in her bad books.'

Her eyes are bright with an intelligence that Skelgill cannot deny; though in typical fashion he retreats behind a pained grimace, as if there is a debate raging for his political allegiance, and his nature knows only independence. His rejoinder dodges the conundrum.

'What about Arthur Kerr? I see you've got a column for him.'

DS Jones inhales sharply, as if she has not finished trying to win Skelgill over – but she relents and moves on to his new inquiry.

'He worked at Broadmoor until six years ago – which means he has overlapped with Briony Boss and Harry Krille at both institutions.'

Skelgill is frowning.

'Are you sure – about the six years?'

DS Jones flashes him a surprised glance. Then she leafs through the pages beneath the chart until she finds the corresponding notes.

'Aha – that's what I've been given – see, Guv.'

Skelgill looks pensive, but does not comment. DS Jones, however, has more to add.

'There are confidential notes on his file, Guv – not the sort of thing we could put in print – it would compromise our source – I haven't even written it out in longhand.'

'Such as?'

'He's known as a bit of a militant. There was a period at Broadmoor when the unions apparently ruled the roost – and worse if the rumours are to be believed – he was one of the leading convenors, *Red Arthur*, they called him. Perhaps that's got something to do with his move away – to Haresfell.' (Skelgill nods in a fashion that suggests this information doesn't surprise him.) 'I wonder if Briony Boss – when she landed at Haresfell – wasn't too pleased to see him?'

'Or the opposite.'

This is a typically oblique Skelgill response – and DS Jones looks hard at him. Is he playing devil's advocate for the hell of it, or in fact is there some basis for his glib quip? His features remain implacable.

'What else?'

'Er – yeah, Guv.' It takes her a couple of seconds to get back on track. 'There's a bit of a blot on his professional copybook. At Broadmoor a patient in his care died unexpectedly. It went to a tribunal and he was exonerated of any blame. Evidently they accepted his defence that the institution was under-resourced, and he was overstretched.'

Skelgill is feeling the stubble on his chin.

'What was the cause of death?'

'It was a heart attack – apparently the patient was awaiting regular medication and the nurses were late doing their rounds. There's some suggestion that they were having an unauthorised staff party, but nothing could be proven. It looks like the workers closed ranks.'

DS Jones glances up from her notes. Skelgill is staring fixedly into his coffee mug; at the same time methodically stirring the residual froth into what little is left of the liquid beneath. When he does not respond to her latest statement, she offers a prompt.

'What are you thinking, Guv – that there might be something more to Frank Wamphray's death – given the Arthur Kerr connection?'

Skelgill jolts out of his daydream and gazes at her, blinking.

'What? No – I was just wondering what confidential notes are on my file.'

DS Jones regards him with a certain amused irony; he forces a rueful grin and consults his wristwatch.

'I need to make a phone call.'

Now DS Jones sits back in her chair – but then she realises he might mean that he wants privacy, and is not prepared to find a quiet spot. She pushes back her chair to indicate she is willing to move away.

'Are you hungry, Guv? I haven't eaten – they only offer a detox tray at the hotel – I don't think they expect their guests to be up in time for normal breakfast.'

Skelgill cranes his neck around to inspect the service counter.

'Do they serve bacon rolls in here?'

'Afraid not, Guv – there's toasted panini – ham and cheese, maybe?'

Skelgill shrugs.

'Aye – whatever looks biggest.'

DS Jones smiles and gets to her feet. As she moves away, Skelgill suddenly calls her back. He is digging in his jacket pocket.

'Jones – here – it's my round.'

She stops and turns and shakes her head.

'It's okay, Guv – DI Smart has got approval for full board expenses – may as well put it on his account?'

Skelgill hesitates for a moment – but just a moment.

'Better make it two of those paninis, then. And get something for yourself.'

DS Jones grins broadly and resumes her mission to place an order. She waits at the counter not only for fresh drinks to be prepared, but also for the food to be heated. By the time she returns bearing a loaded tray, Skelgill has concluded his call and is reading an article in a complimentary tabloid newspaper. He is shaking his head and clicking his tongue irritably.

'This reminds me why I don't get a paper.'

He rotates the periodical so she can read the headline: *"Bonnie & Clyde Confound Cumbria Cops."*

DS Jones raises her eyebrows.

'It hasn't taken them long to come up with Bonnie and Clyde, Guv.'

Skelgill shakes his head, his countenance sour. He crumples the newspaper onto the vacant seat beside him.

'Bloodsuckers. Let's stand on the sidelines with no qualifications and pull down people who are knocking their pans out.' He makes a gesture, pointing alternately with his sandwich to indicate he includes the pair of them. 'Look at us now – on a Sunday morning – in our own time – a hundred and twenty miles from home.'

DS Jones nods.

'What does the article say, Guv?'

Skelgill takes an exploratory bite of his sandwich. The toasted bread is crisp and dry and it takes him a few moments to chew and swallow and he needs the last dregs of his previous coffee to wash it down. He glowers angrily.

'Quotes the Chief – we've apparently got the situation under control – just a matter of time before we locate them.' He makes a sarcastic scoffing sound. 'The worst thing is – the headline writer's got it right.'

DS Jones's brow is furrowed pensively.

'There's probably more we could find out, Guv – from the NHS records. My friend's willing to meet us today – if you think it would help – to give him a better idea of what we're looking for?'

Skelgill is raising his sandwich for the next bite, like a flautist preparing to play. A sudden reticence clouds his eyes. He gives a slight shake of his head.

'I've got an appointment on the Eden – with the *Lady of the Stream*.'

21. FISHING WITH ALICE

'Does one *eat* grayling, Daniel?'
'Some folk prefer it to trout – it's supposed to smell of thyme – but it's pretty similar if you ask me.'
'And is it in season?'
'Aye, you're allowed two fish a day – provided they're between a foot and fifteen inches.'
'Why is that?'
'To conserve the stocks – the lower limit protects the juveniles that are still to spawn – the upper safeguards the specimen fish – that make it through the net, you might say.'
'It is such a beautiful creature – it would be a shame to kill it at all, Daniel.'
'I'm pretty much a catch-and-release man myself.'
'Then go ahead.'
Skelgill slides the silvery lady back into the stream and watches as she slips away with the current, her elegant dorsal fin momentarily slicing through the surface ripple before she submerges whence she came. He washes his hands of slime and dabs the landing net into the river for the same purpose, and then clambers back up the bank from his position as ghillie. Alice Wright-Fotheringham regards him with evident satisfaction. He raises a quizzical eyebrow.
'Except when it comes to criminals, obviously.'
'Well of course, Daniel – I think the *release* part was more my bag – much to your chagrin at times.'
Skelgill shrugs phlegmatically.
'Time for a cuppa, eh?'
With care he relieves the retired judge of his best spinning rod, and secures the hook in the keeper.

'Ah – the contraption. Will it work in the rain?'

'Aye. Some folk call them a storm kettle.' He glances skywards, as though he senses he is tempting fate. 'Or a volcano kettle.'

And now he stops in his tracks – perhaps this postscript has rekindled the image of the last time he used his kit, eight days ago on Bassenthwaite Lake, when the attractive Swedish psychologist Agnetha Walker showed her mettle as a outdoorswoman – perhaps something that will stand her in good stead in her present state of jeopardy.

'I think this must be the best part of being an angler, is it not?'

Skelgill stirs from his deliberation and leads the way to his assortment of kit, heaped beneath a spreading yew where the ground is dry despite weeks of persistent rain. He considers his companion's suggestion with a tilting of his head.

'It's a close-run thing, that's for sure.'

He pulls a couple of sit-mats from a rucksack, and offers a hand to help Alice Wright-Fotheringham lower herself into a recumbent position.

'It was kind of you to take up my plea to fish so soon. And now my first grayling.'

There is a mischievous note in the woman's voice, and Skelgill evidently decides that he will not be well served by beating disingenuously about the bush.

'I have to admit to a professional interest.'

'Your Haresfell case, of course.'

She says this as a statement of fact, and indeed her tone suggests she would be offended if he had anything other in mind. Nonetheless, he manages to contrive a certain look of discomfiture, as he begins to busy himself with assembling the Kelly kettle.

'Aye.'

'It is not so straightforward as the media would have it?'

Skelgill shakes his head ruefully.

'It's like a wind-knot – you know, when you've made a shoddy cast? It's not a true knot at all – just a great bunch in the line itself, and you can see the whole thing – but just not how to undo it.'

'So how does one unravel a tangled wind-knot?'

Skelgill pours a little methylated spirits into the chimney of the kettle, and then drops in a lighted match. There is a whoosh and he jerks his head back and instinctively rubs at his eyebrows. A cloying sulphurous smell now taints the air. Alice Wright-Fotheringham gives an amused chuckle. Skelgill is still thinking about his answer.

'I don't know.'

'But it must be a predicament you face from time to time – even a proficient fisherman such as yourself?'

Now he shrugs with affected modesty.

'Aye, well – you know – I just go at it – I don't think "pull that loop through here, and push that strand through there" – I just sort of do it by feel – working the line from the inside out.'

'And does this method bring success?'

Now Skelgill nods musingly.

'Aye, usually – you think it's never going to clear – next thing, it's out.'

Already the water is beginning to boil, and now Skelgill sets up a pair of tin mugs and charges them with tea bags and milk from a small flask. Then deftly he lifts the kettle from its base and tilts it to fill the mugs. Alice Wright-Fotheringham watches, intrigued – is it his adeptness with the device or his crime-solving simile? She leans to one side and delves into a pocket of her waxed-cotton stockman's coat. There is a rustling sound and she produces a paper bag – and as if by magic two dogs appear silently at her side; Cleopatra, Skelgill's Bullboxer, and Justitia, her own chocolate Labrador Retriever, have spent the past hour curled contentedly on an old tartan rug between the roots of the yew.

'Ah, my dears – to what do I owe the pleasure?'

Skelgill glances up from his stirring of the tea with a smile on his face. For once he looks relaxed, and enjoying the moment, and he continues to beam paternally as the retired judge breaks a stick of shortbread in two and invites the pair of drooling canines to sit. Clearly knowing on which side their bread is buttered, they obey almost instantly.

'Nicely.'

Her second command is also followed to the letter, and the dogs simultaneously with the greatest of care take the pieces of biscuit from her fingers, like trout that nonchalantly sip unsuspecting mayflies from the surface film with barely a show of lips.

'I ought to have you training my team.'

'Oh – I think I can be of more utility as a sounding board, Daniel – and, of course, I still have contacts in the right places – or some them, at least.'

Skelgill makes an ahem-like cough and, at the same time, glancing sideways to see that she is gazing regally across the fast-flowing Eden, with forefinger and thumb he deftly plucks the teabag from her mug and presents it to her, handle first.

'Aye, well – I know you're not one to gossip, Alice – but I was wondering if you could do a little digging among your old acquaintances?'

She turns, a little stiffly, to face him. Then she proffers the paper bag.

'I've done it. Here – have a piece of shortbread – it's home made – in fact, take two.'

Skelgill is looking somewhat wide-eyed, but nonetheless he accepts her offer.

'Don't mind if I do. Thanks.'

'Yes, Daniel – I anticipated your curiosity – particularly after the clumsy hints you dropped when you rather casually appeared at my regular dog-walking spot the other day.'

Skelgill now ruminates sheepishly.

'Was it that obvious?'

'Daniel – when one has spent a lifetime in the courts, hearing the truth, the whole truth, and nothing like the truth – one becomes rather adept at dissecting between the lines, so to speak.'

Skelgill bows his head obediently – then he remembers the shortbread and dunks a baton into his tea and pops it into his mouth. Now he nods with approval, and holds up the remaining piece to indicate his sentiment.

'An old family recipe, Daniel – the Fotheringhams were Scots – from Auchtermuchty, I believe.'

'Keep it in the family.'

'Alas, I am the last of the line.'

Skelgill nods respectfully. He seems reticent about picking up the conversation concerning her contacts, and what she may already have gleaned on his behalf. However, she harbours no such qualms.

'Since you were inquiring about the incumbent Director, Briony Boss, I took it upon myself to fill in a little of the background detail. I am in touch with members of the NHS Board – indeed one of their number is my regular bridge partner.'

Skelgill frowns pensively.

'She's having a bit of a hard time of it right now – what with this sudden avalanche of catastrophes – and she's not getting a lot of support from her lieutenants.'

'And who might they be?'

Skelgill pulls a face, as if to indicate he has perhaps over egged this indictment.

'There's the head security guy, Eric Blacklock – he's none too chuffed – he's blaming their problems on her cost cutting. Then the senior forensic psychiatrist – he seems to be at loggerheads with her, too – name of Dr Peter Pettigrew, husband of the woman attacked on Friday night.'

'Ah.'

'Is there something, Alice?' Her monosyllable has his antennae twitching.

'Peter Pettigrew I know – not socially, of course – but he was vice-chair of the sub-committee that oversaw the recruitment process for Haresfell – the position that Briony Boss was appointed to fill. As I recall he was a very strong advocate of her case.'

'I'm surprised to hear that.'

'You will recall, Daniel – when we touched upon this at Crow Park – that I mentioned there had been some rumour of an affair?' (Skelgill nods dutifully.) 'Peter Pettigrew met with her, in confidence – he established that in fact she was going through a divorce – it is a time when all sorts of false accusations fly about. He convinced me that there would be no problems on that score – and he does have a persuasive manner – with the fairer sex, at least.'

'Aye?'

Skelgill seems caught off guard by her afterthought. Alice Wright-Fotheringham regards him with a twinkle in her eye.

'You might be surprised, Daniel – what it is about certain men that causes women to weaken at the knees.'

She surveys him with a knowing grin. Unsure of how to respond, he averts his gaze and stares out rather blankly across the river. Her next remark seems designed to compound his confusion.

'Take the escapee Harry Krille – a case in point. I found him a most disconcerting and yet engaging adversary.'

Skelgill darts her a surprised glance.

'You knew him?'

'Only in a manner of speaking – back in those dark days – I was the Crown Prosecutor.'

Skelgill bites at his lower lip and nods slowly.

'When you were at the Old Bailey.'

'Harry Krille – you see, Daniel – he was your typical neighbourhood psychopath – a ruthless killer, lacking empathy and emotion, but also a smooth-talking, unselfconscious flirt. Of course – I have not set eyes upon him since his trial.'

Skelgill shifts uneasily, as if the hard ground is discomforting him.

'The trouble with a psychopath, Daniel, is that they know what you are feeling but they don't feel it themselves – so they can use your own emotions against you. One has to be very guarded in one's dealings with such a person.'

Skelgill now makes a deep expiration of breath that is something akin to a sigh.

'You sound like you're describing my boss.'

She responds with a throaty chuckle.

'Now, now, Daniel – you know only too well that she and I are acquainted.'

Skelgill reciprocates with a rueful grin.

'Aye – and you know I'd never say anything I wouldn't tell a person to their face.'

'That may become your downfall, Daniel.'

'I think I'm well past the point of no return, Alice.'

She considers him through narrowed eyes.

'Oh, I hear on the grapevine you are most highly regarded – even if those in authority are reluctant to admit it.'

Skelgill makes a dismissive scoffing sound.

'They won't have to if I don't get somewhere with this case.'

She wags a reprimanding finger.

'Which brings us back to Broadmoor.'

Skelgill looks bemused.

'Does it?'

'Yes – at least as far as Briony Boss is concerned.' Now she delivers a confidential wink. 'I appreciate your observation about my not being a rumourmonger – but one cannot avoid what one hears. Gossiping is the gratuitous passing on of superfluous information. This is not such a circumstance.'

'Aye.'

'Evidently the sub-committee did entertain some reservations over Briony Boss – there was more debate than was finally presented for my approval – and of course sweetened by the silky tongue of Peter Pettigrew. It was noted that her elevation from staff nurse had been somewhat meteoric, entering the administrative ranks and rising rapidly to executive level. There was a suggestion that at certain pivotal moments of her career something more than merit was at play.' Alice Wright-Fotheringham scrutinises him closely. 'You have met her, of course?'

'Aye.'

'Then perhaps you understand what I may be talking about?'

'I reckon I get your gist, Alice. She's a striking lady.'

'There we are, then. It is not difficult to imagine that she might still be a source of disquiet. And, of course, she came with a reputation for stamping out restrictive practices amongst the workers. She is said to have wreaked havoc upon the unions at Broadmoor, and broken up their most militant cabal.'

Skelgill nods, but senses she will continue.

'However, it does strike one as odd that there is friction between her and Peter Pettigrew. From what I am told he has done very well out of Briony Boss's accession – promoted to higher grade and awarded overall control of medical policies for Haresfell. She has given him the platform to become a national authority – with so few similar institutions in the British Isles.'

Skelgill is looking concerned.

'We've not been able to interview him – since the attack on his wife – he's spending a lot of time at her bedside at Cumberland Infirmary.'

Alice Wright-Fotheringham makes to remark – but she checks herself and shakes her head sympathetically. They both sip their tea in silence for a minute or two. The scene is pleasant, despite the drizzle, a wooded gorge lined by gnarled alders and oaks. The motion of the river both mesmerises and lulls – its rocky bed and shallow nature conjure a perpetually changing pattern of sight and sound, ripples and eddies that ebb and flow and splash and swoosh with a certain improvised harmony. A dipper buzzes past, and then performs an aerobatic turn to land upon a half-submerged stone. Small songbird though it might be, it bobs once or twice, showing off its smart evening suit, and then plunges recklessly into the torrent. A few moments later it emerges several yards downstream, popping up onto another boulder, now with its dinner wriggling in its beak.

'Do you catch by logic, Daniel – or is it gut feel?'

Skelgill turns to her, blinking.

'You mean fish?'

'Fish – or criminals. Is there a difference?'

Now Skelgill is forced to contemplate the distinction.

'After I've caught a fish – when I'm thinking about it – maybe driving home, walking the dog, whatever – I can explain how I did it.' He pulls off his Tilley hat and absently combs back his hair with the fingers of one hand. 'I can't honestly say I always see it at the time.'

'But you must be using information – otherwise you would cast upon the main road, or a playing field, or the staff canteen at your police headquarters.'

Skelgill grins.

'Might get a battered haddock.'

'But you see my point?'

'Aye. I guess.'

He sounds as though he is not sure that he does, but he nods with sufficient enthusiasm to satisfy her.

'In my most difficult cases – as a judge rather than as a barrister – I always knew before I understood.' (Skelgill is now watching her closely.) 'When the facts are before one's eyes, it can take a little time before one's subconscious yields up the truth.'

Skelgill seems to be composing a rejoinder – but at this juncture a text alert sounds from his breast pocket. He pulls an apologetic face.

'Leyton – one of my sergeants.'

'On a Sunday – is there no peace for the wicked, Daniel?'

Squinting, Skelgill grimaces as he reads the message.

'Important?'

'Could be – possible sighting of Harry Krille – at least, a place he might have been hiding out – a bothy beside Hayeswater – above Hartsop.'

'That is near Patterdale, is it not?'

'Aye – couple of miles south, before you hit the Kirkstone.'

'What might that tell you about his trajectory, Daniel?'

'If you drew a line from Tebay through Hartsop it'd probably pass by Keswick.' Skelgill scowls doubtfully. 'But this the Lakes – who travels in straight lines?'

Alice Wright-Fotheringham is frowning.

'Then hadn't you better do so – make a beeline – Inspector?'

Skelgill glances about uneasily. His gaze comes to rest on his dog. She is regarding him inquiringly, head cocked on one side, ears pricked, pink tongue protruding by a quarter of an inch.

'Daniel – I shall take Cleopatra – the pair of them seem to be getting on like a house on fire – she can stay the night if you can't drop by before, say, ten p.m. Failing that, collect her tomorrow.'

He casts a loose hand towards the Eden.

'Sure you don't mind, Alice – cutting it short?'

'Daniel – we've had our tea – I've caught my Lady of the Stream – I've told you all I know – I think we'll begin to get bored of one another – that is ample for a first date.'

Skelgill grins – but it is Alice Wright-Fotheringham that has the final word.

'When you call at Keswick – not that I am unappreciative of your builder's brand – but you shall have a decent pot of Earl Grey.'

22. INTERVIEWS

'Shame about that barn catching fire yesterday, Guv – think it could have been a red herring?'

'You mean to put us off the scent?'

'I suppose so, Guv.'

'What about *on* the scent?'

DS Leyton scratches his head.

'How does that work, Guv?'

'If it were Krille – why would he torch it, Leyton?'

Now DS Leyton puffs out his fleshy jowls.

'Destroy any evidence, Guv – that he'd been there.'

Skelgill shakes his head slowly, patently unconvinced – although DS Leyton makes a fair point. By the time they arrived yesterday evening at the peaceful grey-stone hamlet of Hartsop – in the seventeenth century a lead-mining and spinning community – a glum PC Dodd was waiting to intercept them with the news to which DS Leyton has referred: the bothy was gutted. Skelgill had remarked that the inferno had done them out of a nice stroll (a sharp climb beside Hayeswater Gill of around a thousand feet). DS Leyton, for his part, had looked somewhat relieved – knowing his superior officer, he quite likely would have led them onwards and upwards, on the grounds that to be within touching distance of High Street (the fell where once a mountaintop Roman road passed joining forts at Penrith and Ambleside) it would have been churlish not to go the extra half mile, for his sergeant's edification. This would have seemed an even worse prospect were he to be informed – as Skelgill undoubtedly is – by the words of Lakeland's cantankerous biographer Alfred Wainwright, who candidly described the remaining ascent from Hayeswater as "*deteriorating into a dull trudge.*"

'What would he have left behind, Leyton – to give away his presence? He'd realise a sniffer dog would pick up his scent inside or out – so destroying the place makes no odds.'

DS Leyton rolls his shoulders, as if he has slept badly and still bears the stiffness.

'Might have been testing his bomb, Guv – could have saved us a job if he'd blown himself up.'

Skelgill declines to be amused.

'There's no knowing it was Krille, Leyton.'

'But the dog, Guv – the handler reckoned it got something.'

Skelgill shrugs. He leans forwards over the map of the Lake District that is spread out before them. Now he stares at it determinedly, like a person willing form to emerge from a Magic Eye image. DS Leyton sits patiently at his side, but when after about thirty seconds Skelgill makes no move, he checks his wristwatch and shunts restlessly in his chair.

'Want another tea, Guv? We've got about ten minutes before Arthur Kerr's due.'

Skelgill does not respond – as if he is locked in a battle with his senses, and cannot afford to let go of his grip at this precise moment. But then he releases the breath he has been withholding, and pushes himself back into an upright position.

'You know what they say about the Pope, Leyton.'

DS Leyton grins and rises dutifully. They have set up their allocated Haresfell interview room in a more formal style, with their two seats facing a single chair across the table. There are no windows, and Skelgill glances about uneasily while he waits for his colleague to return. He lifts the map, stretching his arms to grab either margin, breaking its back and compressing it like a practised concertina player. The coffee bar is only yards away, and it is just another minute before DS Leyton reverses through the door and shuts it with a shove of one foot.

'Better give me an update, Leyton.'

Now Skelgill refers to the debrief DS Leyton has this morning received from his small team of Detective Constables. DS Leyton deposits the drinks carefully upon the table surface, and then relieves a pocket of two chocolate wafer bars.

'Nice one, marra.'

'Don't tell the missus, Guv – she's been giving me grief about how I need to stop eating snacks between meals.'

Skelgill makes a face – as one who consumes meals between meals and exhibits no side effects, he does not particularly comprehend this logic.

'I'll eat it for you if you like – or go halves?'

DS Leyton reaches rather protectively for his bar.

'Nah – you're alright, Guv – I reckon I'll get away with this 'un. I just need to remember not to keep the wrappers in my jacket. Proper Miss Marple, she is.'

Skelgill is already dunking a section of biscuit into his tea. He shrugs indifferently and pops it into his mouth. He wipes his fingers on his thigh.

'Fire away, then.'

Now DS Leyton retrieves a sheaf of notes from an attaché case. He places them on the table, angled slightly towards Skelgill, but his superior only glances cursorily before turning his attention to his next piece of confectionery.

'There's not a whole lot – but if we take things in chronological order – then starting with the death of Frank Wamphray. Manchester reckon the hospitals they're investigating are admitting to discrepancies in their stock levels, but they're claiming it's down to incomplete reporting when emergencies are taking place.' DS Leyton takes a sip of tea and looks longingly at his chocolate bar, but at the moment there is not time to commence eating it. 'And fair enough, Guv – I mean, if you were the one having a heart attack, you wouldn't want to wait while some geezer fills in a form to get the medicine. Next thing there's another sick patient and the critical response team is off to attend to them. Admin gets done the next day, if they're lucky.'

Skelgill grunts somewhat disinterestedly.

'They've double-checked all their stocks and records here, Guv – and they still insist there's nothing short. But, then again, how would we know if they're covering their backsides? Unless we requisitioned and tested the whole lot, it's irrelevant what it says on the labels. It's impossible, Guv.'

'What about the fingerprint analysis?'

DS Leyton pre-emptively shakes his head as he leafs through the papers.

'Turns out it's just the people that handled the vial afterwards. A cleaner rescued it from the waste, and a pharmacist ran the initial tests – and neither had touched it prior to that.'

Skelgill is frowning.

'Does that strike you as odd, Leyton?'

'Not really, Guv – well, at first, I thought maybe it had been wiped – then someone pointed out that all the staff who handle medicines and give injections and whatnot – they wear these surgical gloves. Everyone carries them – even the security staff in case they get into a bit of a rumble and come into contact with body fluids.'

Now Skelgill grimaces. Still he does not advance any point.

'About Frank Wamphray himself, Guv – we've talked to various people who saw him earlier on the morning he died. The female nurse who was present when he got the injection – the old battleaxe I mentioned – she had the hump because he'd apparently been allowed a trip to the hospital shop. It's mainly tuck they sell, and he must have copped a whole load of chocolate and filled his boat – she reckons that's why he was sick and so they had to give him the injection.'

Skelgill raises an eyebrow. This news, however, does not dampen his enthusiasm for his own chocolate bar.

'Otherwise, Guv – we've tried to verify whether there's any truth in all that guff he told us – the story keeps coming back that he was a serial fantasist.' DS Leyton appears disappointed by this finding and he shakes his head a little dejectedly. 'But I still think there was something in what he said – else why was he done away with?'

'We can't prove that, Leyton.'

DS Leyton slaps his hands down upon the table in a small act of desperation.

212

'I know, Guv – but what? We come here as a favour for Manchester – then the hospital calls us in over those thefts – and next thing all hell breaks loose. There's got to be more to it. You've said it yourself about these coincidences.'

Skelgill folds his arms and slumps against the back of his plastic chair.

'Leyton – if you drained all the water out of Bass Lake you'd be left with a load of mud and thousands of flapping fish. Just because roach would be sharing puddles with pike doesn't make them best of pals.'

An expression of bewilderment crosses DS Leyton's countenance. Whether it is frustration that his superior has now turned devil's advocate, or that his analogy is patent nonsense and perhaps designed to confound, it is difficult to know which troubles him most. He reaches for his snack bar and cracks it open, under the covetous scrutiny of Skelgill. He eats a piece and washes it down with tea. The comforting sensation seems to settle him, and he turns a page of his notes.

'We've not managed to get any further in identifying the last few members of staff that visited the dispensary – but they have now put together the sections of CCTV footage that show Meredith Bale and Dr Agnetha Walker leaving the premises.'

'Aye?'

'To be honest, Guv – I had a butcher's before you got here – there's nothing different to what Eric Blacklock first showed us. You can just see the pair of them walking like they're arm in arm, along a series of corridors and using swipe-cards to get through the doors. There's the red Volvo leaving the main gate from the staff car park – but that just looks completely normal. It must be that Meredith Bale had the doctor under her control one way or another – like we said before, Guv.'

'What about Krille?'

'There's a distant shot of him climbing the rope ladder. You'd have to be eagle-eyed to spot him. You can't make out any detail – like whether he's got a rucksack or not. There was a nearer camera – but they've cut back on maintenance. The lens was covered in spiders' webs and dead flies and all sorts of gunge. Apparently the lights attract insects so the spiders move in. Then birds and bats flock round and guano builds up. It was like trying to look through frosted glass.'

Skelgill shakes his head disparagingly. DS Leyton continues.

'The psychologists' reports show nothing in Harry Krille's behaviour that suggested he was about to do a runner. His gardening plot was immaculate and right in the middle of its season. Seems he's grown competition standard leeks. They say how well he'd been responding to the horticultural therapy. Completely caught everyone off guard, Guv.'

'What about contact with Meredith Bale?'

DS Leyton rocks his head from side to side.

'Nothing obvious. They've been in different wards since Meredith Bale was committed here. There were no activities that they shared – like the drama group or gardening. There's been talks and film screenings that they've both attended – but there's no socialising and they weren't observed trying to make direct contact. Course, it don't say they couldn't get messages passed between 'em.'

DS Leyton drops the sheaf of papers and massages his scalp with the fingers of both hands, as though the effort of recounting these details has strained his faculties. Skelgill stares expectantly across the room, as if he anticipates their first interviewee to enter at any second.

'Aye – but if they have – it means someone's holding out on us, Leyton.'

*

'How long have you been at Haresfell?'

Arthur Kerr's gaze shifts from Skelgill, posing the question, to DS Leyton, and back. He runs a hand through his oily hair, dislodging a few strands from the frayed band that holds his ponytail in place.

'Can't say I've counted.'

214

'Coming up four years, wasn't it?' Skelgill repeats the words Kerr himself had used at their meeting in the Hare's Beck Foot Inn.

Arthur Kerr shrugs evasively. DS Leyton taps a finger on a pad that lies halfway between himself and Skelgill. The page is covered in notes scrawled in Skelgill's spidery hand – a small concession to preparation that mainly consists of a list of items he needs to buy from a fishing tackle shop. But it appears at least that he has briefed his sergeant on DS Jones's findings.

'Says six here, Guv.'

From behind his round-lensed spectacles Arthur Kerr peers furtively at the upside-down notes, although it would seem unlikely that he could decipher Skelgill's writing, even the right way around. Skelgill waits for a few moments, until he is certain Arthur Kerr is not going to reply.

'So you were at Broadmoor at the same time as Briony Boss?'

Now Arthur Kerr's wily countenance becomes creased by suspicion. Skelgill has highlighted a blemish in his account of himself, yet has chosen not to explore the motive for any such deception.

'What if I were?'

'How would you describe your relationship with her?'

'What's this got to do with anything?'

'Just answer the question please, Mr Kerr.'

Arthur Kerr squints accusingly at Skelgill; he could be feeling double-crossed, no longer treated as clandestine confidante, on first name terms.

'She were miles above my rank, man – just like she is now.'

Skelgill stares for a moment at his page of notes, apparently cross-referencing the point.

'That wasn't always the case.'

Arthur Kerr vacillates, as if he is trying to work out what the police might know.

'Mebbes not – but I never had nowt to do with her – whatever she says.'

DS Leyton glances sharply at Skelgill – for in Arthur Kerr's denial there seems to be a contradiction of sorts. But Skelgill seems not to notice.

'Why did you leave Broadmoor, Mr Kerr?'

'To get back to me roots – to me old ma.' His reply comes without pause for thought, and smacks of being well rehearsed.

'You call this close to home?'

'Aye – Broadmoor's in Berkshire.'

Skelgill flashes him a scathing look – that of course he knows this simple geographical fact.

'Sunderland's still the best part of a two-hundred-mile round trip – you can hardly drop in on spec for Sunday lunch.'

Arthur Kerr shrugs.

'It's more within striking distance.'

'When did you last visit?'

Now it is apparent that Arthur Kerr does not have a ready answer; he glances nervously about as though he might glean a date from some stimulus in his surroundings.

'It weren't long ago.'

But Skelgill seems uninterested in this response.

'So the move wasn't due to problems in your job?'

'There's problems in any job – you must know that, man.'

Skelgill's features harden visibly.

'Aye, I'm looking at one now.'

Arthur Kerr, behind his hard-faced façade, seems inwardly to start – a clear sign that tells he is unnerved. He does not reply.

'What role did Briony Boss play in your transfer?'

'Like I say – she were way above my level – happen she signed off some papers – reference, that sort of thing.'

'What did you think when she was appointed as Director of Haresfell?'

'It's not for me to think about – I just do me job.'

'To the best of your ability.'

Arthur Kerr shrugs – but, while he appears uncertain whether Skelgill is being sarcastic, it cannot have escaped his thinking that so far Skelgill has not mentioned their meeting – and in particular his recriminations cast against the establishment under the loosening influence of mild-and-bitter. Perhaps this realisation gives him a modicum of confidence.

'What else would I do?'

Skelgill again leans to scrutinise his notes. He runs a finger down the near-illegible list that includes entries that might spell out words such as *zinger*, *jig head* and *Arlesey bomb* – and something perhaps called *Gink*?

'I believe Frank Wamphray's not the first of your patients to die suddenly?'

Now Arthur Kerr folds his arms and furrows his brow. His prominent jaw juts forwards and his mean lips compress into a narrow horizontal strip.

'That were nowt to do with me, man.'

He stares defiantly, looking from Skelgill to DS Leyton, as if he is challenging them to prove his guilt. But when neither offers a rejoinder, he is prompted to enter a statement in his defence.

'The clue's in the title, Broadmoor *Hospital* – just like Haresfell *Hospital* – patients die all the time, man.'

Skelgill's expression remains obdurate.

'There's a difference between natural causes and negligence, Mr Kerr.'

'You've got nowt on me – I've never done owt like that. If you've found something, it's the organ grinder you want to look out for – not the monkey.'

The watching detectives may have conspired to appear unimpressed, but neither can entirely conceal some degree of intrigue – for in Arthur Kerr's words there is surely a suggestion of underlying knowledge, if not an oblique admission of complicity. Skelgill homes in upon this point.

'It's been said that Frank Wamphray was deliberately poisoned.'

Arthur Kerr does not reply at first – but then he realises he is expected to do so.

'It don't make sense – he were harmless – always inventing stuff.'

Skelgill affects a casual shrug.

'They say there's no smoke without fire.'

'Aye – but what's the fire all about?'

'You tell me, Mr Kerr.' Skelgill's demand must be rhetorical, for he barely pauses. 'Certain malpractices, perhaps – or plans that were afoot.'

Now Arthur Kerr is shaking his head.

'You're talking murder, man. Who'd gan an' do something like that?'

'That's what we're asking you, Mr Kerr.' Now Skelgill grimaces, baring his teeth in a rather alarming fashion. 'Perhaps someone who knew of a reliable monkey?'

Behind his spectacles, the whites of Arthur Kerr's dark eyes widen, a hunted simian that has reached the end of its branch. There is silence that extends to some ten or more seconds before Skelgill speaks again.

'Who do you know in the Manchester area, Mr Kerr?'

And now Skelgill's sudden change of tack further disorientates Arthur Kerr. He wipes his upper lip with the fingers of one hand.

'Never go there – can't stand the place – it's one big traffic jam.'

Much as Skelgill might wish to concur it cannot escape his notice that Arthur Kerr plainly knows enough of the city to share such an opinion. Skelgill picks up his mug and swills the dregs around before swallowing them. He makes a face like the tea is stewed.

'I thought it might be your kind of scene.'

Arthur Kerr darts a suspicious look at DS Leyton – he seems to be checking for some prior collusion between the detectives. But the sergeant remains stoical and so he reverts his anxious gaze to Skelgill. He shakes his head, unwilling to offer any detail.

'No?' Skelgill gnaws tenaciously at a thumbnail and then inspects his handiwork. 'Don't worry – we've got someone looking into all that.'

Again there is nothing forthcoming from Arthur Kerr. Skelgill glances cursorily at the notes, and then at DS Leyton –

who readies himself to speak – but Skelgill turns abruptly back to Arthur Kerr.

'That'll do for now, Mr Kerr. Have a think about what we've said – if something springs to mind, you know where to find us.'

Arthur Kerr is plainly surprised, but he has sufficient wits about him to rise immediately and back away towards the door.

'I'm on a half-day – from one o'clock.'

'Then we'll know where to find you.'

Arthur Kerr swallows and turns and leaves the room. DS Leyton slumps back in his seat, looking a little disappointed at being deprived the opportunity of posing his question.

'He was a lot more cagey, Guv.'

'Aye – now it's on the record, Leyton – he's not so cocksure.'

'Reckon he's holding something back, Guv?'

'I don't reckon.'

Skelgill stares at his sergeant – but his expression promises no enlightenment, and accordingly DS Leyton puffs out his cheeks and shakes his head ruefully.

'Trouble is, Guv – he's canny enough to know if we had something on him we'd already have nicked him for it.'

Skelgill nods grimly. Then he consults his wristwatch. Head of Security Eric Blacklock ought by now to be on standby for the next interview. But Skelgill pulls his jacket from the back of his chair and slings it over a shoulder.

'Leyton – you take Blacklock – I'm going to speak to Briony Boss – while there's a few things fresh in my mind.'

23. BRIONY BOSS

'Would you like a drink, Inspector?'

Skelgill glances uneasily at the glass that Briony Boss has placed on the coffee table in the informal seating area of her office. She appears to notice his concern and adds a rider.

'My PA will bring a cappuccino from the coffee bar, perhaps?'

Skelgill looks for a moment as though he is tempted – but perhaps the idea of the interruption, coming with uncertain timing, deters him.

'No – thanks – I've had my fill this morning.'

The Director smiles sympathetically. For her part, she is certainly more self-possessed than during their last encounter in this office on Friday evening. The casual onlooker would not guess she is captain of a ship that navigates its present troubled waters – or indeed from her appearance that she is captain of any such entity – although pressed for an answer the same might suggest editor of a women's fashion magazine. She has eschewed her regulation charcoal pencil skirt and white blouse, and instead has chosen an ensemble that comprises a sleeveless black cocktail dress with a plunging neckline, sheer stockings and matching heels. Her make up is freshly applied, once again generous around the dark eyes, and her long glossy raven locks spill onto the pale skin of her half-exposed shoulders.

Already seated, Skelgill allows his gaze to follow her movements as she settles languidly opposite him. He too seems unhurried, despite his abrupt decision to abandon DS Leyton. He twists out of his jacket and drapes it over one arm of the sofa.

'Inspector, no news, I take it – of Harry Krille or Meredith Bale?' (With a rueful grimace Skelgill begins to shake his head.)

'And you will have heard that there has been no improvement in Helen Pettigrew's condition? She has not regained consciousness.'

Now Skelgill nods.

'Aye – we got a report early doors.'

Briony Boss arranges her limbs more comfortably, and then casts a searching glance towards the windows.

'Of course – it is Dr Walker's safety I fear for – along with anyone else upon whom they may have preyed.'

Skelgill frowns a little.

'That assumes they've teamed up. There's no evidence for that. If anything it looks like Krille might be at large in the countryside.'

Briony Boss is still gazing beyond Skelgill. Her tone becomes somewhat wistful.

'If only she had taken her planned half day – the Friday staff meeting had been cancelled earlier in the week – she has paid a high price for her diligence.'

The furrows in Skelgill's brow deepen – but any rejoinder he may be shaping is overtaken by the Director's supplementary question.

'And how are your investigations within our four walls progressing?'

It takes Skelgill a second or two to set aside the point he would make – and then he contrives an expression that speaks of his regret to be the bearer of unpalatable intelligence.

'There seems to be a bit of an undercurrent – that the senior management are out of touch with the day-to-day running of the place – I'm alright Jack, you might say.'

A flicker of her eyelids betrays Briony Boss's alarm – for in Skelgill's pithy analysis is bundled a whole gamut of charges. In response, she homes in upon one aspect of these, which is perhaps revealing in its choice.

'But, Inspector – look at me – I live modestly – in accommodation provided on the site – I work longer hours than almost any other employee – and I do not get paid overtime.'

Skelgill holds up his palms in a conciliatory gesture – as if to say he appreciates this, of course, but that perceptions are as much reality as the truth.

'Aye, well – maybe it's because you've got the likes of Dr Pettigrew with his Jag and his big house and his bairns at private school – you know what folk can be like.'

Briony Boss might well be relieved that Skelgill has shifted the onus onto her colleague, so it seems rather paradoxical that she offers an explanation in his defence.

'Peter Pettigrew is well remunerated, that much is true – and he derives additional income from his consultancy services in Manchester, and his court work – but what you refer to is another matter.'

'Aye?'

'Certainly, Inspector – does the name Bulkington mean anything to you?'

'The glass makers that went bust?'

'That is correct. But Helen Bulkington inherited a sizeable fortune before that event. And then she married and became Helen Pettigrew.'

'I see.' Skelgill purses his lips. 'So it's not my taxes paying for the Jag after all?'

'Nor mine, Inspector.'

Now Skelgill could almost be disappointed that there is a legitimate explanation.

'Makes you wonder why she wanted a job here – I mean to say – why she wanted a job at all.'

Briony Boss appears a little surprised by his comment.

'I suppose we all need to find fulfilment in our waking hours.'

Skelgill is looking directly at her, but an unblinking countenance hints that his thoughts are elsewhere. It would not take a highly qualified psychologist to predict that an image of a lake, a boat, a rod and a pike is quite likely at their forefront. Still, he wrestles his mind away from the prospect, and re-sharpens his focus.

'You'd think the husband might have something to say about it – with property and family and whatnot to run.'

'Quite the contrary, Inspector. Peter Pettigrew was very supportive. He pushed for the drama project from the outset and – the present tragedy excepted – it is probably true to say it has been beneficial for all concerned.'

Skelgill is listening implacably.

'I believe he's done well career-wise since you took over.'

She shoots a wounded glance at Skelgill, as though she feels this is an unfair question. It takes a moment for her to provide an answer.

'I like to run a meritocracy, Inspector.'

Though her statement is constructive there is something distinctly rueful in her tone.

'I gather he put in a good word for you on the NHS recruitment committee.'

Now Briony Boss bites at her lower lip.

'It seems you have spies in high places.'

Skelgill affects an affronted grin.

'I wouldn't call it that – just a little bird that told me.'

It is apparent that Briony Boss is now just a touch on her guard – that Skelgill has been prying into her background – though she must understand that this is what the police do. With a strained smile she leans towards him and slides her hands from her lap to fasten them over one knee.

'I should like to think that was on merit, also.'

Skelgill shrugs casually.

'If you don't mind me saying – from the meetings we've been in – the pair of you don't seem to be hitting it off.'

'Inspector, as George Bernard Shaw put it, all progress depends upon the unreasonable man. I rather expect my senior managers to offer a conflicting opinion and to stand their ground. I imagine you encourage such a culture in your own team?'

Skelgill stares uncomprehendingly – and appears ready to gainsay this proposition – but then it must strike him that to do so would be to become diverted.

'I don't know about unreasonable – but he's not a happy bunny. I'm just wondering if Meredith Bale's attack on his wife is retaliation for something he's done that we don't know about.'

Briony Boss reaches for her glass and swirls its contents. Skelgill's suggestion appears to have stimulated a moment's reflection.

'Well, of course – as I mentioned previously – Peter Pettigrew chaired the panel that recommended Meredith Bale should be committed to this institution –'

Abruptly she stops speaking, and stares at Skelgill with a sudden light of realisation in her eyes.

'What is it?'

'You will be aware that Meredith Bale has consistently maintained both her innocence and her sanity?'

'Aye – I've heard that said.'

'There were several specialists seconded onto the forensic panel – each with their own distinct area of expertise.' She pauses to brush a strand of hair from her cheek. 'Key amongst them was Dr Agnetha Walker.'

Skelgill nods, his face stern. Briony Boss continues.

'If you are talking about Peter Pettigrew being targeted – then Dr Walker could surely fall into the same category? And now she is a hostage.'

Skelgill sits back against the settee and folds his arms. He does not need to reveal his knowledge of the investigation – but clearly this information supports the line reflected by DS Jones's findings about the connections of several of the actors in the case. After a few moments' consideration he settles upon a question.

'Why was Dr Agnetha Walker appointed to come and work with Meredith Bale?'

Briony Boss makes a hand gesture that indicates a caveat.

'I should stress that Meredith Bale was not her only patient – but certainly her experience on Meredith's case made her a good candidate for the job. Peter Pettigrew came to me with the proposal – I'm sure you are aware it is not easy to attract the best people to this far flung corner of England – but Agnetha Walker had lost her husband some months before, and he felt she might be amenable to the change of scene. We positioned it as a temporary assignment – although Peter had in mind that it could be made permanent if it proved to be a success.'

As Briony Boss recounts this history, it seems that a note of unease creeps progressively into her voice, and disquiet mists her dark eyes. Skelgill, at first both listening and watching attentively, allows his own gaze to wander and he stares out through the windows on one side of the office. From a sitting position there is not much to see – just an undulating line of brown fell tops and a blanket of low grey cloud, albeit the latter is showing the bluish hints of breaking up. He faces the Director.

'So what might either of them have said or done to wind up Meredith Bale?'

Briony Boss strives to shrug off whatever preoccupation has stolen upon her. She gathers herself, though she responds with excessive formality.

'By being associated with her committal to Haresfell instead of prison. Such an outcome interposes a significant hurdle to a judicial review of her case. Subsequently, I suppose Meredith Bale would regard any attempts at treatment or therapy as a further denial of her belief that she is a victim of a miscarriage of justice. I am aware she objected to the regime of medication prescribed by Peter Pettigrew, and among other things disliked Dr Walker's use of hypnotherapy.'

'Hypnotherapy?'

'That is correct. I am led to understand Dr Walker is a highly skilled practitioner. I cannot comment upon its efficacy, I'm afraid. But given Agnetha Walker's remit – in assessing the veracity of a patient's claimed condition – one can empathise with the Meredith Bale's interpretation that it is a somewhat clandestine method.'

Skelgill is plainly discomfited. He rubs his chin and shifts position on the sofa. His gaze darts about his feet and the legs of the coffee table. When he looks up he finds Briony Boss's probing eyes upon him.

'She told me that Meredith Bale is a sly operator – not easy to get behind the mask. Refused to speak about the letters she wrote to Harry Krille. I didn't realise she'd tried hypnosis on her.'

Briony Boss nods.

'It may have backfired.'

'She also said that if there had been some communication between Meredith Bale and Harry Krille – as a kind of experiment – it would have needed your authorisation.'

Briony Boss seems to start at this suggestion, and her features harden.

'That is certainly correct – but I cannot always guarantee that the correct protocol is followed.'

'Are you saying they may have had organised contact?'

The Director meets his inquiry with a level gaze.

'Simply that I don't have eyes everywhere, and that if a person were to initiate some interaction, I may not find out about it.'

'But that couldn't just be any old nurse?'

She gives a confirmatory shake of her head.

'No. It would need to be a senior member of staff – someone with jurisdiction over both of the patients concerned.'

'Such as Dr Peter Pettigrew?'

'Certainly at his level it would not raise any eyebrows – my own excepted.' She tilts her head to one side inquisitively. 'But you have no actual basis for this idea, Inspector?'

Skelgill shrugs with affected casualness.

'Only that Harry Krille escaped on Thursday – and Meredith Bale escaped on Friday.'

Now she plies him with a distinctly submissive expression.

'You must be thinking that the escapes occurred too easily, Inspector.'

Skelgill seems to be disarmed by this trick of body language.

'I'm not sure I'd say that about Meredith Bale. Hers seemed a pretty high-risk strategy to me.'

'And Harry Krille?'

He gives her a rather old-fashioned look.

'Aye, well – with hindsight it was put on a plate for him. And a convenient blind spot in your security.'

Briony Boss still has her head bowed.

'You are aware of the views of Eric Blacklock.'

Skelgill makes a scoffing sound.

'Happen I'd be calling him Eric Buckpass if I were in your shoes.'

Briony Boss forces a grin. However she lays a palm upon her breastbone. Her nails are varnished in a dark ochre that matches her lipstick.

'It stops here, I'm afraid.'

'Can't be easy when you've got a simmering mutiny on your hands.'

Again she seems inwardly to reel – Skelgill's erratic approach mixes expressions of sympathy with sharp critical jabs – however, she maintains her outward calm.

'I'm not sure I'd put it as strongly as that, Inspector – with almost nine hundred staff there will always be little areas of local difficulty.'

Skelgill nods, though in a non-committal manner.

'We were just speaking to the primary nurse for Frank Wamphray and Meredith Bale.'

He watches her closely.

'Arthur Kerr, yes.'

Now she waits for him to elaborate.

'I gather he's been a bit of a troublemaker in his time – like when you were at Broadmoor.'

She regards Skelgill evenly.

'Thankfully those days are past now.'

'He seems to have done alright out of his transfer – considering some of the allegations that were made against him and his cronies.'

It is plain that Briony Boss is becoming increasingly anxious, as if she suspects Skelgill of feeling his way towards some dark corner of her curriculum vitae that she would rather remained undiscovered.

'I suppose you could say everyone deserves a second chance, Inspector.' She gives a nervous laugh and bats her eyelashes. 'If I, of all people, weren't to champion that, what sort of place would this be?'

Skelgill's stare is penetrating, and he does not respond to the ambiguity implicit in her statement. But gradually his concentration wavers as, rather musingly, Briony Boss takes a slow sip from her glass. She leans back against the sofa and her body slips down by a couple of inches, causing the hem of her skirt to ride up and reveal bare thigh at the top of her hold-ups. Now she is watching the tracking of his eyes – in a prolonged and deliberate movement she uncrosses and re-crosses her legs. There is a moment of silence – punctuated only by the faintest hiss of their breathing. Skelgill's gaze travels back up to meet hers.

'Can I ask you a personal question?'

'I am at your mercy, Inspector.'

Sharply, he inhales.

'Did you have a fancy for Harry Krille?'

24. THE LUNE

'Guv, I've been looking all over for you.'

'I stepped out for a breath fresh air – I needed to think.'

'Where are you, Guv?'

'Not far.'

There is a pause as DS Leyton considers to what degree he may quiz his superior. In the end, he opts for a less contentious question.

'What shall I do, Guv?'

'Just carry on, Leyton – I'll be with you in a bit.'

'Right, Guv.'

DS Leyton inhales as if to speak again, but Skelgill chooses to interpret the pause as the end of the conversation and terminates the call. He returns the phone to a breast pocket of his gilet. In his left hand he grips a fifteen-foot salmon rod and now he draws back the line that has floated downstream, until the rod is perpendicular to the river, the Lune. Working two-handed, with a smooth action he crosses his forearms and touches the rod against his right shoulder, lifts it back across his chest to 'present arms', pauses for half a second, and then fires the shooting head through the air: with great precision the leader unfurls to drop the fly gently above a deep pool that runs a slow black under the far bank. He watches hawkishly as the current takes the line; he mends when necessary and when it begins to swing around he retrieves with jerky movements of his right hand. Finally he takes a couple of steps downstream and sets himself to repeat the whole operation. The classic double Spey cast with a Skelgill modification or two thrown in.

The rain has stopped and bright patches of blue sky have begun to appear with increasing frequency, allowing the sun to turn the clouds white for the first time in what seems like weeks. The temperature is rising and beneath his gilet Skelgill wears just the shirt and trousers he dressed in for work, though these garments are protected by an old pair of somewhat corroded olive-green bootfoot chest waders. He stands about a third of the way across the river, the water lapping around the tops of his thighs. His location is a mile or so north of the bridge from which he and DS Leyton have observed Haresfell Hospital, and quite close to the hamlet of Hare's Beck Foot – indeed the confluence of Hare's Beck with the Lune is just a couple of hundred yards upstream, and quite likely has influenced his choice of beat.

His expressed "need to think" would appear to remain as yet unfulfilled, since he and DS Leyton have much to do back at the hospital – a packed timetable of interviews – but he shows no inclination to return to such duties. There is of course an alternative explanation: that he has the scent of a salmon in his nostrils. Indeed, there have been one or two likely rises – tantalising glimpses of silver scales glinting in the sunlight – easily sufficient to divert his focus. And though he is a self-professed "pike man", there is a quality about salmon fishing certain to ignite his competitive instinct: just how do you catch a fish that does not want to feed?

Either way, compulsion appears to have the upper hand and in a slow tango at one with the stream, methodically, metronomically, he continues to cast, retrieve, step and repeat. And then his phone rings again.

'Jones.'

Perhaps surprisingly under the circumstances, his greeting lacks any particular note of censure.

'Hi, Guv – that's us on the way back.'

DS Jones's use of the collective pronoun warns him that she is in the company of DI Smart.

'Driving?'

'We just set off. The satnav's saying ninety-six minutes to Penrith.'

In the background there is some unintelligible quip from Alec Smart – probably to the effect that he will do it in a lot fewer. DS Jones affects a polite laugh.

'I shan't ask how it went.'

'Pretty successful, thanks, Guv.'

It is clear her response is for the benefit of her companion. Skelgill grunts his disapproval.

'Pass on my congratulations. Not.'

'Will do, Guv.' She inhales and pauses for a second – it would seem she is composing a suitable form of words for her primary message. 'Remember last week, before I left – you asked about my contact in the NHS?'

'Aye?' Skelgill sounds briefly amused – she is evidently massaging the facts in order to conceal their clandestine rendezvous.

'I've received an email – there was a piece of information I thought I should pass on.' (Skelgill does not respond – though he has one eye on the river.) 'He came across a mailing address in the Manchester area for Dr Peter Pettigrew – it related to an expenses claim for professional literature that was delivered, a couple of years back.' She pauses again. DI Smart has evidently turned on the radio and now she is competing with rock music. 'The thing is, Guv – the expenses claim was all above board – but the apartment's address – it's the same one on record as being Dr Agnetha Walker's home address.'

Skelgill remains silent. Now his line has wrapped itself around a raft of sticks trapped by a cluster of exposed rocks.

'Guv?'

'Aye – I was making a note. Two years ago, you say.'

'Where are you, Guv?'

'Just by Haresfell.'

'Right.' She hesitates, but Skelgill offers no encouragement. 'Want me to follow it up when I get back?'

'Maybe – I'll let you know.'

'Sure.'

Skelgill ends the call and puts away his phone. He makes a curious face – something of an unbecoming gurning expression if the truth were told. Then he resumes his fishing. After a few minutes his staccato progression downstream brings him opposite a break in the bankside vegetation. There is a raised area of short-cropped lawn upon which stands a small plain-looking stone lodge, of the sort that once would have been the residence of the gardener or gamekeeper on a large estate. The property is in good repair, with newly pointed joints and a bright coat of maroon paint on the woodwork of the windows and the bargeboards below the gables. Skelgill does not pay particular attention, concentrating as he is, until some sixth sense must raise his hackles. He glances sharply to see that, from a position beneath the steep grassy bank, almost at water level and only half a dozen yards away an elfin boy is perched on a rock watching him.

'Alreet, marra?'

The boy evidently does not understand Skelgill's colloquial greeting, but he has not lost his tongue.

'Caught owt, Mister?'

Skelgill grins.

'Just about to, lad. Next cast, maybe.'

'Can I try?'

Now Skelgill lets out a little chuckle.

'Even if I could wade through that deep pool – this rod's way too big for you, chum – get your Dad to buy you a starter kit. Six footer max, you want.'

The boy makes a face of resignation.

'Me Mum and me Dad are divorced.'

There is a moment's silence as Skelgill searches for the right words. His gaze falls upon the water streaming relentlessly between them – but before he can speak they are both startled by a scolding voice that emanates from the direction of the cottage.

'Johnny! You mustn't disturb the gentleman – people pay a lot of money to fish. I've told you before. Now go inside and watch television, there's a good boy.'

Approaching them across the grass, Skelgill sees a woman of around his own age. She is of medium height and slender, and looks ready to exercise, since she wears trainers and black calf-length yoga pants, and a close-fitting fluorescent pink vest top. Her long brown hair is drawn back into a tight ponytail, ringed by a set of neckband headphones of the sort used by dedicated

232

joggers. Her red lipstick stands out at a distance, as though it is freshly applied. There is something of the catalogue model in her appearance – toned, tanned, trim – and Skelgill might be speculating that she seems unlikely to stay divorced for very long.

The boy glances ruefully at Skelgill and scrambles up the bank, to scuttle obediently around the corner of the building. A cloud unveils the sun, which angles dazzlingly from behind the woman, as she seems to teeter on the edge of the embankment. Skelgill narrows his eyes and is obliged to raise a shading hand in salute. She is well spoken, and addresses him apologetically.

'I'm sorry – he can't help it – he'd love to fish but I don't know what to do – and it's very expensive, of course. Sorry he disturbed you.'

Skelgill, grimacing into the streaming rays of sunlight, must look rather fierce, for the woman clasps her hands apologetically to her bosom, and brings one knee forwards in front of the other, in a semblance of a curtsey. It is the kind of body language that would work on Skelgill in most circumstances, but on this occasion there is no such need.

'No worries, love – it's not easy to spook a salmon – even if there's any to be spooked – and I've just got a local angler's permit – only costs a couple of quid.'

'Oh, well – that's good to hear.' The woman smiles with relief and lowers her hands, placing her palms on her haunches, her hips pushed forwards in an athletic stance. Skelgill's comment, together with his accent, has probably revealed sufficient of his provenance, but she takes the opportunity to make conversation. 'Are you from this area?'

'Cumbria, aye – North Lakes.' Now Skelgill hesitates, perhaps assessing how much he should say – and not forgetting that he is a Detective Inspector presently on duty (on lunch break, at a stretch), and that it behoves him to uphold the good reputation of the force. Then he evidently decides it is better if he asks the questions. 'How about you – do you live here?' He directs a tip of his head towards the small property.

'Oh, no – if only – no, we are on vacation.' She turns her upper body to consider the cottage with a longing gaze. Skelgill notices her supple movement and the curves of her figure, highlighted by the sun that glances off her sheer outfit. She looks back at him. 'It's a holiday home owned by my boss – he kindly let me borrow it for the week – it's a bit of a hideaway, really.'

She observes Skelgill for his reaction – there is a glint of intrigue in her eyes, and she smiles again, displaying even white teeth. But Skelgill – though he is looking directly at her – does not respond. Indeed, she might reasonably think she has offended him in some way – or even that he has suddenly been caught short and is embarrassed to be trapped beneath her gaze. Moreover, if this latter scenario were to have crossed her mind, his next action would reinforce the notion. Without a word he begins to back away, and then he seems to realise he ought to offer some explanation. He makes a brief hand gesture that might be a wave.

'Must rush – I'll see you later.'

And with this he rotates completely and begins to splash with indecent haste towards the far bank. If salmon were spookable, now they are being spooked. The woman watches with a bemused expression; she might be wondering if his farewell is meant literally, or is simply the ambiguous northern British version of goodbye. Skelgill meanwhile has reached the opposite bank and is frantically reeling in his line. He secures the hook in the keeper, and sets off in an upstream direction, at something resembling a jog, though running in bootfoot waders that have been leaking for the last hour is not to be recommended. As he goes, he fishes in his top pocket for his mobile phone, and somehow contrives to tap out the instructions to make a call.

'Leyton.'

'Guv?'

'Get your car.'

'Righto, Guv.' It is clear to DS Leyton, from Skelgill's urgent intonation and heavy breathing, that this is not an instruction to be queried.

'Leyton – phone the estate agents in Keswick – Parish & Co, they are now – find out exactly when Dr Agnetha Walker took that cottage. Then call Jones and tell her to be ready to meet with us. Smart can drop her off. Maybe Tebay.'

'Got it, Guv.' DS Leyton pauses, while Skelgill's gasps come down the line like he is working a pair of bellows. 'Er – where I am going, Guv?'

'Meet me at Hare's Beck Foot. Wait by the inn. If I'm not out in five minutes, come in swinging.'

'You're onto something, Guv?'

'I think I understand, Leyton.'

*

'You okay, Guv?' DS Leyton has an anxious note in his voice. 'I was just about to saunter in for a pint.'

A dishevelled-looking Skelgill hauls his lanky form into the passenger seat of DS Leyton's car.

'Aye, fine.'

But Skelgill, stone-faced, begins sucking at the knuckles of his left hand. DS Leyton watches doubtfully, and it takes a few moments' observation before he is satisfied they can depart.

'Which way, Guv?'

'Get on the motorway – northbound – I need to look at the map.'

'Roger.' DS Leyton jams the car into gear and cuts a tight semi-circle into the gravel of the pub car park. 'What went down, Guv?'

Skelgill lowers the side window and spits into the wind. Then he takes a handkerchief from his pocket and binds it around his fist.

'Just knocking a couple of heads together.'

DS Leyton makes a series of odd facial expressions – as though he is rueing his absence and acting out a little cameo in lieu.

'Anyone I know, Guv?'

'Arthur Kerr.' Skelgill runs the fingers of his right hand through his hair in a cursory attempt to restore some order. 'And Eric Blacklock.'

'Cor blimey, Guv – what were they doing in there?'

'It's Kerr's local – and I reckon old Blacklock's no stranger.'

'Proper little works canteen, Guv – what made you decide to join 'em?'

Skelgill is purposefully unfolding his large-scale map of Cumbria.

'An address he was able to supply me with. Holiday cottage.'

'Who's on holiday, Guv?'

'That's for us to find out.'

'Right, Guv.'

Skelgill is glowering and does not deign to elaborate. Instead he fires off a question.

'How did you get on with Parishes?'

DS Leyton wavers, as though he is not content with Skelgill's answer to his previous query.

'Er – what they said, Guv – the property at Bassenthwaite has been leased to Dr Agnetha Walker for six months – the tenancy agreement was signed two weeks ago today – that'd be the first Monday we came down to Haresfell.'

Skelgill lowers his map and stares out through the windscreen. They have reached the nearest junction of the M6 motorway. DS Leyton accelerates up the on-slip and weaves through a convoy of trucks that labours on the incline like a herd of overburdened oxen.

'I take it we're in a hurry, Guv?'

It is a couple of seconds before Skelgill snaps out of his reverie. He checks his wristwatch. His reply is somewhat oblique.

'What's the score with Jones?'

'She ought to be at Tebay by now, Guv – they were past Lancaster when I spoke to her.'

Skelgill makes a scoffing noise.

'About time Smart did something useful.'

DS Leyton chuckles.

'So we'll pick her up as planned, Guv?'

'Aye. Then we'll take the back roads.'

This prompts Skelgill to return to his map. He holds it out at arm's length, blocking his view ahead. He curses and anguishes over something or other – perhaps he bemoans the Lake District's irregular topography, which has defied all but the Romans (and even them at times) from travelling as the crow may fly. For his part, DS Leyton is becoming fretful. Skelgill's taciturnity seems designed to unsettle – and now he has them heading into the unknown. After a couple of minutes during which nothing more is forthcoming, DS Leyton ventures an inquiry.

'Guv – I take it we're on the trail of Meredith Bale?'

Skelgill offers a grudging reply.

'Aye.'

'What about Harry Krille, Guv?'

'Maybe.'

'But, Guv –' DS Leyton takes a hand off the steering wheel to rub the top of his head. He flashes a worried glance at his superior. 'Hadn't we better organise some back-up?'

Skelgill is scowling at the drivers of vehicles whom they pass, taken by surprise and sometimes plainly irked when stared at by a wild-eyed passenger in a speeding car.

'Let's not get ahead of ourselves, Leyton.'

This appears to be all he has to say on the matter. He settles into his seat, the map draped over his thighs like a travel rug. He folds his arms and closes his eyes, and gives every indication he is about to take a catnap. Then without warning he produces his mobile phone and calls up a number. He introduces himself with his official title and requests to be put through to "the Director" – it is evidently Haresfell. There is a short hiatus while he is transferred via Briony Boss's PA. Once connected he does not beat about the bush.

'Two more questions.'

The Director must invite him to continue.

'First – on Friday night when we discussed Meredith Bale's disguise – you said it wasn't unusual for Dr Walker and Dr Pettigrew to leave together.'

It appears she affirms his statement. Skelgill's rejoinder is blunt.

'Who did you mean?'

He listens intently – though his stern features reveal no clue to any feelings evoked by her response.

'Second question.' But now Skelgill falters. He lowers the handset and glances uneasily at DS Leyton, who makes a face of innocent concentration – in fact a counterproductive attempt to suggest that he is not eavesdropping. It leaves Skelgill still dissatisfied. After a moment's thought he raises the phone. 'I'll text it to your mobile – you can give me a verbal yes or no. I'll put you on hold.'

DS Leyton steals a suspicious glance at his superior: not only does he have Briony Boss's private number, but also he is giving her the opportunity to answer some question unwitnessed – and blatantly off the record. Skelgill taps out a message using the index finger of his injured hand. He transmits with a final decisive poke and then retrieves the call.

'Got it?'

Now he waits while Briony Boss considers his request. He sits in rigid anticipation, breathing heavily through his nostrils. The answer seems to take a disproportionately long time – but come it must, for with a single word – "Thanks" – he ends the call.

DS Leyton exhales heavily, as if he has been holding back, eager to speak.

'Here's Tebay, Guv – look – there's DS Jones by that picnic area. No sign of DI Smart's motor. That's her luggage beside her.'

Skelgill sniffs.

'Looks like he's got the hump, Leyton.'

'Looks like DS Jones has got the burgers, Guv.'

25. SADGILL NOOK

'Turn right, Leyton!'

There is a screech of brakes and a squeal of tyres, and the dull thump of passengers being flung against the interior of DS Leyton's car.

'Take it easy, man!'

In truth, Skelgill brackets this complaint with a pair of colourful adjective-noun combinations of Anglo-Saxon origin.

'Leave it out, Guv – you said turn right!'

DS Leyton – reasonably taking offence that the latter of these choice phrases was of a somewhat personal nature – responds with an unprintable postscript of his own, though it is one aimed at injustice in general, rather than directly at his capricious boss.

'Aye – but let's not kill us before we get there.'

DS Leyton bristles with discontent. He has a fair point – had Skelgill given him any less warning he would not have been able to make the turn at all – and, once committed (by instinctively trusting his superior's imperious command), it was a case of all or nothing. The manoeuvre had to be completed, or a ditch beckoned. What must be additionally galling is that, while the route is new to him, it cannot be to Skelgill, who boasts of knowing every byway in the county. He might have mentioned that this particular charted course begins with a one-hundred-and-eighty-degree hairpin off the main Penrith to Kendall highway.

Skelgill cranes around to check upon DS Jones. Such concern is uncharacteristic, so it may be deduced that it is an additional oblique swipe at DS Leyton's driving, to make doubly sure he fires the final salvo in the argument.

'Alright, Jones?'

'I'm fine, Guv.' But she has lowered the window by a couple of inches, perhaps anticipating the onset of carsickness. 'What is this road?'

Skelgill frowns in mock censure – that she is a local lass and should know her geography – but it is a chance to show off his knowledge of Lakeland.

'Longsleddale. Runs up to Harter Fell – two-five-three-nine.' He refers to the summit height. 'The road stops short – dead end at Sadgill.'

'What is it – a village, Guv?'

Skelgill shakes his head.

'There's not a hundred folk live in the entire dale – Sadgill's just a farmstead.'

'With a holiday cottage?'

Skelgill nods forbiddingly.

'Reckon so.'

They fall silent as they anticipate what might be to come. The tiny hamlet of Sadgill – the one-word address extracted by Skelgill from a squealing Arthur Kerr – is one of Cumbria's more isolated spots, which is saying something given the rugged nature of the region. Located at the navigable limit of a five-mile-long single-track straight, it sits a good six hundred feet above sea level, just below the source of the aptly named rushing River Sprint.

Initially, clipped hedgerows that threaten to scour the sides of the car hem them in; occasionally, low whitewashed properties flash by, their frontages perilously close to the road, and rusting pickups are jammed into improbably tight strips of verge. However, DS Jones's worries of queasiness prove unfounded – the route might be direct, but at regular intervals small bends restrict a driver's visibility, and DS Leyton is obliged to set a steady pace for fear of meeting an oncoming tractor with zero wriggle room. As they gradually gain altitude, the dense hawthorn gives way to dry stone walls, and the view opens out. Narrow enclosures lie on either side, butting up to rising fellsides dappled by the shifting shadows of clouds. To port streams the river – by no means wide, indeed more of a beck – but clearly running with considerable force of water at the limit of its banks, and beginning to converge with the lane as the valley floor tapers. Skelgill is eyeing this feature with a critical eye.

'The Sprint's the fastest-rising river in England.'

DS Leyton frowns.

'What does that mean, Guv?'

Skelgill casts him a disparaging glance.

'It flows uphill, Leyton.'

'Is that right, Guv?'

Now Skelgill makes an exasperated gasp.

'No, Leyton, you dolt – it means it floods quickly – look for yourself.'

Indeed at this juncture the road dips and they come alongside a section of waterlogged meadow. DS Leyton glowers, though it may be the reflection of the sun as much as Skelgill's casual insult that exaggerates his apparent displeasure. He looks to be seeking a suitable retort – until a timely cough from DS Jones reminds him that diplomacy is generally a better tactic with their boss. He opts for a more productive complaint.

'Don't like the look of that, Guv – what do we do if the road's flooded?'

Skelgill harrumphs.

'We'll cross that bridge when we come to it, Leyton.'

Knowing his superior's erratic temper, this curiously literal idiom may well be intentionally flippant – but then DS Leyton's fears are literally realised before he can respond. They round a curve to be confronted by water streaming across the tarmac. As far as is visible – perhaps fifty yards to the next bend – the road is inundated. DS Leyton slows to a halt.

'Keep going, Leyton – what are you playing at, man?'

Now DS Leyton looks pleadingly at Skelgill.

'Struth, Guv – what if the engine stalls – and then we're stuck and the flood rises – you know me and water, Guv.'

Skelgill carelessly flicks a hand in an onwards direction.

'Just take it easy – you'll be fine.'

'But, Guv –'

Skelgill seems unconcerned.

'Leyton – we'll know how deep it is – we can wade out if necessary – anyway, it's also the fastest falling river in England – and the water's receding.'

DS Leyton does not look convinced – quite likely Skelgill has plucked this dubious claim from the fiction section of his extensive mental library of 'convenient facts of Lakeland'.

'How can you be sure, Guv?'

In a superior manner Skelgill now points to a wire mesh fence that fills a gap in a wall. About thirty inches above the water level is a tidemark of trapped straw and twigs and fronds of bracken.

'See that? The worst of the rain was Friday night and Saturday. That's where it would have peaked last night. This could be our best friend.' He elbows DS Leyton like he is spurring a reluctant horse. 'Step on it, Leyton.'

DS Leyton swallows and without enthusiasm selects first gear. He enters the flood at a crawl, and lowers his window to watch with trepidation as the water begins to creep up the walls of his tyres.

'Gawd 'elp me, Guv – the missus'll go snooker loopy if this motor gets ruined – if I'd known we were doing this I'd have booked out a pool car.'

Skelgill suddenly guffaws – and although the laughter sounds affected, he thumps his sergeant convivially between the shoulder blades.

'Very funny, Leyton – that's the spirit – now go for it – and once you've got a bow wave don't slow down.'

DS Leyton's baffled expression suggests his pun is unwitting – but Skelgill's exhortations seem to do the trick, and setting his jaw determinedly he takes on the flood. His misgivings, however, are soon corroborated as the peaty water rises above the sills, and only the integrity of the door seals stands between DS Leyton and a good tongue-lashing. Skelgill, meanwhile, makes various unintelligible but enthusiastic-sounding noises to offset DS Leyton's tormented groans.

'Just get round the bend, Leyton – I know the lie of the land – this is always the worst spot.'

DS Leyton is too preoccupied to speak – or perhaps even to listen – but, sure enough, Skelgill's prediction proves to be accurate, and his sergeant lets out a gasp of relief as he sees the level ebb.

'It's dropping, Guv!'

'Nice work, Leyton – you've cracked it.'

DS Leyton looks pleased with himself, and even accelerates triumphantly, raising great arcs of spray as they emerge from the shallows. His mood lightens immediately.

'What happens to the fish, Guv – I mean, when it floods – do they swim off on a little adventure?'

Skelgill looks suddenly pensive.

'Happen they do, Leyton – it's a common enough sight to find dead salmon dried up in depressions in a floodplain meadow.'

DS Jones has been leaning forwards between the two front seats for a better view of this amphibious stage of their journey.

'That section would have been impassable, Guv – anyone living above here would have been cut off until now.'

Skelgill nods grimly.

'That's why plenty of folk drive Defenders.'

Their conversation dwindles as DS Leyton pilots them uneventfully the last mile to Sadgill. Just as Skelgill has foretold, the route directly ahead crumbles into gravel – this is a disused mining track that once served Wrengill green slate quarry beneath Harter Fell. The metalled lane itself hangs a left across the Sprint, bounding over an ancient packhorse bridge to its terminus at the farmstead. They draw to a halt in the shadow of a great old stone bank barn, traditionally used for fattening drove cattle from Scotland, but now more likely to be pressed into service for lambing and the keeping of sheep. Skelgill lowers his window and listens keenly – but at the moment there are no farmyard sounds, either animal or mechanical.

'Where exactly are we, Guv – I mean, on the map?'

It is DS Jones that poses this question, her voice hushed by the atmosphere of uncertainty that has descended upon them. Skelgill stretches his arms and produces a nonchalant yawn – but it is not convincing and hints of pre-match nerves.

'If you'd carried on up that track – on foot, like – go three miles due north over Gatescarth Pass and you're into Mardale – you come down by the southern tip of Haweswater.'

DS Jones nods; however DS Leyton chips in with an eager declaration.

'That's where the bothy was, Guv – that Harry Krille torched.'

Skelgill regards his sergeant with eyes narrowed. He shakes his head slowly.

'That was Hayeswater, Leyton – it's to the north-west – maybe five miles.' He points a finger in approximately the right direction. 'Still no distance, though.'

DS Jones is looking thoughtful.

'What about Tebay, Guv – how far is that across country?'

'As the crow flies, seven miles, I'd say.'

'So, Guv – the suspected presence of Harry Krille – we're kind of at a midpoint between those sites?'

Skelgill shrugs. His features suggest only a limited interest.

'It's one way to think about it.'

'But places that are quite easy to reach from here? And vice versa.'

'Aye – provided you're prepared to stick your walking boots on.'

There is another silence as they contemplate the implications of DS Jones's analysis. Skelgill has been no more forthcoming on what they may expect to encounter here in Longsleddale, and thus there is ample scope for his subordinates' imaginations to range freely. On this basis, it is not surprising that it is DS Leyton who pipes up anxiously.

'What do we do, Guv?'

'Find the cottage – I reckon it's beyond the farm, couple of hundred yards, at the edge of a little brake – I remember it being a ruin. They must have done it up.'

DS Leyton drums out a restless beat with his fingers upon the steering wheel.

'Wouldn't this be a good time to call for back-up, Guv – just in case? We're right out in the sticks – it might take them a while to get here.'

Skelgill takes out his phone, consults the screen, and looks from one to the other of his colleagues with a curiously contorted facial expression. He makes a short, rather hysterical laugh.

'Anyone got a signal?'

*

'Crikey, Guv – there's the red Volvo, right enough!'

'Hush, Leyton – and keep your head down.'

Skelgill has led them on foot through the apparently deserted farmstead, and then tangentially across a boggy pasture to skirt an adjoining broad-leaved copse. Hidden from sight on the north side of this nestles an old shepherd's cottage, single storey, with a heavy roof of local green slate. The building appears to have been restored to a decent standard, although a tumbledown structure to one side serves as a rudimentary log store and carport. A stone wall encircles the property – the standard first line of defence against voracious Herdwicks – and a muddy track from the farm swings around to meet a five-barred gate. The garden is mainly given over to lawn, although borders of rosemary and lavender line a narrow gravel footpath that connects the front door to a small gate cut into in the wall. The grass is in need of a trim, and the borders of a good weeding, although the overall impression is of a quaint Lakeland cottage. Around the door is an open porch, painted green, with a triangular canopy, from which hangs a hand-painted sign, 'Sadgill Nook'. There is a chimney pot at either end of the house, and from the right-hand of these a weak column of smoke rises for a dozen feet before drifting away on a light westerly breeze.

Skelgill jerks a thumb over his shoulder.

'I've kipped here – when it was abandoned. We used to do exercises down this way. There's a mountain rescue post in the wood.'

'What's that for, Guv?' DS Leyton sounds hopeful.

Skelgill manufactures a macabre grin.

'You never know when you might need a stretcher, Leyton.'

'Forget I asked, Guv.'

But Skelgill is already craning to get a glimpse of the property.

'There's a room each side of the entrance, and that's about it. Maybe they've got bunks in the loft. Going by the smoke, I'm guessing they've made that the kitchen on the right.'

All three detectives crouch behind the wall to one side of the gate. There is a silence while Skelgill seems to be debating with himself as to the optimum tactics. DS Leyton, perhaps swayed by the proximity of their quarry, now seems resigned to their acting alone.

'What do you reckon, Guv – take 'em by surprise?'

Skelgill appears to nod.

'Unless they've changed it, there's no windows or door at the back – but we'd better check.' Without taking his eyes off the cottage he lays a hand upon DS Jones's upper arm. 'Jones – sneak round the wall and have a dekko. Leyton, you wait here – stay hidden.'

'What about you, Guv?'

Skelgill grimaces.

'I want to get a look inside.' He taps DS Jones to indicate she should move. 'Let's go.'

DS Jones sets off commando style, bent over so that her head remains below the uneven crest of the wall. Skelgill is right behind her, but he halts as soon as he reaches the plane of the front of the building. He hisses an instruction to his colleague.

'Meet back at the gate beside Leyton.'

DS Jones raises a hand in affirmation and continues on her way. Skelgill cautiously rises, but when he sees the coast is clear he swarms decisively over the wall and darts across the lawn to the corner of the cottage. Now he presses his spine against stone and edges along the frontage as if he is traversing a narrow ledge on a rock face. He reaches the left-hand window and in slow motion leans to peer through the glass. The room must be empty, for now he slides across without ducking. He has taken maybe two more steps to reach the angle of the porch when the front door suddenly opens and a woman emerges. In one hand she dangles an empty log basket – and in the other a shotgun. It is the unmistakeable ginger suedehead, Meredith Bale.

DS Leyton has been observing Skelgill's progress through a slit in the warped planks of the gate. Now he sees his superior stiffen, spread-eagled against the cottage wall like a gnarled wisteria. Meredith Bale's gait is ponderous – she is a big woman and carries excess weight. Her beady black eyes fix disconcertingly upon his hiding place – although she cannot possibly see him. However, rather than cross to the log store she takes several paces down the path towards his place of concealment. Then she halts and swings around. Her movements are robotic. Seeing Skelgill, she drops the log basket and raises the gun. Behind her, DS Leyton noiselessly pushes open the gate.

There now ensues a prolonged standoff. Meredith Bale is statuesque, her expression implacable, her eyes glazed. And so it falls to Skelgill to make the first move. But just when he might be expected to stoop for a stone or a handful of soil (or, more sensibly, complete a sideways roll and a zigzagging dash for safety), he detaches himself from the wall, thrusts his hands into his pockets, lowers his gaze to the ground between them, and begins to saunter casually towards her. He might even be whistling. DS Leyton can restrain himself no longer.

'Guv – she's a serial killer!'

'Is she.'

Skelgill's muttered retort carries no hint of a question. He walks directly up to Meredith Bale, takes hold of the twin barrels, and gently tilts the gun until it points skywards. Meekly, she releases it into his possession. He smiles graciously and steps even closer. She is almost as tall as him and they are face to face. Suddenly, she begins to blink – she looks most disconcerted – it as though he has just roused her from a confusing daydream. Skelgill addresses her in a matter of fact manner.

'Where's Harry?'

'He hasn't come.'

Skelgill looks past her to DS Leyton, who strides up the path, his features a confusion of alarm and bewilderment. Skelgill flips the gun and presents it stock first to his colleague. Meredith Bale looks on benignly. Skelgill turns on his heel and stalks into the cottage.

The front door opens directly into the right-hand room. It has been knocked through from the entrance hall to create a reasonably spacious living kitchen. There are several well-worn easy chairs, a square oak farmhouse table and matching carvers, a log-burning stove in the hearth and, against the back wall an array of kitchen appliances, including a modern take on the old-fashioned range cooker. Beside this, in one of the carvers, sits a frantically writhing Dr Agnetha Walker. There is a sweatshirt discarded upon the flagged floor and she wears only a translucent white bra and faded blue hipster jeans – her blonde hair is unkempt and she grimaces beneath a gag improvised from an elasticated hairband – she is struggling frantically to liberate her hands from behind her. As Skelgill enters she wrenches herself free, arises awkwardly, and hauls down the gag from her mouth.

'Oh – Dan – thank heavens!' She stares at him with great intensity. 'When you think of the fishes.' There is a curiously imploring note in her voice, bordering on prurient.

Skelgill's trajectory seems momentarily disrupted – but he lurches forwards with indecent haste and she topples willingly into his arms. His palms slide down to her buttocks and he pulls her hard against him – but then there is a curious metallic sound and he steps away. Dr Agnetha Walker seems frozen; she gazes at him, her distinctive eyebrows high with alarm, her mouth open – but words fail her. Now she looks down to her side with disbelief: she is handcuffed by one wrist to the solid stainless steel towel rail of the cooker. Skelgill regards her for a moment, and then without a word turns and stalks away.

DS Leyton is standing guard beside Meredith Bale. They both squint into the sunshine as Skelgill approaches. The sergeant now has the shotgun broken over his right forearm.

'It wasn't loaded, Guv.'

Skelgill holds out his bandaged left fist. He unfurls his fingers to reveal two live cartridges.

'The safety was on, Leyton.'

DS Leyton exhales deeply and shakes his head. He has overheard Meredith Bale state that Harry Krille is not here – but now he has the presence of mind to realise they should make doubly sure.

'I'll just have a quick butcher's, Guv.'

Skelgill nods, understanding his sergeant's intent. For good measure he hands him the cartridges.

'Where's Jones?'

'She's legged it to the farmhouse, Guv. She said she'd noticed telegraph poles along the lane – they must have a landline.'

DS Leyton disappears into the cottage, leaving Skelgill alone with a subdued Meredith Bale. He seems disinclined to restrain her – not that she would get far in this terrain. He frowns in a companionable way, rather as though they were two passengers on a platform when it has just been announced that their train is indefinitely delayed.

'I never wanted this. They brainwashed me.'

Skelgill nods slowly, his brow still furrowed. It is hard to discern if he is affecting sympathy or mulling over the meaning of her statement.

'So what's our friend Harry up to?'

Meredith Bale shrugs somewhat helplessly.

'Unfinished business. That's all I know.'

She makes it sound like she is quoting directly from her fellow inmate. But something suddenly dawns on Skelgill. He curses under his breath and turns away. He sees DS Jones running athletically along the uneven track that leads from the farm. She clears puddles and dodges ruts with a succession of graceful leaps and bounds. Leaving a stationary Meredith Bale, he strides away to intercept his colleague at the five-barred gate.

'What's the story?'

'We're in luck, Guv.' DS Jones rests her forearms on the gate and dips her head while she gulps air. 'There was a patrol just passing the junction where we turned off. They're in a 4x4 –

they'll be here in ten minutes – fewer. And two more units on the way from Kendal. They reckon twenty minutes.'

Skelgill nods. His face is grim and there is an uncharacteristically harried look in his grey-green eyes.

'As soon as the first car arrives – we fly.'

DS Jones lifts a surprised face; her cheeks flushed pink with exertion.

'Where to, Guv?'

'Keswick. And we need to find Pettigrew.'

26. EARL GREY

'Which house is it, Guv?'
'The one on the end.'
'At least we can get round the back.'

Skelgill makes a pained face – he seems now to doubt whatever is his hunch, and is uncertain of what should be their course of action. Perhaps drained by their dramatic discovery at Sadgill and their abrupt departure and ensuing dash to Keswick, the detectives sit rather becalmed in DS Leyton's car. They are parked in The Heads, a pleasant airy street of triple-storey slate-built Victorian guest houses with ornate porches and balconies, and multiple gables, and narrow terraced frontages that overlook the grassy expanse of Hope Park, beyond which is Crow Park, Derwentwater, and the undulating backdrop of the Cumbrian mountains. Skelgill gnaws at a thumbnail and gazes at the distant skyline. The fells look inviting today, swathed in verdant summer vegetation, their colours and contours picked out by the burgeoning sunshine. He squints and can see tiny figures, antlike, wending their way up the path to Catbells' distinctive pike. Down here in the town, tourists have shed their cagoules, and to some extent blend with locals as the latter go about their business. Though tourists tend to walk with a more aimless gait, wear small backpacks, and sport smears of chocolate ice cream on their faces.

'Look, Guv.'

DS Jones brings their attention to a courier van that has drawn up just ahead. Its livery advertises a private healthcare provider, and a woman emerges from the driver's side. She holds a clipboard and wears a smart white overall and a nurse's cap that bears the company logo, and attached to a lanyard around her neck is an ID badge. She opens the rear doors, selects a package from within, locks the vehicle, and strides purposefully up the front path of an adjacent property. The

251

detectives watch in silence as she rings the doorbell and, after a short delay, exchanges the medicine for a signature from an ageing male resident. Briskly, she trots down the steps to the sidewalk, and returns to her vehicle. Skelgill looks questioningly at DS Jones. She nods decisively.

At the end house the garden is more extensive. There is a small plateau of lawn, and matching ornamental conifers that stand sentry on either side of the front door. The nurse seems a little unfamiliar with the workings of the antiquated brass bell-pull – but she gets it after a couple of tries. From within comes a tinkling, and the more distant bark of dogs. She waits patiently. In time footsteps shuffle closer, and then a faint scratching – someone is looking through the peephole. Finally there is the clunk of a mortise lock.

The elderly woman that opens the door does so only to the extent of a safety chain. Despite the time of day she wears a long flannelette nightgown beneath a thick towelling dressing gown, and carpet slippers upon her feet. Her face is heavily lined, and although her skin is tanned, her features are drawn and her eyes bloodshot, as if through lack of sleep. She seems alarmed by the presence of her caller, wary and on edge. The health visitor, however, takes this in her stride.

'Good afternoon, Mrs Wright-Fotheringham – your diabetes medication to be signed for.'

The older woman's eyes widen – she appears confused – she takes a deep breath, and rather nervously glances over her right shoulder. There is a moment's delay and she looks back at the nurse and nods – perhaps she is feeling self-conscious in her nightclothes – but she unfastens the door and opens it a little wider. The nurse offers the clipboard and pen for signature, balanced upon it a little packet marked with a printed sticker – however, two high steps mean she is out of reach and the householder has to lean outwards and downwards. And thus at this very second two small boys cycling past must think they have chanced upon a scene being played out on a movie set.

It is the old lady's shriek of alarm that stops them in their tracks – thrown astride their crossbars they gape to see her grabbed at the wrist by a younger woman in a nurse's outfit and hauled unceremoniously down the steps and across the lawn to collapse into a heap. Simultaneously two men rush out from behind the conifers. The first – decidedly stocky, with a mop of flopping dark hair – hurls himself at the door. There is an almighty crash and from within an agonised cry of surprise. The first man loses his balance but the second – taller and more agile – vaults his associate and disappears into the hallway. The human battering ram now scrambles to his feet and follows suit. While the two females begin to untangle themselves – the younger woman now tending to the older – a brief sequence of yells, grunts and thumps emanates from the house. A moment later the invaders emerge with another man held between them: he is short and wiry, with close-cropped grey hair and the grizzled stubble of several days going unshaven. He appears dazed; though his captors have his arms twisted in what might not be the most comfortable of positions. There is a distinctive swelling in the centre of his forehead, already beginning to turn blue.

Awestruck, now the juvenile spectators are almost mown down by a marked police car that slithers to a halt in front of them. Three uniformed officers burst out, casting off their caps and abandoning the vehicle with its doors akimbo. They sprint up the path – it must be an action movie – and promptly relieve the arresting officers of their charge. They handcuff the felon, feed him unceremoniously into the back of the car, and speed away. The taller of the two plain-clothes men notices the boys; he marches rather menacingly towards them, digging into a trouser pocket as he does so. For a pistol? Have they witnessed an unlawful kidnapping? But when he holds out a bandaged hand it is to reveal a couple of two-pound coins.

'There you go, marra – hop it and get some mint cake – something to tell your pals about, eh?'

He grins at them and ruffles the hair of the nearest boy. Then he turns and jogs back up the steps of the front garden. Alice Wright-Fotheringham, apparently none the worse for her ordeal, sits upon the grass, reunited with her dog. It seems DS

Leyton – who has disappeared inside the property – has freed the canines from confinement. The exuberant Justitia is plainly delighted to see her mistress. Her temporary stable companion, Cleopatra – gambolling generally about the lawn, having recognised there is some cause for celebration – now detects Skelgill's approach and intercepts him with her trademark cannonball-to-the-midriff greeting, chopping him to his knees beside the retired judge. Skelgill wrestles his dog to the ground and addresses the dishevelled householder.

'So you were Harry Krille's unfinished business.'

'I think he merely wanted to talk to me, Daniel. You were rather rough with him. He bore no grudge that I was his prosecuting counsel. And it seems he is a dog lover.'

Skelgill flashes her a malevolent glance.

'Just as well for him.'

She frowns with mock censure.

'Well, I suppose it was providential that you invited your colleagues along for that pot of Earl Grey. Shall we have tea?'

She does not wait for an answer, but rises with a helping hand from DS Jones and marches indoors. The dogs bound ahead of her. Skelgill and DS Jones exchange helpless simpers, but do not protest (though DS Jones must first return her disguise). And thus, along with DS Leyton and their host – still clad in her nightclothes – they are soon seated around a coffee table in a pleasantly bright conservatory at the rear of the house. Skelgill needs little invitation to begin tucking into home-made treacle scones, thickly layered with brandy butter.

The detectives are no doubt keen to hear Alice Wright-Fotheringham's account of her uninvited guest – but with the Haresfell fugitives back in custody, and recognising that the elderly lady must be shaken by her ordeal (despite her pretensions to the contrary), they skirt diplomatically around the matter. But when Skelgill mentions that Dr Agnetha Walker has also been arrested, it is the retired judge herself who makes the running. Her shrewd pale-blue eyes narrow, and she gives him a portentous shake of an index finger.

'You know, Daniel – when I heard of your little fishing arrangement – I was sorely tempted to warn you. And although my intuition has perhaps been borne out as correct, I felt at the time that I must adhere to my schooling that a person is innocent until proven guilty.'

Skelgill stops eating. His sergeants stare at him in surprise.

'What are you saying, Alice?'

But there is something in his demeanour that suggests he already understands.

'I heard word of her – Dr Walker – through a former colleague on the NHS Appointments Board. There was the unexpected death of her husband – he had no history whatsoever of coronary illness. I understand it caused a few raised eyebrows in some circles. Although of course nobody was willing to go beyond the rumour.'

Skelgill stands up.

'What is it, Guv?' DS Leyton braces his elbows on the arms of his chair, ready to rise.

'Dr Peter Pettigrew.'

'But we've got everyone looking for him, Guv – like you ordered.'

Skelgill regards his sergeant with some desperation.

'What about the hospital – Carlisle – where his wife is?'

'There's an officer at the main entrance, Guv – round the clock.'

'Aye – but he could get in through the staff channels. No one would bat an eyelid. He's more senior than most of their top people.'

Skelgill pats his pockets – but anticipating some rough and tumble, all three detectives have left their mobiles in DS Leyton's car.

'Alice – may I use your phone?'

'Unfortunately my visitor tore off the cable.'

Skelgill grimaces and makes a move for the door, pausing only to sweep up his remaining portion of treacle scone.

27. THE LUNE

'Think he would have done it, Guv?'

Skelgill shrugs.

'He must have had plenty of chances. I reckon he lost his bottle. Away from her influence.'

DS Leyton shakes his head rather disbelievingly.

'Still, Guv – just as well it occurred to you – else she might have been a goner – and now they're saying she should make a full recovery.'

Skelgill stoops for a flat pebble and sends it skimming across the surface of the river. The trio have returned to collect his car from its parking spot beside the Lune, a short distance from Hare's Beck Foot. It is early evening, and the recent rains could be a distant memory as slanting rays of sunlight filter through leafy bankside alders and a blackbird makes up for lost time with a virtuoso performance, its rich fluty lazy song the quintessence of English summer. From the nearby inn Arthur Kerr and Eric Blacklock have been taken into custody to assist police with their inquiries. They may sing, too. It is the Pettigrews, however, to whom DS Leyton refers. Dr Peter Pettigrew – now under arrest – was apprehended at his wife's hospital bedside; in his possession was an ampoule of epinephrine. Though he maintains his innocence, already through its batch number its origin has been traced to a Manchester hospital.

'What Mrs Wright-Fotheringham said, Guv – about the death of Dr Agnetha Walker's husband – what do you reckon?'

Skelgill is staring grimly at the river, its surface shimmering mesmerically. He turns and regards DS Leyton through narrowed eyes.

'I reckon it's got to be looked into. Consider the sequence of events. She and Pettigrew meet on the panel for Meredith Bale's case – that's what, two years ago? They're both away from home. On the quiet he's a bit of a ladies' man and she's on a power trip. Let's say they start an affair. Then it escalates – and they hatch a lovers' plot.'

'But what's in it for them, Guv – why not just leave their spouses?'

Skelgill again stares pensively over the Lune.

'For one thing it might blow their careers – who knows what kind of stink their former partners would kick up – they might have thought so, anyway. But I reckon there's a lot more to it than that. Helen Pettigrew is a wealthy woman – and I bet her husband stands to inherit the lot. If so, Dr Agnetha Walker gets a rich and influential new husband – he gets a younger model. Plus.'

DS Leyton is shaking his head.

'He never struck me as the murdering kind, Guv. That he'd agree to a plot like that – a top consultant and all.'

DS Jones is watching Skelgill closely. She realises he has something to add. But Skelgill replies to DS Leyton, his tone contrary.

'Who says he *did*?'

'What do you mean, Guv – that *she* was the driving force?'

'Think about it, Leyton. She's got a reputation for getting what she wants. She's got looks on her side – not to mention that she's an expert in hypnosis. When she asks him into her parlour, he's easy meat.' Skelgill breaks off, a worried grimace momentarily tearing at his features. But he re-gathers his thoughts. 'So she fixes her fangs into Pettigrew – one way or another – and starts to mess with his head. The affair gets serious – she's working in Manchester and he's regularly visiting – then her husband conveniently dies. Maybe that's as much of a shock to Pettigrew as anyone. But before long she's relocated to the Pettigrews' flat in Didsbury – very handy for them both. Looks like he's been handling the family properties with the rental agents – so there's no need for anyone to know the new tenant's also his lover. Next thing she's moving in closer – there's a proposal for her assignment at Haresfell. Everyone thinks it's Pettigrew's idea – but what if it's hers? – now he can see her every day. She even gets friendly with the family. Then comes the last act – remove the final obstacle – the wife, Dr Helen Pettigrew. He sets up the drama therapy job – and, bingo, they've got her in their sights.'

Skelgill steps away and scoops up a handful of pebbles and begins to throw them one by one into the water. It is as though he is relieving himself of the burden of the many pieces of a jigsaw that did not fit the pattern, and now he knows they are superfluous: red herrings sinking without trace into the Lune. DS Leyton claps his hands together almost joyously.

'Cor blimey, Guv – it all makes sense now I can see it – but what put you onto them?'

Skelgill turns to face his subordinates.

'That first time we went to Haresfell – I got a glimpse of Dr Agnetha Walker – I didn't know who she was – I thought she was a patient – in fact she was with Meredith Bale.' He stares at the remaining stones in his right hand, and weighs them broodingly. 'Maybe she was preparing her for the interview. And then when she came to Peel Wyke – I knew I recognised her – but I didn't know why – I remember, straight away, like this tiny alarm bell – but then she kind of won me over.'

DS Jones flashes a wary glance at Skelgill – it prompts him to revert to his stone throwing. DS Leyton, however, gives an abrupt laugh.

'Maybe she hypnotised you, Guv!'

There is something unnatural about Skelgill's stance, and he keeps his back to his colleagues, eking out his ammunition. DS Jones, too, seems uneasy; she takes a tentative step towards him.

'Do you think, Guv – her involvement in the fishing trip – there was more to it – remember the feedback from the auction – that she outbid everyone to get the prize?'

Skelgill rotates slowly on his heel, his eyes downcast and his expression one that admits to suffering a reverse. It seems likely DS Jones has learned this detail from DI Alec Smart, whose motive for imparting the information would likely bear little relation to solving the case.

'Aye – happen she saw the chance to get an inside track. That's the brass neck of a psychopath. They knew we were starting to investigate Meredith Bale – and they knew what they were planning. Looks like she even rented the cottage at Bassenthwaite to keep herself on the spot. Let's take up fishing and get into bed with the local cops.'

Skelgill's cheeks suddenly begin to colour, and again he walks away, down to the water's edge. It must irk him as the realisation grows that here was his very own *Mata Hari*, subtly inquiring as to the progress of his investigations, seeding his perception of Meredith Bale as dangerous and scheming and secretly triumphant, and being craftily evasive whenever his own questions might expose the conspiracy. And, to do so, she brazenly employed her full armoury of resources.

There is a lull in the conversation – it seems all three officers need a moment to absorb the impressions that swim thick and fast into their respective streams of consciousness. DS Leyton is the first to speak.

'Guv – what made them think they'd get away with it?'

Skelgill regards his sergeant with a rather blank expression.

'Look, Leyton – my head's spinning, too. But if I were to put it in a nutshell, they – or she – intended to kill Dr Helen Pettigrew and frame Meredith Bale as the culprit.'

'But, Guv – she'd deny it – surely that would be too risky?'

'Not risky when she's dead, Leyton.'

DS Leyton looks even more perplexed.

'But why did Meredith Bale have the gun at the cottage, Guv?'

Skelgill shrugs.

'To make sure her fingerprints were all over it – that's my guess. If she were under some influence, she'd probably cart the gun around without questioning why. Remember – Dr Agnetha Walker had the cartridges in her back pocket. I don't doubt she can handle a gun as well as she does a fishing rod. Pretending to be tied up was a last ditch smokescreen.'

DS Leyton begins to shake his head in wonderment. Skelgill continues to elaborate.

'But I reckon the flood saved Meredith Bale – they were cut off at the cottage – they couldn't get out to drive to wherever it was they planned to kill her. Nor could Dr Peter Pettigrew get in to Sadgill – if that were part of the plan. But they obviously couldn't do it there – they'd attract attention to him as the owner. They'd tell her they were going to rendezvous with Harry Krille.' Skelgill takes a deep breath and sighs as he exhales. 'Course – that wasn't the only fly in the ointment. Dr Helen Pettigrew surviving the attack meant they had to resort to plan B – to kill her with the adrenaline and make it look like natural causes. So that delayed them, too.'

'Handy gaff to keep an unlicensed gun tucked away, Guv – I bet the regular local bobby never gets near the place.'

'If he even knows it exists.' Skelgill darts a glance at the river, for a salmon has breached with a sizeable splash. 'Perfect to hide out – they probably had Meredith Bale believing they were waiting for Harry Krille to arrive cross country. Then when he never showed they'd have the excuse to go and meet him. Next thing – find a quiet spot miles from there – roadside scuffle as the "hostage" tries to escape – the gun goes off – the police roll up – Meredith's lying in a layby with her brains blown out – no need for anyone to mention the cottage.'

Now DS Leyton is looking a little troubled.

'Why would Meredith Bale go along with all this, Guv? Surely she couldn't have hypnotised her that well?'

Skelgill shrugs.

'Who knows, Leyton – it's a powerful tool – especially when what's on offer is your heart's desire.' He affects an imploring voice. 'Hey, Meredith, Harry wants to marry you – we'll spring you both from Haresfell – we'll give you cash, our passports – you'll be safely out of the country before anyone knows about it.'

'So Harry Krille escapes and she believes it?'

Skelgill grins ruefully.

'You've got it, Leyton.'

'So his escape was a put-up job?'

Skelgill nods.

'It was Dr Peter Pettigrew that relaxed his conditions – the gardening, reduced supervision – and the failing security just played into their hands. Permission to roam outside – nice view of the fells. Talk about letting the dog see the rabbit.'

'So there never was any plan for Bale and Krille to meet up?'

'Leyton, I doubt if Harry Krille knew the first thing about it.'

'Struth, Guv – and his escape soaked up a load of resources – took our eyes off the ball. Not to mention we already had our hands full with the death of Frank Wamphray.' DS Leyton scowls, screwing up his face in a puzzled manner. 'What do you reckon about that, Guv? I had Arthur Kerr down as the prime suspect – and maybe Briony Boss behind it.'

Now Skelgill smiles benevolently.

'Aye, I trod that road myself, Leyton. But I think we know what happened – probably not so far off what we deduced in the first place. Poor old Frank's chucking all sorts of mud at the wall – sooner or later something's going to stick. Dr Peter Pettigrew and Dr Agnetha Walker were getting close to executing their plan and got the wind up. Remember – Frank Wamphray was in the drama group, too. He might easily have put Helen Pettigrew on her guard – that was a chance they couldn't take. So they switched his medication for the contaminated vial. Engineered it so he was sick with eating too much chocolate. Events took care of themselves. Suspicion falls on Meredith Bale – it's her MO, even though it seems impossible she could have done it. Failing that, there's a ready-made scapegoat in the shape of Arthur Kerr – who could have been doing someone else's dirty work in return for a nice little payday.'

'He seems to have his finger in a lot of pies, Guv.'

'He's made it his business, Leyton – all the way to the top.'

'Do you include the Director in that, Guv?'

After a moment Skelgill nods, but he remains taciturn.

'That question you asked her, Guv – on the phone in my motor – that seemed to make your mind up about something.'

Skelgill considers his response.

'Let's say that was about her and Dr Peter Pettigrew – and leave it at that.' However, he immediately contradicts himself by revealing more. 'You can imagine them crossing paths when she was in charge of hospitals in Manchester – he was consulting in the district. So by the time she applies for the post at Haresfell they're well acquainted. Too well. He's on the appointments board – she gets her job. Next thing, he's promoted – quid pro quo. And probably everything's hunky-dory until Dr Agnetha Walker comes onto the scene at Meredith Bale's assessment panel. She sees off the competition, but the competition doesn't know who it is that's seen her off.' Now Skelgill sighs. He is speaking in such a way that requires his deputies to read between the lines. 'What I learned, Leyton – it explained a few things – about Briony Boss, aye – but more importantly about Dr Peter Pettigrew.'

DS Leyton nods, his countenance rather grim. He must suspect that his superior is protecting Haresfell's Director – and that it may not matter. That she seemed prepared to allow the death of Frank Wamphray to be put down to natural causes – albeit in ignorance of the truth, on the advice of Dr Peter Pettigrew – might be regarded as unprofessional. But the unfortunate patient was something of a loose cannon and not shy of iterating problems she would rather were swept under the carpet. As a former nurse with medical knowledge she could even have been considered in the frame for the murder. And yet it was she who called in the detectives to investigate a series of petty thefts that ordinarily would not have merited such attention – and risked the lid being lifted on a troubled regime that could only have shown her in a poor light: out of her depth and at the mercy of her own excesses, and consequently vulnerable to manipulation and mutiny from below decks. Perhaps it was a cry for help? By good fortune, in Skelgill she struck upon someone who is not such a distant relation in the soulmate stakes.

DS Jones has fallen silent during this long exchange. As a spectator for much of the investigation, obliged to follow its progress at a distance, and piecemeal, she has been unable to grasp fully the implications of the findings she has contributed. However – though she may have tended towards the wrong conclusion (that the conspiring doctors were targeted by Bale and Krille acting as a latter-day Bonnie and Clyde) – it is clear that her input has been vital in leading Skelgill to recognise the clandestine relationship that has been the beating heart of the case. Whether Skelgill will give her the credit for such is a moot point – and not one she shall lose sleep over – and indeed already her alert mind is turning in a new direction. Now, a little apprehensively, she takes the floor.

'What do you think, Guv – about the idea that –'

'Aye?'

Skelgill senses she is about to say something of significance. DS Leyton, too, detects the signs and watches her with interest. She clears her throat and continues.

'About Meredith Bale's claim that she didn't kill all those patients.'

Skelgill's immediate reaction seems to be one of resistance – that this is a step too far, the lifting of the lid of a Pandora's box from which they may quite justifiably retreat, having already succeeded beyond the call of duty. But his features reveal a little battle is taking place in his mind. It is his internal gatekeeper, his inherent sense of justice as a man of the fells, that for all his maverick ways guides him in times of need. It wins the argument. Slowly he nods.

'She reckons she's got a hidden dossier that will clear her name.'

DS Jones's eyes light up.

'When you think about it, Guv – it would be an overwhelming motive to eliminate her.'

Now DS Leyton interjects; there is a note of excitement in his voice.

'So, what are you saying – that Dr Agnetha Walker committed the hospital murders – and Meredith Bale knows about it?'

His colleagues each turn their solemn gaze upon him. After a moment's uneasy silence, Skelgill steps towards his sergeant and delivers a friendly left jab to his shoulder.

'One for the Greater Manchester boys, eh? They'll regret the day they got us country bumpkins to do their legwork at Haresfell.' He grins broadly. (Of course, he employs a somewhat coarser expression than "country bumpkins", one that might unfairly pertain to Herdwicks and their owners.) 'Come on Leyton, get that boot open – you've got my jacket in there.'

The tension released, DS Leyton grins and shrugs, and then he checks his watch. He might even get home in time for some leftover dinner and a bath-time soaking. He ambles to his car to do as he is bid. Skelgill, however, lifts the tailgate of his own vehicle, and begins to rummage noisily amongst the extensive jumble of fishing tackle and outdoor gear that covers the flatbed. DS Leyton calls out to him.

'Staying for a spot of fishing, Guv?'

Skelgill is shaking his head – although he has produced a small rod with a spinning reel attached, rigged with a silver Toby and ready for instant action. He walks over to DS Leyton's car. He holds up the rod – it is perhaps only five feet in length.

'I'm just going to pop down the river – there's a family staying at a cottage – this is for the little lad – to return a favour.'

DS Jones has drifted to join them, and now she looks inquiringly at Skelgill. There is something plainly self-conscious in his manner. DS Leyton glances from one to the other.

'Emma – I can give you a ride back up to Penrith – to get your motor from HQ.'

She smiles graciously at her colleague, and glances again at Skelgill, and then away across the water. But Skelgill suddenly leans into the trunk of DS Leyton's car and snatches up the holdall that she has brought back from Manchester. He thrusts the rod into her hands.

'Come on, Jones – keep me out of mischief, will you?'

***

Next in the series...

THE MISTS OF TIME

One week after the death of his 93-year-old twin brother, the reclusive Declan Thomas O'More is found murdered in his study at the ancestral family estate, rambling and isolated Crummock Hall.

Suspicion immediately falls upon his five great nieces and nephews, who between them stand to inherit the considerable proceeds of their grandfather's will – along with a valuable library of antiquarian books, a collection that is Declan's lifetime work.

And yet each member of this generation – which includes a famous actor and a successful author – is apparently wealthy in their own right. Why would any of them murder their great uncle?

DI Skelgill and his team must unravel a mystery that not only harks back to the tragic drowning of the children's parents in Crummock Water in the 1980s, but may also have its roots in the despicable Triangular Trade that enriched so many British and Irish merchant families in the eighteenth century.

'Murder at the Wake' by Bruce Beckham is available from Amazon

Made in the USA
Coppell, TX
26 October 2022